TRIVIUM

BY

AMBER NGUYEN

TWO **SPARROWS**
Publishing

Oklahoma City

Published in the United States by Two Sparrows Publishing, Oklahoma City.

Publisher's Cataloging-in-Publication data

Names: Nguyen, Amber, author.
Title: Trivium / by Amber Nguyen.
Series: Trivium Trilogy
Description: Oklahoma City, OK: Two Sparrows Publishing, 2018.
Identifiers: ISBN 978-1-7320559-2-6 (hc) | 978-1-7320559-0-2 (pbk.) | 978-1-7320559-1-9 (ebook) | LCCN 2018902384
Subjects: LCSH String models--Fiction. | Space and time--Fiction. | Friendship--Fiction. | Family--Fiction. | Dystopian fiction. | Science fiction. | Love stories. | BISAC YOUNG ADULT FICTION / Science Fiction / General
Classification: LCC PZ7.N498 Tri 2018 | DDC [Fic]—dc23

Amber Nguyen
Visit my website at www.TriviumBook.com
Cover design by EBookLaunch.com

Printed in the United States of America

*For my favorites: Tj, Trinity, Aidan, and my
mother, Jan.
My life is a beautiful story. Thank you for helping me write it.*

CHAPTER ONE

I dreamt of a time when there were no predetermined choices; an ancient society that focused on living a life of freedom. A man was there, with his eyes darting often from his book to my face, stealing quick glances from above the pages. We were lying in a hammock—feeling the breeze gently sway us back and forth as we faced each other side by side—reading. *Pride and Prejudice* for me. A Bradbury short story about a butterfly for him. His face was mostly hidden behind the paperback, and all I could see was his dark hair ruffling slightly in the breeze as it made its way across his forehead and into his eyes. He pushed it away—tucking it behind his ear, although it wasn't long enough to stay there. In the dream, I knew he was mine. Somewhere in the depths of my being, I knew he was supposed to be there. I inhaled deeply and breathed in the smells of fresh cut grass. Birds were chirping, hidden in the surrounding trees and bushes. Somewhere in the distance was the sound of waves crashing on the shore. The silence between us was comfortable and pure. Words unspoken filled the air with a thick essence of longing. I snuck glances of this familiar stranger, searching for any information as to who he really is. I looked for anything that would lead me to his identity, and to answer the question as to why he haunts my dreams so often. Just as he decided to put his book down and lean toward me, the hammock turned over suddenly and dropped us into a tangle of limbs. I heard myself laughing and yelling his name, but it was muffled like an underwater echo . . . and then I woke up.

The dreams are happening more often, and I'm not any closer to discovering who this mystery man is. Perhaps he's just an amalgam of every literary hero I've ever read about. My own Mr. Darcy. You can do that in your dreams, right? Make someone up? Surely you can't dream up a person you've never met. That's a pretty outlandish idea—even for the world I live in. I'm left with that thought as I roll over and realize the clock says 7:00 a.m., and I'm already running late for school. Normally I would be panicking—as the importance of punctuality has been drilled into my brain by my parents, but this week is the last week of school and the countdown till my visit to the Trivium. I slide my hand over the back of my neck and feel for the small, raised square nestled under the skin that we call the "D.B."—the microchip that computes our futures and tells us how our lives will end. The current world is very different from the liberated one of my dreams. Here, we have a choice of predetermined futures. There is no mystery to life and what the future entails. The past holds an air of romance in its innocence and unawareness. I read the history books feverishly trying to understand how they could handle each day not knowing how it would end. The outline of the microchip is faint, and I forget it's there most of the time. It tracks our response to every decision we've ever made, and stores that data until we go to the Trivium at eighteen years old and make our official choice.

Until now, I've never wondered if it's able to read our thoughts and dreams. Does it know the man whose name flows inaudibly from my lips?

A blaring car horn belting out a Morse code SOS startles me back to reality. I grab my messenger bag that's weighed down with school books and test notes, pull my long blonde hair into a ponytail, and make haste down the stairs and out the door.

"Are you feeling okay? You're never late. Stay up all night studying? Worried about your birthday? Boyfriend problems?"

My best friend Verity is always chipper first thing in the morning. I'm used to her rapid-fire questioning. "Overslept. I'm fine." I sling my bag into the back seat as she takes off fast enough to squeal tires. She starts telling me about some conversation she had with her new boyfriend, Jason, and there are bits and pieces of a new movie thrown in with something about a double date. My mind is wandering back into dream territory—pondering my future and the tough choice that lies ahead—before I realize I inadvertently agreed to see a new action movie tonight with her and Jason. I should tell Gunner what I signed us up for. It wouldn't be the first time Verity conned Gunner and me into a double date with a new boyfriend, but I can already picture Gunner rolling his eyes when I tell him.

School and study for finals occupy my mind for the rest of the day, and I hurry out of my last class at the sound of the bell and head straight toward Gunner's car. His last hour is spent at baseball practice, and the team's final game is only a few days away. He saunters toward me, gear slung across his back and sporting a wry smile when he catches my eye.

"I take it you already heard about tonight?" I force a fake smile and give an *I'm sorry* shrug.

"Yep. Verity caught me this morning after first hour. Who's the new flame?" His blond hair resembles a dull shade of gold, and his bright blue eyes reflect a mischievous sparkle. Standing there—towering above me—he resembles a modern Prometheus. Incredibly charming while simultaneously disarming. He's the kind of guy you want to be friends with because he's enigmatic, but also one you fear. There's always an undercurrent of thought beneath those blue eyes, like he's quietly plotting world domination. For me, he's an oversized teddy bear, and my longtime boyfriend. I have always been on his good side.

"Jason something-or-other. I don't know, I wasn't listening to her this morning. That's how I ended up agreeing to a movie. You know, the nod-your-head-say-yeah when there's a pause in the conversation and you weren't listening kind of thing. I'm sorry Gunner. I don't even know what movie it is."

"No worries. Just means I'm spending tonight with you. That's worth the price of admission."

I can't help but beam at him while looking away, turning a slight shade of pink. He knows I hate cheesy lines like that, but it's bewitching coming from him. I have a pretty amazing best friend, the perfect boyfriend, and a bright medical career in front of me—assuming I pass my tests. Seems like every choice I've made so far has been the best one. My D.B. chip must have it easy. This is the life I've been planning for myself. How could two other options compare? I've been very strategic in my choices, so why does the thought of the Trivium put my stomach in knots?

We ride with Verity and Jason that evening to the local theater on our side of suburbia. It's not a small town as far as size and population, but it's as small as you can get when it comes to mentality. There aren't many dreams of grandeur. No breaking the status quo. It doesn't matter how many people are in this city, it never fails that you'll run into someone you know or who knows your parents. A small part of me would appreciate living with a slice of anonymity occasionally, but the other part feels tethered to this place. Not that it matters as I have no plans of leaving. I'm a planner. I could chart every decision I've ever made to get where I am today. I'll go to the local university after graduation. After that is medical school. I'll fit in nicely at my dad's practice. I'll marry Gunner. We'll live in the historical district downtown in an early 1900s bungalow reminiscent of Frank Lloyd Wright's early work. It may seem presumptuous to create such a detailed list in a time where we can see the future, but I'm confident that this is what the Trivium will show me. Verity isn't so sure of what she wants from life—which is why I think she flits around with different boyfriends and invests in a new hobby every week. Either she's trying to test the efficacy of the D.B. chip in her neck, or honestly doesn't know what she wants so she tries everything and dates everyone.

I do my best to follow the story line, but I can only handle so many explosions and cliché one-liners before my mind drifts off and I'm back to floating in a world of my own making. I can't help but contemplate what lies ahead of me in just a week's time. There is still so much I don't know about the Trivium. I don't fully understand how the D.B. chip works. No one talks about it, other than the basic idea of what we learn in school. I guess since you already chose your perfect life, why dwell on the past? But why just three choices? Are we not able to change our course once we choose? Has anyone tried changing their fate? Even though I think I'm comfortable with what lies ahead for me, I do worry a little for Verity. She is always trying new things and never really nailing down any specific passions. After everything she's been through, I want so much for her to have the happy ending that her mother never had. I get so caught up in my musings that I don't realize the end credits start playing.

As we leave the smells of buttered popcorn and the pinging sounds of the digital arcade games, a brief flash of brown hair gets caught in my peripheral vision. As I scan the crowd for the source, I catch a brief glimpse of the boy sporting the tousled brown hair, but not enough to figure out his identity or see his profile. The thought creeps in that it's him—my dream guy—but I wave that thought away quickly as it's not plausible that he even exists.

"What did you think of the movie?" Gunner's looking at me with a crooked smile. I have a feeling he knows I wasn't paying attention. One of his favorite pastimes is quizzing me on things he knows I don't know. My answers are almost always snarky. I don't like being made to feel unintelligent, especially from him, but I usually brush it aside.

"Fine. Good. Lots of explosions, car chases, and guns. Action. Quippy phrases. Everything I look for in a quality film." The sarcasm wasn't lost on him. He laughs, but Verity is giving me the death stare look she has that tells me she isn't amused. I always thought she picked these movies to impress her dates. Now I'm curious if she's quite the fan. With all her passions, it's easy to miss *action films* being one of them. The three of them become instant movie critics on the ride back to my house, and I listen half-heartedly—mostly so I know what the movie was about. Turns out, my commentary wasn't far off. I know as soon as she gets home she'll be calling me to discuss my thoughts on Jason. And like clockwork, thirty minutes later my cell rings.

"Hey, so what do you think about Jason? He's great, right?" She blurts this out before I've even finished saying hello. She may try to live a life of unpredictability in what she does, but she's completely predictable in her behavior.

"He seems like a really nice guy. He doesn't go to our school, does he? I don't remember seeing him around before."

"Oh no, he goes to that private school on the north side. The one for arts. He's a very gifted poet and painter. Granted, I don't know my Shakespeare from my—I don't know—Eliot? But I've read some of his work and I love it. I think you should read it sometime. You're into that stuff. You'd be a better critic."

"So, he's sharing his poetry with you? Is that a clever ruse to get you to date him, or is this a serious thing? Because you need to prepare me for potentially serious relationships so I can grill him interview-style next time I see him."

"Cassia, you kill me. Am I ever serious with anyone? He's fun. He's talented. But I'm not betting my future with him or anyone right now. I just want to have fun while I can. Only a few weeks left for me, I'd hate to fall in love and then get my heart broken if he wasn't my future . . ." Her voice falters, and then she's silent. There's an air of sadness that has crept in, and I'm finally piecing her together like the puzzle I know she is. My fiery, red-headed beautiful friend that has always lived her life with abandon, carefree and lighthearted, has just admitted her biggest fear. I can't remember ever having a moment of vulnerability with her. I've known her since we started school at age six, but all throughout our lives, she's never been truly open with her feelings. Uncomfortable with this revelation, I try to ease her worries.

"Verity, you're going to end up with a perfect life fit for you. You know that, right? You'll be living the life you've always wanted, where you want to live. I don't think the Trivium has ever been wrong."

"What if I don't know what life I want? I know you have your life all planned out and that I've never really mentioned what I think my future will be or should be, but I'm really worrying, Cassia. What happens when you can't decide? What if there's not a future I see myself in? Then what? I'm at a loss right now and it's all I think about. Sorry to throw this on you suddenly, but I guess I'm at that point where reality hit me. I can't continue to live carelessly anymore. At some point, I've gotta grow up and think about my future and be serious, and I just don't think I can handle it."

Her voice grows quiet again. I'm so caught off-guard by her sudden serious demeanor that I struggle for the right words to say. I have planned my life out just like she thinks, but she still doesn't know that I'm beginning to have doubts myself. I want to be supportive and say all the right words to comfort her, but it wouldn't be sincere. For the first time in my life, I have no words.

"Cas, are you okay? Is this too much?" Her eyes are clearly holding back tears; I hear it in her voice.

"No, no not at all. I'm just—" I'm grasping for the right words to say so that I don't reveal my own fears, especially since I'm still struggling with what the root of that fear is. "I don't know many people that aren't happy. Or at least they all *seem* happy. Have you ever heard someone say they made the wrong choice?"

"Well, no. I don't think so. I've never asked before though. I mean, my dad—" She breaks off into silence abruptly. Verity's mother was in a car accident several years ago and was on life support for several months before they lost her. I know what she's thinking. Did her dad know it would happen? Did he see that far into his future and still choose it? Or was it her mom that chose? I can't imagine Verity asking her dad much about her mom and their past. He hadn't been the same man since, and no one faulted him—least of all his children. The worst of it was that he checked out on being a father—so much so that Verity ended up raising her brother, Jordan. Sure, her dad has always faked a cheerful demeanor and recognized his kids' accomplishments. He's been to every sporting event and award ceremony. On the outside, it seems like he's a great father, but you can peel back the façade and see how much pain he's still in. He's emotionally checked out. I have never experienced that kind of loss. Is it deep love that would make a person choose a fate where they die young? It's something I've never put much thought into, but now I can't help but wonder. Did those in the past worry every day if it would be their last? "Ver, I just have to believe that everything works out in the end. Call it choice, call it fate, call it destiny or whatever you want, but if all options have us still being best friends when we're older, it can't all be bad, right? As long as you're in my life I know that everything will be fine." She does a half-laugh-half-sigh and I know it means she's rolling her eyes and shrugging her shoulders. When you're this close to someone for so long, you pick up the slightest details—even over the phone. Maybe it's your best friend that is your soul mate sometimes. When everything else falls apart, it's your friends that put you back together. We end on a better note, and as I close my eyes, I wonder if I'll see him again. Verity may be the person I share my secrets with, but a part of me is still too scared to share something that isn't real.

CHAPTER TWO

"We are an impossibility in an impossible universe."
—Ray Bradbury

I'm walking in a garden with my sandals in my hand and the feel of the soft, lush grass under my feet. The light, fresh scent of impending rain colliding with the sweetness of roses lingers in the air, while the wind is softly kissing my cheek. Up ahead is a gray gazebo peeking out beneath a covering of beautiful candy pink rose blooms, and beneath it is a cast stone bench with lions carved into the legs. As I walk closer, my breath catches in my chest when I realize it's him that sits on the bench—book in hand. I'm drawn closer to him as if an invisible thread binds us together, and he looks up and smiles when he realizes I'm approaching. He speaks to me, and all I can do is search his lips to make sense of the words, but they are just beyond my reach. Frustrated, I ask him if he can hear me, but before he responds, a crack of thunder disrupts us and a sheet of rain comes pouring down, blowing sideways, and pelting us with sharpness. He grabs my hand quickly, and we're racing away from the gazebo and out of the garden. We reach the back porch of a small cabin—soaked and disheveled. He's laughing as he embraces me tightly—shirt sticking to his skin and so cold that I try to break away, but he doesn't let me go.

My eyes open and all I see is my ceiling fan above me. The sound of droplets hitting my window grows louder and thunder is rolling in the distance. Just a dream. Another dream. No answers just more questions. I want to recall every detail of the garden and the cabin, so I grab the notepad beside my bed and rummage through my nightstand for a pen. As quickly as I can, I write down everything I remember in vivid detail so that nothing escapes my memory. I want to know where this place is. I want to know if it exists. There must be a link somehow; maybe I have a defective D.B. chip or some repressed memory I can't recall. Either way, I want answers.

I have three of my final exams today, and two of them weigh greatly on my medical school aspirations. All our exam scores get stored in the D.B., making them a factor in our future career options. Our schools allow us to choose different electives so we can find what we're talented in. I chose to take multiple science classes in preparation for being a doctor. Verity thinks my schedule is boring—she filled her schedule with various art classes—but I don't mind the demanding work and lectures. Gunner mostly takes athletic courses: kinesiology, sports psychology, physical education, and the like. I'm not sure what his career aspirations are besides trying out for a league sports team. To be honest, I know so little about baseball that I don't even know if he's good. I had hoped he'd join me in the medical practice and maybe specialize in sports medicine. He didn't seem that interested though. I hop out of bed and get ready quickly enough to beat Verity to the horn blowing. I'm completely focused today, no mindless wandering. My first two tests went by easily. The last one was tough, but I'm confident I did well on it. I've always had high marks in school—and I'm toward the top of our class—but I still stress about my test-taking skills. Gunner has a late practice today, so if we get a chance to we'll meet up later, but I'm not thinking much of him momentarily. My brown-haired guy is slowly taking up space in my thoughts that were previously occupied with chemistry and physics. I opt to do research at the library, so I walk that direction. Verity has something at home to take care of after school so I'm on my own.

The local library is only a few blocks away from my school and not much farther away from my house. It's nice to have a bit of alone time with my thoughts as I make the trek. I don't have my own vehicle yet, so I walk or take rides everywhere. My part of the city is a small suburb, but the stores and buildings are sprawled out miles from each other. I don't walk to many places even though it's safe here. Another Trivium advantage, or so the pamphlet reads. A decrease in crime since its installation into the fabric of our society. The creators of the Trivium also claim they're responsible for world peace. I eye roll to myself. I've always questioned that claim.

The town library is an older historic building, one with tall columns and a dome, and you can imagine a world so long ago of finely dressed patrons strolling up to the front steps in summer dresses and parasols. Every other library in the state was demolished and replaced with contemporary architecture featuring sharp concrete and glass. I like that this one was kept intact. The coffee bar they added inside is the only proof of modernity. I've spent enough time here that the librarian, Ms. Ann, knows me by name and knows what section she's likely to find me in. The card catalog is contained on computer tablets that you check out and take with you. They're the size of a postcard and easily slip into your pocket. I get mine and walk to the section of scientific journals.

I haven't thought through exactly what I want to look for. On the one hand, I'd love to get online and look for English-style rose gardens and cabins, but I doubt mine exists in the real world and decide the chance of finding it would be slim. My family doesn't own a computer tablet with internet. Those are reserved for the wealthy and educational facilities. I've read that in the past, cells were like miniature computers. All mine does is make calls and sends short messages. I can't prove it, but I believe the Trivium officials were responsible for restricting the flow of information so that only the elite, or bookworms like me, would seek out knowledge beyond what's taught. Why they'd do such a thing, I can only guess. At least the library doesn't seem to censor information, but then again, how would I know any differently?

I slowly walk down the row of ancient-looking tomes, sliding my fingers along the spines until something catches my eye. I stop when I come to a rather slim book called the *Journal of Quantum Theory and Mechanics,* and I sit down on an overstuffed chair nearby. Gingerly leafing through it, I scan every page as quickly as possible in the hopes that something jumps out at me. There's an abstract titled, "String Theory and Its Impact on Future Decision-Making," and I think I've found something. I know I've heard mention of this article—possibly in my History of the Sciences class in school—but I can't remember ever reading about some of the details it mentions. We're taught that just a few generations ago, society was left making life choices without knowing the impact it would have on the future. You could marry the wrong person and end up divorced, you could choose one day to change your routine, and the after-effects would ripple till it resembled large waves of change. The flapping of a single butterfly's wing would drastically change fate. Cause and effect. Choice and consequences. At some point, humanity was tired of seeing its own destruction wrought by complete recklessness and sought to use science to decide the future. They argued that, if we knew we could be happy and avoid pain by seeing what lay ahead, we could choose that life, and therefore live in complete peace and happiness. It doesn't mean you won't see something bad in your future because it largely depends on the current choices you make right now—and continue making up until the point of choosing—but you could choose which life you wanted out of three. Society has improved. Statistics back up that claim. The divorce rate dropped off to almost nonexistence (if anyone does divorce, you never hear about it). Crime is low, morality is high. My parents absolutely adore each other. Verity's did too until her mother died.

String Theory was introduced to us as a fact. Whatever you choose today, splits off into multiple futures. Just because you choose a future where you marry a certain someone, doesn't mean that person chose you. They just exist in the parallel world. If you both did choose each other, that would be what we call a "soul mate." I've heard that's rare, and no one knows if it's even real, because our choices are sealed to the public once made.

I keep looking for answers in this article, but I come up blank. It's nothing I don't already know, other than the details of the equations used and the name of the researchers who discovered it. Perhaps we just don't know what happens if you choose wrong. Perhaps I do just have dreams that mean nothing. Maybe my mind makes a collage of every face I've ever seen that was attractive and throws it together into one perfect person. It doesn't explain away the realness of these dreams, but science apparently can't or won't explain it either.

I leave the library feeling deflated though I'm not sure what I wanted to find. Am I wanting an out? Am I afraid I'll make the wrong choice and regret it? Is that possible? I resolve to do something I've never done before: I head home to question my parents.

My family lives on a relatively quiet street—save for Verity's endless blaring of her horn. We've lived in this house my entire life. And yet, walking up to the front door, it seems distorted, distant, and unfamiliar. I once knew every single nook and cranny, where the paint was peeling, where the foundation had a slight crack. But I never once looked at it through the lens I'm seeing it through now. Why this house? Why this future? What mysteries are there about my life and my world that are yet untold? What secrets would I unearth if I dug a little deeper?

I walk in and I'm greeted with the smells of fresh basil and garlic, and a soft humming coming from the kitchen. My mom is a talented cook, she's probably running her own restaurant in another life.

"Cassia! Dinner is almost ready. Would you set the table?" I smile, nod politely, and grab the plates and silverware. Everyone is taught proper place setting etiquette in grade school, so I take care to have the fork and knife in their proper place. We still have traditions we hold onto.

"Mom, may I ask you a question? I mean, I'm just curious since I'll be going to the Trivium shortly and I need some answers."

"Well, sure. I think. I mean, that was years ago. Are you nervous or something?" There's unease in her voice, and she turns her back to me and starts stirring whatever it is causing that delicious smell on the stove. Normally she's very calm and relaxed. This may not end well.

"No, nothing like that. I just wanted to hear about your experience. What was it like when you saw Dad in your future?" I do my best to stay the nervousness in my voice, hoping she won't be deterred. *Casual and flippant, Cas. Nonchalant.*

"Oh!" She looks both relieved and elated. The knots in my stomach loosen. "Well, all I remember is going to the Trivium. There's really not much more to say. Haven't you read the pamphlet, Cassia?"

"Of course, I have," I say with an eye roll. "It's required reading, mom. You really don't remember seeing your choices? You don't remember seeing dad?" The words come out like rapid-fire—both from anxiety and just wanting to get the question out there in the air. She hesitates. A stern look comes over her face. Uh-oh. My questioning obviously crossed the line.

"No, Cas. I don't remember any other choice there was, and I don't need to remember any because I know I chose correctly." At that, she turns away again with her shoulders tense and starts heaping spoonfuls of pasta on the plates. I know I need to diffuse the situation quickly; I don't want to have her upset with me like this.

"Mom, I'm sorry. I was just thinking of Verity's dad the other day . . . and well . . ." Her shoulders soften and she turns back around.

"Oh honey, I'm sorry. I know it's got to be tough to imagine that someone would choose a future if they knew they'd die young and leave their kids and husband behind, but I don't know how that works either."

"Do you think she knew?"

"It's possible she didn't know. Or maybe she did and didn't care. Maybe in all possibilities, she would die young, so she chose the way she'd go."

"Is that what true love is, mom? Being willing to die young to be with the person you love?"

"Love is many things, Cassia. Don't put much thought into it though. That doesn't mean your future is filled with tragedy. We don't know everything that will happen to us. If we did, would we ever be able to make a decision again?"

I leave the inquiry at that and stay mostly silent during dinner. I didn't have anything else to say.

That night I make sure my notepad is next to my bed with a pen on top, just in case. It's wishful thinking that I will dream when I should be focused on the world in front of me.

CHAPTER THREE

Thoughts are racing through my mind at warp speed, and I can't distinguish one from the other. I toss and turn all night. Listening to the sounds of the crickets and locusts outside, my restless mind refuses to shut down and sleep. I spend the night in a half-stirring half-asleep stupor so that when my alarm goes off, I'm jolted awake so quickly that I can't tell how much of the night I was sleeping. A wave of disappointment comes over me and takes me aback. Normally I would be upset that I didn't wake up rested and would have to rely on coffee to get me through the day, but this morning I'm surprised that I'm more aggravated that I didn't dream. He wasn't there. I had started to draw comfort from such beautiful scenery and tranquil happiness in my dreams that I forgot they all *were* just dreams. A burning frustration seeps through my body. I'm not sure which I'm angrier at, that I didn't dream, or that I am upset about not dreaming.

The last of my tests are today, and then the countdown to graduation and the Trivium begins. Celebrations will be thrown all over town for each graduating senior. My parents have spent all week organizing a party for me, and the house is covered in streamers and filled with balloons of blue and silver—the school colors. There's a cake box with a "Do Not Open" sticker on top in the fridge, but I'm not tempted to see what's inside. I know it probably has a picture of me on there with *Congratulations Graduate!* written in icing—just like most every other graduation cake out there. And I'm sure it's my favorite flavor—chocolate. My parents are predictable.

The more I think about what awaits me when I head to the Trivium, the more anxious I get. I like details and knowing what I'm walking into, but the technology is top secret and guarded by the government officials assigned to it. Few know much about what's inside, and those that do aren't talking about it. Our culture doesn't like the idea of dwelling on what could have been when you've been given your best options. I had hoped my mom retained something, anything from her time there. I guess she didn't. It was too much to hope for. They must wipe your memory of the experience for safety reasons. But is it for our safety or theirs?

Soon, this chip in the back of my neck will be gone. Almost like parting with an old friend, but I won't miss it. I worry a little about what kind of information it gathers. I'm concerned it reads my thoughts and dreams. Not that it would matter much—since dreams aren't real, and the people in them don't actually exist. It's not some great threat to my future. Still, it's a little unnerving thinking about what that chip knows, and I get a cold chill that passes through my body.

Verity and I head out to school for the last time together. She will more than likely be off to college somewhere else as the medical school and art schools are in separate locations. And Verity is nothing if not artistic and creative. She may not read poetry, but she does like to do crafty things. She's great with clothing design. It's one of her many hobbies. The school upstate has a great fashion design program. I wonder if Verity considered that as an option for her. Or she's just too wrapped up in the idea of not choosing anything. The college I'm going to is local, and I know she wants to get out of here and start with a clean slate. If it's a choice given to her. It will end up being a friendship that's based on weekends if we aren't too far away, and we can each handle the course load and aren't stuck inside doing homework with no social lives. I hope not. I hope she ends up being my roommate. That would require her staying here though. Maybe she won't want to leave her family after all. She's the only thing tethering and grounding me in my life, that I can't imagine life without her. The odds of Verity going to medical school are beyond slim though. It wouldn't suit her.

We talk about our boyfriends and our respective parties happening later today, all the while subconsciously knowing this is our last time to ride like this together and talk about things this way. Sure, we have the summer and we aren't saying goodbye or anything, but we're leaving the realms of comfort that high school has given us and are entering adulthood. Things are about to change, I feel it in the air. Verity only has a week until the Trivium—with mine soon after—and then there's no telling what that will mean for our friendship.

My semester tests are officially over and done, and I feel confident that I did okay. Gunner meets me after school with a carefree look on his face, and I know he's confident he passed too.

"So, everything go okay like you thought? Because you look pretty pleased with yourself." He cocks a crooked smile at me and I can't help but smile back at him.

"Why yes, I am pretty pleased with myself. I'm sure I scored higher than I thought I would. Those weren't my most difficult classes. You seem pretty confident in how you did too."

"Yeah, but my classes were easy. No big deal. Want to go get something to eat? Before the party?"

I don't have a lot of time between now and when I'm supposed to be home for my graduation party, but I accept since I hadn't eaten much at lunch. Nerves get to me every time a test is involved—no matter how well I know I'll do—and my stomach had hurt so much that I couldn't eat. The graduation ceremony isn't until tomorrow night, but families know their kids will be out celebrating together, so everyone has a large family party on the last day of school. I have cousins and grandparents traveling from the towns nearby because to everyone it's a big deal. Another rite of passage. I just want cake.

Sitting across from Gunner at the local diner—in a booth we've sat in multiple times—no longer feels the same now that school is over. I can tell he senses that I'm drifting into my own world, so he asks about my party and what gifts I hope to get that will help in college. There's a strangeness in the air. Of change. Of endings.

"A car. That's all I want. At this point, I'll take whatever they throw at me as long as it has wheels and a motor. Bumming rides off you and Verity gets old. Not that I don't love spending time with you both, but sometimes a girl just wants to go somewhere without help."

"So, you'd take a scooter? You didn't specify how many wheels." He tilts his head back and laughs. "I kind of like you having to depend on me for rides."

"A scooter would be a step up from walking and a bicycle so—yeah, smart guy—I'd take a scooter. And while I appreciate the gesture, a girl's gotta have some independence. What about you?"

"Independence is overrated. Anyway, I'd like a new cell, but I'm pretty sure all I'm getting is luggage. Something about a standard gift for graduation is luggage and its symbolism of a new adventure or whatever. It's ridiculous. They're just ready to have me out of the house." There's a tinge of sadness in his voice. I don't know much about his parents now that I think about it. I've only met them once, and it was brief. They both seemed pleasant enough, so I can't tell if he's joking or being serious—or a bit of both.

"Yeah well, my parents have earmarked my bedroom for a new home gym so . . ." He reaches across the table and kisses me so quickly that I lose my train of thought.

"Cas, you're the best," He stares into my eyes intently and I feel my heart pounding. "I won't miss you though."

Startled, I start stammering, "Wait, wh-wh-what?"

He does his head-tilt-and-laugh thing again and then looks at me with those impish eyes. "How can you miss someone you're not letting go of?"

I just shake my head at him. "Jerk." I walk away in a pretend huff but I'm just getting a refill of tea. I glance back at him and he has a smile spread across his face. I bite my lower lip and attempt to stave off a return smile and look away, but I notice a shock of brown hair as I do so and I instantly freeze. *Stupid Cassia, lots of guys have brown hair. What is wrong with you? Just glance around inconspicuously and see who it is. Because really, it's not going to be him. He doesn't exist.* I fill up my cup and take deep breaths, and as I walk back to my table, I casually look around the diner—but I don't see him. *Great, now I'm hallucinating.* I sigh softly and then notice a guy walking out the door. A guy with brown hair. The girl at the bar calls out for him and runs after him saying he left his sunglasses, and when he turns toward her, I go weak and my body stiffens and I can't breathe. A trembling panic courses through my veins and my heart feels like it's stopped in my chest.

It's him. It truly is *him.*

He sees me staring at him and nervously smiles at me, and then quickly walks back out the door. My cheeks flush and my heart starts beating again, but I'm still stuck in the same spot.

"Cas, you ok?" Gunner jumps up and heads toward me, a look of concern on his face. "What happened?"

I try to breathe at a normal rate, slow my heartbeat down, and shake off all the emotions running through my mind.

"I'm fine. Sorry, I was just thinking and thought I forgot something my parents needed tonight. It's good though, I didn't. I panicked."

He doesn't look completely convinced, but he lets it go and doesn't press further.

"Ok, well, if you need anything for tonight—or want to stop somewhere—we can on our way to your house. Ready to go?"

"I don't need anything, I was being silly. Yeah, I'll meet you at the car, going to run to the restroom." He grabs his keys out of his pocket and steps forward, kissing my forehead gently, then walks out the door. As soon as he's out of sight, I walk up the counter to the lady that had given the guy his sunglasses.

"Ma'am? That guy that just left—the one who left his sunglasses—do you know his name? Does he live around here?" She looks at me curiously for a second, probably thinking I'm a boy-crazy girl with a crush on a guy I just met. She would only be partially right.

"I've seen him before in here, but no I don't remember his name. Why?"

"Well, did he pay with a card by chance? Where he'd sign his name?" Now she's looking at me warily like she's about to tell me off. I'm desperate and it's showing. "I'm sorry, I'm pretty certain that's the guy that hit my mom's car and took off without leaving his insurance, and we're really struggling financially right now—and it'd be a huge favor and tremendous help if I at least had a name to go find him." Wow, what a quick lie. What is it lately with the lying? This isn't like me at all.

"Oh, I'm so sorry to hear that!" She leans in closer and lowers her voice so I lean in toward her too. "We aren't supposed to give out customer information like this, but if it's the guy I hope you catch him. No good jerks with no integrity anymore. Gah." She walks back to her station and looks through the signed receipts, till she finds the right one, and discreetly hands to it to me. I take a glance at the name on the bottom, and all I make out through the sloppy signature is the name Ethan. *Ethan.* I thank her, hand it back, and walk quickly to the car.

"Girls. Always taking their sweet time in the bathroom. What do y'all *do* in there? Shower? Compose poetry? Save the world and then come back and change into your everyday disguise?"

"If I told ya, I'd have to kill ya." He laughs and I wink at him, and on the way to my house, he talks about what superhero identity he'd have and his abilities. I think to myself I'd like to be invisible. At least this very moment I wish I could be. I need time alone with my thoughts.

Gunner isn't staying since he has his own party to get to, so I give him a quick kiss and head inside. The interior of my house looks like a party store threw up on it. Confetti on the table, balloons tied to the staircase and chairs, streamers have multiplied and are now across the entry and living room ceiling. A lot of my relatives arrived early to help, so the house is a boisterous flurry of activity. I guess my skills of invisibility are working because I manage to sneak up the stairs without anyone noticing and shut myself in my room. I only have a few minutes to change clothes and fix my hair. I know there will be a lot of picture-taking as soon as I present myself downstairs. I change into a blue V-neck top and my nice jeans and quickly smooth out my hair. Just because there are pictures doesn't mean I'm wearing a dress. It takes a lot to get me to put one on. I prefer comfort, and something about a skirt or dress leaves me uncomfortable. Unfortunately for me, my mom already picked out a dress for me to wear for graduation. I had no choice in that decision. I see the dress staring me down from the hanger on my closet door. I stare back to let it know it won't break me. Not today, dress. Not today.

I spy my notepad on the nightstand and grab the pen. I write "Ethan" and "Castletown," hoping that I can search at the library soon for those terms together and that there aren't many of that name in this city. There's a knock at my door and I quickly hide the notepad under my mattress just in time for my mom to walk inside.

"Cas, I just knew you would be up here. Sneak in, did you? Are you ready to join us?"

"Yeah, I'm ready. I had to come up here and change. Didn't want to meet family without looking my best, you know?

She eyes me up and down, probably wondering if jeans and a tee are really looking my best. I know she'd rather I dress up and be a little more girly, but her look is more of amusement than exasperation. She's been through many fights over my wardrobe over the years. At this point, it's not exactly a shock to her anymore.

"So, this is your idea of looking your best?" She raises one eyebrow and smirks. It's her go-to facial expression for subtle disapproval.

We walk downstairs, and before we even reach the last step, a loud cloud of congratulatory shouts echo in my ears. I feel like a small leaf being tossed around violently in a tornado as each member of my family takes turns spinning me around and hugging me and taking pictures. Flashes of red dots are singeing my eyes as cameras are positioned everywhere. I knew this would be a huge affair for my family, but I didn't realize it to this extent. The night wears on, and there are the predictable chocolate cake and gifts, and the promise that my future is bright and happy. The last of my family trickles out one-by-one around eleven, and I spend an hour helping my parents clean up. Finally, at midnight, I manage to pry myself away from them and head back to my room—where I shut myself in and recharge. Being around that many people wears me out after a while. As I slide into bed—my eyes heavy with the weight of today's revelations and excitement—I nod off into a dreamless sleep once again.

CHAPTER FOUR

School is over. I realize something is off when my alarm doesn't wake me up. I roll over to notice it's already late morning. A little groggy from last night, I rub my eyes and sit up. As I look around my room, it strikes me that everything feels different. Or maybe *I* am different. It's the same room I have always lived in, but today—the morning of my graduation—it doesn't feel like mine anymore. Maybe this is what growing up feels like. It won't be long till I make my choice and then move off to college. I'll be living on campus—even though it's not far from here. I'll be starting a new life in many ways. Seeing my room through a different lens today wakes me up even more. No more car horns blaring. What a bittersweet moment to behold.

Verity and I have plans to meet up later before we head downtown to the large convention center where our graduation is held. Before that, I had planned on visiting the library to search for

Ethan. Nervousness and excitement mix together uneasily in my stomach.

Pulling on some comfortable jeans and a soft tee—and grabbing my long-sleeved cardigan—I head downstairs, kiss my mom bye and walk out the door. It's a beautiful sunny day today. Perfect day for a walk.

The library isn't busy, and the quietness is welcoming. I grab a tablet and find an empty aisle of fiction novels. I can't help but feel paranoid, although I know no one is going to look over my shoulder to see my searches, let alone would they care. Still, the butterflies in my stomach flit around, and I don't want to look suspicious. I pull up the search function and type in "Ethan" and "Castletown," and hold my breath as I await the results. *Over forty Ethans in Castletown. Ugh.* I grit my teeth and decide that I'm too frustrated to dig any deeper. I turn my eyes to the row of books, thinking I should get lost in a story instead. It may help calm my nerves. I scan the fiction section and beginning with the As, slide my fingers slowly across each book until I know it's the right one. *Emma.* An Austen novel. How befitting. As much as I love Miss Emma Woodhouse, I politely decline and scan again. *Persuasion.* While still an Austen novel, I haven't read it yet, so I take it off the shelf and open it to scan the pages while walking back to the lounge area of the library. With my nose in the book, I don't realize I am walking right in the path of another person until I bump right into him and we both drop our books on the floor.

"Oh, my goodness! I'm so sorry! I wasn't paying attention whatsoever." I kneel to pick up the fallen books and stand back up again to hand the book over. *The Martian Chronicles.* Interesting.

"It's ok, I had my nose in a book too. I didn't see you either." He laughs, and the sound startles me. I know that voice.

I look up and hand him the book and am caught speechless. *Ethan.* No. Yes. I realize I'm staring, and I quickly look back down at my book and try to tell myself to breathe.

"I've never read *The Martian Chronicles.* Is it pretty good?"

"Well, so far it's good enough that I didn't see a pretty girl walking in my direction." There's a smile on his face and I feel myself blush and my heart beating heavily in my chest. *Breathe, Cassia. He doesn't know you like you know him. Well, you don't really know him, do you? Stupid random dreams.* "So, *Persuasion* I see. You have a thing for Jane Austen or just tragically romantic novels set in Bath?" He's still smiling and it's warm and comforting, and at the same time, I can't think straight.

"A romantic novel set in a bath?" My hand instantly goes to my forehead and I close my eyes once I catch the words I just said. *You idiot! Oh geez, Cassia, what are you doing?* He starts laughing again, but he doesn't sound like he's mocking me. I open my eyes and slowly lift my chin till I see his chest and stop there. I can't bear looking into his eyes. The slight definition of his chest and stomach show through his shirt and my face feels hot. "Yes, yes, sorry. I don't know why I said that! I like Austen. And you must like Bradbury a lot."

"Well, I don't really know. It's my first time to read anything of his. Perhaps I'll like him well enough." Again. So stupid. But he was reading Bradbury in my dream. How's that for coincidence? How's that even possible? I peel my eyes away from his body, and I catch a look in his eyes like he knows something he isn't telling me. Like maybe he knows something about me that I don't. I wonder if he dreams of me. Maybe it's all in my head. "My name is Ethan." He reaches his free hand out for me to shake.

"Cassia." I take his hand and quickly let go as if electricity just shocked me. I can't keep my eyes on his. It's too intense, so I look away and back at my book and then back to his chest. He's taller than me by several inches, but I'm relatively short so that doesn't mean much.

"So, were you headed to the chairs over there?" He points in the direction of the lounge and I nod quickly. I am barely breathing. "I was planning on going that way, but I got turned around. There are two chairs over there next to each other. Is it too presumptuous to ask you to join me?"

I can barely concentrate on anything but the pounding in my chest.

"No, not at all. I'd love to." I'd love to? Really? Am I living in my Austen novel? Get a grip, Cassia. Now.

He leads the way to the two chairs off on their own by the back wall. A few people have come in to read and the main sofas and chairs are taken. The ones by the back wall are more private though, so there's less of a chance of disturbing someone if you have a conversation. He plops down with such coolness and ease and opens his book back to where he left off. I carefully sit down in the chair next to him—feeling stiff—and attempt to get my limbs to cooperate with me so I can get comfortable. I try to readjust myself slowly, but these chairs are so plush that you sink into them—and it's easier to move quickly around than try to look proper. There is a slight chill, as the chairs are under the air conditioning vents, so I stand back up and put on my cardigan and then mimic him when I sit back down. I don't know him. I have a boyfriend. No need to be weird. I have graduation tonight and college in a couple months and a boyfriend I'll end up marrying. Why am I worried about Ethan? I should talk to him so I can see he's nothing like I was hoping he would be, that way I can move on with my life and chalk up my dreams to some weird twist of coincidence. I mean, I could've just seen him around before.

"So, where do you go to school?" It's an easy enough opening question to ask someone you just met. *Play it cool, Cassia.*

"I go to the Fine Art Academy. Or did. Our graduation is tomorrow. You?"

"Castletown Prep. Our graduation is tonight. So, are you an artist?"

"Oh, no. Writer. Well, hope to be. I've done short stories, but I'd rather write novels. Science fiction. Suspense. Mysteries. Anything like that. Maybe some screenplays. I have a good friend that's a poet though, and artist. I'm going with him to a graduation party for Castletown tonight. What do you do?"

He's going to a Castletown party? Tonight? Whose? "Oh, I'm planning on going to medical school. I've wanted to be a doctor since I was little."

"Wow. Hats off to you. You must be very smart. Nice to meet a smart girl. Course, I guess most girls you'd find in a library are. Smart *and* pretty. So, tell me, Miss Bennet, what pray tell flaws you must have? Because I doubt there is a single one."

I get caught off guard at the mention of Elizabeth Bennet, but I try to conceal it.

"Well, Mr. Darcy I presume? A weakness for tragic romantic comedies set in England for starters." He smiles again, and it's just like the one I dreamt about that it's simultaneously soothing and off-putting—if there is such a thing.

"And witty. I like that. So, Miss Bennet, do you have any gentlemen callers?"

Butterflies bursting through their cocoons in droves in my abdomen. "Why yes, Mr. Darcy. A certain Mr. Wickham has come calling." He smiles widely and his toothy grin is charming.

"Well, we'll see about that. I've reliable sources that say Mr. Wickham is a terrible scoundrel." He looks at me in the eye, causing me to look away. "In all seriousness, Cassia, do you have a boyfriend? Is that too forward to ask? I mean, we just met."

I hesitate. I don't know how to answer him. I mean, yes, I have Gunner. And if anyone else had asked me, I would have blurted that out quickly because he means a lot to me. But I want to get to know Ethan better and I'm afraid to scare him off.

"Actually, yeah. I do. We've been dating awhile now. You?" His entire countenance seems to darken instantly. Not good.

"No, not really. I've dated a little here and there, but just haven't really found anyone that perfect for me. Austen heroines are hard to come by—even in a school with dramatic actors." He shifts anxiously in his chair. "So, where are you going to college? The local medical school or one in another city?" His eyes soften, and whatever darkness had come over him previously is quickly wiped away.

"Yeah, that's the plan, anyway. Assuming I passed all my tests and it's a choice for me."

"Ah, that's great though. Good for you. I'll be going out of the city if possible. Upstate. There's a university there with a great creative writing program. It's not too far from here though, about an hour or two."

"Oh yeah, I know which one. I have a friend that may go there for fashion design. If she ever decides what she wants to do."

"Well, when does she choose? I go to the Trivium next month." He instinctively puts his hand behind his neck over his chip like I do.

"Next week. Then I go a week after. She teases me that I'll have it easy because I've had my life mapped out for a long time. She is always all over the place, so there's no telling at this point where she'll end up."

"Oh yeah? You planned your life?" He looks inquisitively at me like he doesn't believe me. Or is perhaps surprised. "I thought I had my life planned out too, now I'm not so sure though." His eyes meet mine with an intensity I've never known before, and then he quickly looks away this time. There's a silence between us that's thick and heavy and seemingly impenetrable. What did he mean by that?

"What changed your mind? I mean, what is it that makes you think . . ." I can't get the words out. I want to ask him if he knows me. If maybe he dreamt of me in the hammock beside him. If that's why he referenced *Pride and Prejudice*, and if perhaps maybe everything he ever knew about his life changed because of something as simple as a dream. But I can't. He might think I'm crazy and have no idea what I'm talking about. He stares at the book in his lap and doesn't meet my eye.

"Sometimes I wonder if we know all the facts behind the choices we're given, I guess," he shifts uneasily in his seat, moving from the center of the chair toward the side closest to me. "I had a girlfriend for several years until a few months ago. I liked her. I really did. I thought perhaps she was my future. I would go to school and become a writer or teach writing, and she would study art and work in a gallery or museum. But then one night, things changed, and I can't really explain it, but . . ." He is still looking away from me, forehead creased, and he's biting his lower lip. He turns to look directly into my eyes, and a lump forms in my throat. "Do you think the universe knows something we don't?" My breathing is shallow and I'm very aware of the pounding in my chest. I can barely speak above a whisper.

"Honestly, I don't know." His entire body relaxes, and he sinks back into the chair. He laughs somewhat loudly, which startles me but makes me smile, and I feel my body ease the tension that had been forming throughout my chest and shoulders.

"We just met, I'm sorry to even ask you that! Wow, I brought the mood down quickly." He brightens back up, but his eyes are still brooding. "So anyway, any grand plans for graduation later? Any fun parties you're going to?"

The shift in tone is sudden but welcome. "My friend is making me go with her to one, but I have no idea where. Someone's house I guess, and her boyfriend will be there. I'm not big on parties. I'd rather stay home and read. Sad, right?"

He smiles so warmly that it's hard to believe he was so serious just seconds ago. "Well, I cannot comprehend the neglect of a family library in such days as these." He looks at his watch and back at me and stands up abruptly. "I'm sad to say I must be going. Meeting my friend for dinner before we head out tonight to the party. It's been very nice finally meeting you, Cassia. I mean, meeting you. Today. For the first time." A look of shock washes over his face and then an attempt at recovering. I stand up to shake his hand, but when I take it, he turns my hand over—palm down—and kisses it sweetly. "You have bewitched me, body and soul, Cassia." He smiles but his eyes are full of sadness, and again I'm left standing there—stupefied.

"Nice to meet you too, Ethan." With that, he turns quickly and walks away, leaving his book on the small table beside his chair.

I watch him leave, wondering if he'll glance back. He doesn't. After he walks through the doors, I sit back down and feel myself take in a deep breath and hold back the onslaught of tears forming behind my eyes. I need to go somewhere and process what just happened, somewhere other than the library. My normal place of refuge no longer feels like it's mine. I want to walk to the park nearby, but Verity sends me a message that she's ready to get together. Thinking will have to wait. I'll need to push Ethan out of my mind for a little while longer.

But how?

I run back by my house to change for the ceremony. I stare down my opponent for the evening one last time: a teal, sleeveless dress with a flared skirt. I feel the softness of the fabric and give points to my mom for choosing something that won't itch. With my hair curled and my makeup on, I almost don't recognize myself. Verity pushes her way into my room in a beautiful red dress—looking stunning. Getting all dressed up is easy for her. She makes it look effortless.

"Cas, you ready? I want to go by the diner and grab something to eat before we have to get there."

"Yeah, pretty sure I can't do much else to myself to look decent at this point. It will have to do."

"Whatever, Cas. You look amazing. Gunner will love it. You should wear that dress again on a date." I make sure she sees me eye roll. She eye-rolls back.

We make our way to the diner, trying hard to not mess up our outfits in the process. Verity grabs a booth by the window and I slide in across from her. I breathe in the greasy smells of burgers and fries and take in this moment as much as I can. It's the little things I'll miss the most. The routine. Our casual days pre-Trivium are dwindling.

"So, are you ready for the party tonight?" Verity is glowing with excitement, she loves parties. Any chance to be social. In many ways, she is my opposite.

"Not really. But you know how I am."

"Yeah, I know. Still, I think it will do you some good to spend time with everyone before we all head off in different directions. Jason is meeting me there after the ceremony. Then tomorrow he's graduating and I'm going with him to another party. Wanna go?"

"I don't know. Maybe." I'm thinking of Ethan and if I would run into him if I went with her. Do I want to see him again? A part of me wants answers, and another part is conflicted. Getting to know Ethan so close to the Trivium doesn't really make sense to me. He may not even be a choice. He may not even be interested in me. But, what if he were? Would it change anything? Is it possible the dreams are more than what they seem?

"I honestly expected you to say no. What changed your mind?"

"Just want to spend more time with you is all." She doesn't look entirely convinced, but she's not pressing me for more information either.

Graduation is a blur of streamers, confetti, and bullhorns. I barely remember walking across the stage and hearing my name called. I'm sure my family cheered, but the sounds were so loud they were drowned out if so. The best part of the night was sitting behind some of my favorite teachers and listening to their quips and jokes. Caps raining down from the ceiling in a shower of blue and silver—balloons flying all around. It's a celebration of a milestone, and everyone is laughing and excited. I am too, but there's a feeling nagging at the back of my mind that things are about to change drastically. Of course, there is change after graduation, but this feels like a foreboding force that I can't shake. And just like that, the ceremony is over and it's time to take pictures with family and head on to the celebrations. Verity has already stripped out of her graduation gown and fixed her makeup by the time I make my way to her car.

"Ready to get outta here and go have some fun?" she yells as she sees me heading her way.

"I think I just might be! Where are we going?"

"Athena's house. You know Athena, right? Jackson?

"I know who she is, I don't think I ever had a class with her though."

"Oh, well she's super great, you'll like her! That's where everyone is going. Hurry up and get in!" We leave downtown and start back toward the area we live in. Athena's house is in a nice subdivision I hadn't been in before—where all the houses are more upscale with finely manicured lawns. It took a while to find somewhere to park—seems like everyone beat us here—but we walk up to the door and Athena greets us. I'm not a fan of crowds, or at least, not when a lot of people are in cramped spaces. I hold onto Verity's arm as we make our way through the house and to the backyard. Jason had messaged her saying he was here already and waiting for us. Verity informs me that Jason and Athena knew each other because of their families being on some art board—so they've been friends a long time. Scanning the backyard, we find Jason sitting on a lounge chair by the pool. He stands up as we walk to him, and he kisses Verity before handing her a drink. I message Gunner that I made it to the party, and since Jason and Verity are now locked in intimate banter, I'm hoping he shows up quickly. I walk around the backyard—scanning to see if I know anyone else—and to give Verity and Jason some privacy.

"Cassia?" Recognition hits me and something within me lights up. I turn around quickly to see Ethan behind me with a drink in hand, and a curious but pleasant look on his face.

"Ethan, hi! Well what do you know, we managed to be at the same party. Strange coincidence, huh?"

"I don't know, lately I'm beginning to believe coincidences are disguised as fate." He smiles sheepishly and then looks back at Jason and Verity. "I take it Jason's girlfriend is your friend?"

"Yep. That'd be Verity. My lovely friend that forgot I was here. I was regretting coming."

"And, now?"

"Well, now I'm thinking I have a reason to stay. Perhaps." I gently bite my lower lip, feeling slightly ashamed of what I just said.

"Do you want something to drink? I can grab you something."

"Sure, that would be really nice of you."

"As you wish, milady." He grins and turns away from me and walks toward the house. I look around for a place to sit and find a couple of empty chairs under the pool cabana. I feel my face flush, and suddenly I'm hot and feeling like I need a cool breeze. My heart rate is quickly increasing, and I'm aware that I'm taking shallower breaths. *Calm down, Cassia! Get control of yourself!*

"Well, hey there beautiful, I've been looking for you." I look up and see Gunner and I'm startled back into reality. *Gunner. Oh no. How did I forget about Gunner?* I stand up and he wraps his arms around me in a tight hug. I see Ethan walking back toward me. He notices Gunner embracing me and the smile on his face dissipates. He stops—obviously trying to decide if he wants to come back. I want to yell for him, but I stop myself. He waves at me and decides to walk to Jason instead—since he and Verity are finally apart.

"Cas, did you want something to drink? Pretty sure that's boyfriend duty. I can—"

"Oh, that's ok. I'm fine." He eyes me suspiciously. He knows I don't like parties though.

"I saw Verity with her boyfriend, but she didn't seem to notice when I was asking her where you were, so I gave up. She's really into that guy."

"Yeah, tell me about it. I was ready to leave."

"You couldn't have left, knowing I was on my way to save you. Your knight in shining armor coming to whisk you away from the party I know you don't want to be at."

"Actually, I don't think I want to go anywhere just yet. Let's do the crazy and unexpected thing and stay awhile." I hug him again and feel somewhat guilty for how I reacted earlier to Ethan. Besides Verity, Gunner's my best friend. I'm not always at ease with Gunner, his temper with others can be startling. But he's always been sweet to me, and there's a level of comfort there. Gunner wraps his hand around mine and we walk together toward Verity. I'm consciously aware that Ethan has his eyes on me, and part of me wants to pull my hand away. That thought unsettles me and the shame creeps back in.

"Hey, you two! Glad Gunner could make it. Cassia, where did you go?" Verity bounces toward me and she's radiating happiness.

"Oh, I just thought I'd leave you two alone for a bit to talk."

"Ooh, yeah. Sorry about that." She laughs and walks with us to where Jason and Ethan are standing. "Cassia, I want you to meet Jason's friend, Ethan. Ethan, my best friend, Cassia."

Ethan puts his hand out to shake mine and does so firmly but quickly. Very different from the kiss on the hand I received earlier.

"Nice to meet you, Cassia. And this must be your boyfriend . . ."

"Gunner. This is Gunner." Gunner looks Ethan up and down before shaking his hand firmly, and then puts his arm around my waist, pulling me tighter to him. I don't know why Ethan decided to act like he doesn't know me. Maybe because he doesn't want to explain how we met or doesn't want to feel awkward, but I'm suddenly aware that the tension is thick and I feel cheated that there are words we have left unsaid. What would we have talked about? More book innuendos? Coincidence and fate? Or would we have kept talking about things in code to not bring up that perhaps we really know each other better than we let on? There's a sadness washing over me that I can't quite explain; I feel like I'm missing out on something important. A detail I can't quite put my finger on.

"So . . . Gunner, what college do you want to go to?" The way Ethan says it sounds like he's interviewing Gunner. Or testing him. I can't help but wonder why.

"Oh, I'm just staying local. I don't really have any set goals. I figured I'd let the Trivium decide it all for me. Just as long as it keeps me close to Cassia. Can't let her get too far away, you know? I play sports, maybe I'll make league. How about you? You don't seem like you're a sports guy." Gunner squeezes me tighter around my waist, making me uncomfortable enough to politely push his arm off me. He crosses his arms across his chest instead, a motion that doesn't go unnoticed by Ethan. Do I see a hint of mischief in his eyes? I feel like I'm stuck between two peacocks dancing for my attention. It makes me uneasy.

"I'd like to go upstate. Creative writing. How about you, Cassia?" He looks at me nonchalantly and without emotion. Is this a game to him?

"Local. Medical school." I give him a furrowed brow for a second. He notices but retains a look of ambivalence.

"Wait, you want to be a *writer?*" Gunner laughs. I feel my face grow hot.

"Cassia is super gifted. She's going to be an incredible doctor." Verity chimes in unexpectedly. I'm not sure why she's building me up to Ethan.

"Is that so?" Ethan looks at me with a wry smile.

"Oh yeah, she's one of the smartest people in our class!" Verity smiles at me and winks.

"No, I just study hard. Hard work. Anyway, writing, huh? What do you plan on doing?" If he's going to act like he doesn't know me, then I plan on deflecting the conversation back.

"Well, writing. Maybe teach. I could go either way fate takes me." Coy. That's the way he's playing it. Also, he's a bit of a smart aleck. No one has acknowledged Gunner's snide remark. He fidgets next to me. "So, Verity, Jason tells me you'd like to come to college with us in the fall? Is that right?"

She looks at me sheepishly. "I haven't said anything to anyone yet, but yes! I'm hoping the Trivium lets me choose fashion design. And the program there is great. Crossing my fingers I can choose that and not like, uh, some non-artsy career." She beams at us and Jason leans over and kisses her cheek.

"My girlfriend, the fashion designer. She'll be a big hit someday in New York." Jason is clearly smitten with Verity, which makes me wonder what her thoughts are about him. She was so confused the last time we really spoke, and neither of us has brought up the conversation since. Is she embracing life, or is this what she truly wants?

Ethan tosses his drink in the trash can behind him and puts his hands in his pockets. "Well, I hate to leave so soon after arriving, but I must be going. Jason, I'll see you tomorrow. Guess I'll see you too, Verity. Gunner, nice to meet you. Cassia, a pleasure."

"Wait, you're leaving already?" Verity looks at me curiously. "I mean, you just got here. We were planning on going out for dessert in a bit. Don't you want to join us?" I can see that he's conflicted.

"Oh, no, I really should get going. I don't want to be a fifth wheel. Maybe I'll see you around though?" He winks at me and waves at everyone as he turns and walks away out of sight. I watch him, hoping this time he'll turn back—and just before he walks into the house, he does. Everyone else has already gone back to a conversation and doesn't notice like I do. He smiles a sad smile, pretends to bow, and walks into the house—leaving me standing there in his wake. I do my best to act like nothing is wrong as I feel sadness creeping in. No one would understand. Right now, even *I* don't understand.

We head to a local café to stuff ourselves full of pastries and coffee, and though on the outside I'm smiling and laughing and following the conversation, on the inside I'm slowly falling into an indescribable despair. It's unlike me to sulk over someone I don't know. But that's just it. I'm not sure I *don't* know him. Perhaps I know him better than I do myself. Maybe I know exactly what it's like to embrace him and feel him next to me while running in the rain, laughing together, reading side by side, and loving each other fully. Maybe it was all a dream, but it felt real—and that's the part I'm stuck deliberating. I have two weeks before the Trivium, and for the first time in my life, I am only certain of my uncertainty. It's unsettling and scary and exciting all in one. There is a sick feeling taking over my gut, and I suddenly feel heavy—like a thick fog has surrounded my mind and a weight has attached itself to my heart. Gunner gives my hand a squeeze under the table, and I snap back into the life now before me. It's selfish of me to be brooding about someone else when this great guy that I care so much about is sitting beside me. We've talked about how convenient it would be to go to college together next year, and how easy of a choice we'll have if we choose each other. How would he feel if he knew I was conflicted about my future? And not only that, but it's because I had a dream about some random guy and then coincidentally ran into him in a library? He wouldn't understand. It could ruin everything between us. For the first time in weeks, I'm looking forward to the Trivium—if only so I can hurry up and choose and get on with my life. I haven't changed my mind about Gunner, but if I'm faced with a choice that doesn't include him— and does, in fact, include Ethan—then what? Would the choice be harder or easier? I'm turning into that desperate heroine in fiction novels that I hate so much, with all this indecision.

Gunner drops me off at home and kisses me goodnight. Verity hasn't called to gossip since I got home, but I still plan on going with her to Jason's graduation tomorrow. I guess it's also Ethan's graduation. His name alone causes me anxiety. It's odd how one day can make you question everything you've always known.

CHAPTER FIVE

"One's philosophy is not best expressed in words; it is expressed in the choices one makes . . . and the choices we make are ultimately our responsibility."
—Eleanor Roosevelt

The rain is pouring down outside, and I hear it tapping loudly against the window. A fire is blazing wildly in the fireplace, and the smell of cinnamon is permeating the air. I'm sitting on a soft and worn sofa, wrapped up in a throw and holding a piping hot mug of cocoa. It's quiet except for the crackling of the fire, but it's warm, cozy, and serene. A manuscript lies in front of me; I've been reading it for the past hour and making edits. I'm confused as to why I'm editing a manuscript, but it feels natural. Or at least, this version of me feels at home reading and editing books, poetry, and screenplays. I think about my life and how much I enjoy reading, and how it makes sense that this is the path I would be on. Why hadn't I thought of this before? What in me made me think I would be truly happy as a doctor? The front door bursts open and the wind howls inside. A dark figure is balancing an umbrella in one hand and a paper bag of groceries in the other. He puts the bag down and hangs up the umbrella on a black wrought iron stand while pushing his rain boots off with his feet. As he takes his coat off, his profile comes into the glow of the fire, and I know at once that Ethan is home. It's at this point that I realize I'm dreaming again. It's surreal to feel awake in a world that doesn't exist. He grabs a bottle of wine out of the bag and goes into the kitchen for an opener. He comes back into the room with a couple of wine glasses and the bottle and sits them down on the coffee table in front of me. He plops down on the couch beside me—the same way he did when we first met in the library—and wraps his arms around me so tightly that I protest and quickly put my mug down or else fear it spilling all over me. He laughs and then pulls me closer and kisses my cheek. He smells of leather, bergamot, and rain, and it's intoxicating and familiar. This dream is all too real and longer than normal, and I see both above my body while experiencing it firsthand. This is where I want to be. He kisses my cheek again, with more passion, and then I'm woken abruptly by the sound of thunder outside my window.

I don't understand how these dreams can be so real and so dreamlike at the same time. My heart is racing, and I feel tears welling up in my eyes. I'm upset that it's over and yet startled by my intense emotions. I really must call Verity. No matter what, I need to see Ethan again.

Verity answers her cell after several rings—sounding groggy—and I realize I never paid attention to what time it is and that it's Friday.

"Hey, Cas." She answers, a dazed and tired voice—clearly unhappy with being woken up so early. "Is everything ok?"

"I just realized what time it is. I wasn't thinking. Want me to call you later?"

"No, that's ok. I really should be getting up anyway. Supposed to get my hair done and then meeting Jason for lunch. I forgot about setting my alarm. Good thing you called. I'd hate to miss my appointment."

"Well, I just wanted to know if you still wanted me to go with you to Jason's graduation tonight. I thought about it and remembered we never actually made concrete plans. Like, what times we'd go and whatnot." I'm trying to sound as nonchalant as possible.

"You really do want to go? I figured you and Gunner had plans tonight so I didn't want to ask you again. But yeah, I'd love to have you go with me. I really didn't want to go alone. I'm kind of shocked you really want to go when you won't know anyone there. You don't even like going to parties where you *do* know people." She pauses, probably trying to figure me out. I'm hoping she doesn't connect Ethan to my reason for going.

"Gunner has something tonight with his baseball buddies. End-of-year party or whatever. I'd rather hang out with you than stay at home. Want to pick me up when you head toward downtown?" All graduations around here take place in the same convention center—it's the only place large enough for most of the schools here.

"Yeah, that sounds great. Probably around four? Jason is eating dinner with his family, so you and I can grab something and then meet him there."

"Sounds like a plan. I'll see you then!"

"Hey, Cassia?" Verity's voice is somewhat quieter. "Does this by chance have anything to do with Ethan?"

"Ethan?" I feel my pulse quicken. *Oh no.* "Why would you think that?"

"It's not a big deal, I was just wondering. It just seemed like you two were having a private conversation without saying anything at the party last night. But, I could be mistaken. You two don't know each other, do you?"

I'm not sure how to react. On the one hand, I want to tell her everything: the dreams, meeting him in the library, everything I've been keeping secret. But I don't know what to say. Ultimately though, she's my best friend for a reason, and she deserves to know she's not alone in being confused about life. Especially since she's always thought I've had it all together. Granted, before the dreams started, I did.

"How about we talk when we go out to eat? It's kind of a long story."

"Okay." There's curiosity in her voice that I knew would happen, eventually. I knew she had seen and read the emotions on my face last night when I was so desperate to hide them. "Well, we'll talk later. See you at four. Later, Cas." We hang up and I fall back onto my bed. I need to think about what I'm going to say. I don't think she'll judge me; she and I are too close and have been friends for too long for that. But I feel like my own thoughts are jumbled and nonsensical as it is. How do I explain what I can't make sense of? My own heart is betraying me.

I fall back onto my bed and stare at the ceiling. I'm not sure what all I want to do until Verity picks me up. Maybe go for a walk. Perhaps go read in the library. I need to clear my thoughts—and after mulling it over—I throw on some comfortable clothes, pull my hair up into a ponytail, and walk to the library.

The rain has ceased for now but the dark clouds are threatening to unleash more anytime. It doesn't bother me, walking in the rain. I love the smell of the air after the rain—it's tinged with freshness and purity; the slate is wiped clean. I need the fresh air of the walk, but I also want to lose myself in some fiction. A mind-wipe for a few hours.

I walk down the fiction aisle, going past the AUS and instead look for something a little less romantic. *Frankenstein*? No, not in the mood for gothic horror. I settle on Vonnegut's *Slaughterhouse-Five* and make my way to the same chair I sat in yesterday. The same space I shared with Ethan just a day ago. I scan the library and there isn't anyone around. Even though school is over, most likely people are still celebrating or heading to the lake for the weekend. Rain or shine. A library wouldn't be a popular summer choice when there isn't research to be done.

Vonnegut successfully takes my mind off everything that's been going on. I try to imagine what a world during war looks like. We've had peace for decades now, and government officials are more than happy to give the Trivium creators full credit for it. Each major metropolitan area has a Trivium, even third world countries have at least one. Smaller rural communities make the trek to visit it as it's required for all. Everyone is happy—or at least content. I let those thoughts go and get sucked into Vonnegut's world of time travel and war. I don't even notice when someone sits next to me.

"That is a far cry from romantic fiction." I snap out of my trance quickly and look up to see Ethan beside me. After how he acted last night, I'm not sure how to respond to him.

"I needed a break from love stories."

"Oh, really? Love got you down?" He looks at me questioningly.

"No, not really. Just not in the mood." I'm not interested in playing coy like he did, but I don't want to come off the wrong way toward him either. "Just have a lot on my mind right now. Speaking of which, why did you act like you hadn't met me last night?"

He takes a moment before replying, shifting in his seat. "I'm sorry. I honestly didn't know what to say. I saw you with your boyfriend, and I just felt awkward. I mean, I know you said you had a boyfriend and all, but I thought it might get weird if we acted like we knew each other." I can tell he's sincere but also uneasy.

"Yes, well, now Verity thinks there is something going on with you that I'm not telling her about."

"And Gunner?"

"Gunner never said anything to me. I don't think he really paid that much attention. But now I have to explain to Verity that we actually met yesterday and make it seem like I'm not hiding something. Which, I'm not. There isn't anything to it, really." I feel flustered and it makes me a little angry at myself.

"Cassia, may I ask you something?" His voice is lowered now. He's hesitant, and I'm afraid of what he'll say next. "Okay, I realize this is a weird thing to ask you since we just met, but . . . do you believe in fate?" He's visibly nervous, and he's wringing his hands and won't meet my gaze.

"I don't know?" I can't answer his question truthfully because I've been mulling that same question over and over in my thoughts without an answer. Tension is slowly forming between us, and I want so badly to pierce it. "It's possible. Maybe I do. Right now, I don't know what I think."

He takes a deep breath and exhales slowly. "Do you like hot cocoa with cinnamon?"

I freeze. My breath catches in my throat and I can't speak so I just nod.

"Well, I know it's been off and on raining today—and it's not really that cold outside—but would you want to go to the café with me and get some? I really need to talk to you, and I don't feel the library would appreciate us conversing so much." He smiles sweetly, but there's still nervousness there. Without thinking I answer "Yes," and we stand up and put our books away. I'll have to come back another day and finish. *And so it goes.*

I follow him out the door and we run to his car parked close by. The rain has begun coming down fiercely, and neither of us has an umbrella. Despite this, he opens the car door for me—ignoring just how soaked he is now getting. Minutes later we're drying off in the café, and we've already ordered some hot cocoa and cookies. He starts fidgeting in his seat, and I figure it's because he needs to get something out but not sure how to word it. I know the feeling, which is why I've stayed relatively silent. I feel like I can read him so well, considering we just met.

"So, Cassia, how was the book you were reading?"

"Pretty good. I didn't finish it," I reply, wondering why he's making small talk.

"I'll have to add another book to my reading list then." He keeps looking away and I can tell he's nervous.

"So, what did you want to talk about?" I ask him, trying to draw him out and put him at ease. I'd rather blurt everything out and get it all out in the open and be done with it. Unless what he's going to say is vastly different from what I'm wanting to say.

"Well . . ." He looks down at his mug, biting his lip. "It'll just sound crazy to you."

"You'd be surprised what I think is crazy lately." I smile and he smiles back, but he's still anxiously biting his lip.

"Okay, well. You eat at the diner, right? Several days ago, I came into the diner and met a friend and I saw you there . . . with Gunner." Not what I was thinking he'd say, but I'm kind of glad he saw me too.

"And?"

"Well, I saw you sitting there and just thought you were the most beautiful girl I'd ever seen." He takes a deep breath and exhales loudly and then goes back to looking into his mug. This is definitely not what I was thinking he'd say.

"Thank you?" I say with an eyebrow lifted and a grin on my face. Even though he wasn't mentioning any dreams, he was still flattering me. "I saw you there, too."

"Wait, you did?" He looks up at me again and sits much straighter on his seat.

"Yeah, I saw you leaving. I was getting a refill. You looked familiar when I ran into you in the library."

"I think I want to finally come clean with you. Complete honesty . . ." He trails off, leaving me wanting to complete that sentence. I don't risk it and instead stay silent. "I actually saw you in the library and I wanted to meet you, so I purposely got in your way." He laughs nervously but there's a twinkle in his eye that wasn't there before.

"Wait, you did? You really did that? I felt horrible!" I laugh with him this time, but there's also a feeling of despair creeping in because he isn't admitting to any dreams. I'm disappointed, but at the same time relieved. They were just dreams. Weird ones, but just dreams. "Did you also know I'd be at that party with Verity?"

"No. I really didn't. Which is why I thought it was such a strange coincidence. Like fate." And there is the nail in the proverbial dreamland coffin. I don't know anything about him. He only just started reading Bradbury, there is no English garden, and there is no shared home with a fireplace. My subconscious is crazy.

We continue chatting about the futures we have planned for ourselves, and it's warm and fun, and I'm not ready to leave—but I know soon Verity will be at my house, so I ask Ethan to take me home. He walks me to my door, and neither of us knows what to do. This wasn't a date. He politely tells me he'd see me later at his graduation, and maybe we can hang out more afterward. Just before he turns to walk off the porch, he reaches for me and pulls me into a very snug embrace, and I catch the slightest whiff of rain and bergamot and leather—and even as he lets go and walks back toward his car, I'm left standing in shock with no idea what to do next.

I must've been standing there awhile because Verity drives up and honks at me and I jump. I hadn't changed my clothes yet, so I motion for her to wait a second. I run inside and up to my room, grab a fresh shirt and umbrella, and then head back. I race back into the rain, heart pounding—and when I jump in and close the door, Verity is looking at me with big eyes and an excited expression.

"What were you doing outside? Even better question, I could swear I passed Ethan on my way here!"

"You probably did. We ran into each other at the library and he offered to drive me home." She isn't putting the car in reverse to back out and leave, which tells me she wants more information than I gave her. "It was nothing! He's just a nice guy." She flashes a toothy grin my direction and we drive off.

"Okay, Cas. Spill. What is going on with you two? And don't say 'nothing,' and don't tell me you just met because I don't believe it."

I hesitate on how much I really want to reveal. Since Ethan doesn't know about the dreams, I'm not sure I want to talk about them.

"We actually met yesterday in the library. I ran into him and we talked for a bit. He just felt awkward at the party being the fifth wheel."

"And?" She glances at me, eyebrow raised. "That's it?"

"Well, yeah. I mean, that's how I met him. Turns out that he had seen Gunner and me in the diner the other day and thought I was pretty, so he orchestrated running into me in the library. He's a nice guy, but that's the story." It's the truth, although it's also omitting quite a few details.

"So, he likes you, huh? He's pretty cute, too. Not in the same chiseled perfection sort of way like Gunner, but *definitely* in a very broody, romantic sort of way." She flashes a cheesy grin.

"Yeah well, he's really sweet and easy to talk to. Pretty witty. Not that it matters. I mean, we're wanting to go to different schools next year. We are definitely not on the same path."

"And you have a boyfriend."

"Yeah, and that."

"I know this sounds like a weird question, with your life all mapped out and everything and you're like, one hundred percent sure the Trivium will agree, but have you considered going to college upstate with me? We could be roommates!"

I wasn't expecting that from her. "I have actually, but you know there isn't a medical track there. I'm not sure what career I would even be suited for if I'm not supposed to be a doctor."

"I know, I was just thinking how much fun we'd have, and how much I'm going to miss you." I don't even want to think about not seeing her every day right now. Having a relationship relegated to phone calls and video chats, and maybe the occasional free weekend. It's not what I pictured when we were younger, living apart. "Although, you'd be great at anything you know. Maybe even writing. You did win an English award. And you *love* reading."

"Be a writer like Ethan? I mean, I can string sentences together, but I'm not sure I have the talent to tell stories. I'm more analytical. I think that's scarier than being a doctor." Verity giggles. "Have you thought about staying here?" I know the answer is no but I ask anyway.

"I did. One time. I know it'd help my dad out, and I'd be around for my brother more, but there isn't fashion design here, and at some point, I need to live my life. Or at least, whichever life I end up choosing. So, you never know, maybe things for each of us will change in a week or so."

She's right about that. Depending on what the Trivium shows us, things could change dramatically. I've never reacted well to spontaneity, and I think that's why I've been so rigid about knowing what I'll see and which choice I'll make.

We get to the convention center, and we cheer for both Jason and Ethan when they cross the stage. After it's over, we head down to the floor and catch up with Jason and his family—but Ethan isn't around anywhere that I can see. I was curious what his family would look like, or if he had a brother or sister. Those are things he never mentioned, and honestly, we didn't have much time to talk about it. Jason notices me looking around, and clues me in that Ethan and his family left as soon as it was over. I'm caught off guard that he knows I was looking for him. Did Ethan say something about me? I wonder if they talk like Verity and I do. I don't know how much boys share with their friends. I feel a little self-conscious wondering what he may have said. I'm gutted with the information and instantly want to go home, but I'm here for Verity and Jason, and technically stuck here till they're ready to leave. Ethan mentioned a party, so my hopes are lifted once I realize I'll still see him. I just feel sad that I couldn't see his parents.

We head to the party at some friend of Jason's, and I'm surrounded by people I don't know. It was bad enough at our party last night where I knew people and still felt out of place—let alone going to a party where I'm basically by myself and knowing no one. Verity and Jason do their best to introduce me to some more of his friends and keep me included in their conversation, but I'm thinking about calling Gunner and finding a ride home.

"Fancy meeting you again." I turn toward the voice, not even trying to conceal my excitement.

"Ethan! Hey!"

"Sorry I didn't see you earlier, at graduation."

"Jason said you left early. Everything okay?"

"Oh yeah, just my family needed to get home. They had set up a surprise for me there. I know I just got here and all, but do you want to get out of here? I'm honestly not into parties. They're loud." My heart skips a beat.

"I'm not a party person either. What did you have in mind?"

"Well, my family has a cabin at the lake—not that far from here. It's nice and quiet, and the perfect place to get out of the rain. I mean, if you'd want to do that. I know we barely know each other, but I promise I don't bite. And I'm a perfect gentleman." He winks at me and displays that wry, charming smile of his.

"You sure about that?" The idea makes me nervous, but I know local restaurants will be closing, and there isn't much to do around town after dark. "I have to be home before midnight. Is that okay?"

"Absolutely. To both. Maybe even have you back early so it looks good on me."

"Trying to get in good with my family already? You just met me." I cock my head to the side and he laughs, his face flushing a little.

"You just never know what path life takes you on. May as well make sure everything is perfect as you go."

We tell Verity and Jason goodbye, and I make sure to tell her where we're going. She raises her eyebrow at me, and I reassure her it means nothing and to check in at my house later. I want to make sure we both are home and safe. Ethan holds the door open for me again and then slides in on the driver's side. There's classical music streaming from the speakers, and he explains that he listens to it when he needs help to sort out his thoughts. We make small talk about our families, friends, and hobbies, and next thing I know we're at the cabin. It's not as secluded as I pictured—as there are some other cabins nearby—and the lights are on outside. He heads inside first to turn all the lights on and start a fire in the fireplace, and when I walk in my heart feels like it stops beating. That fireplace. That couch. I know this entire place even though I'd only dreamt about one room. I didn't realize I had frozen in place until Ethan asks me if I'm okay. I take a deep breath before walking forward and seating myself on the rocking chair next to the fireplace. I don't think I can handle sitting down on the couch.

"Do you want something to drink? Hot cocoa with cinnamon perhaps?"

"No, water is fine." I can't fathom recreating my dream in the present. He comes back with a bottle of water and hands it to me and then plops on the couch like I knew he would.

"You sure you're okay?" I don't know how to answer that. No, I'm not. I'm far from okay, but I can't him tell why.

"I'm fine. Really."

"That's your second use of fine in two sentences. Pretty sure at this point you need to look up some synonyms to replace it with."

"Yeah, okay funny guy. I'm great. Cool. Okay. Fantastic. Wonderful. Excellent."

"I didn't realize you were a walking thesaurus." He shakes his head and disappears back into the kitchen, returning with a mug topped with whipped cream. It looks delicious, but I can't imagine having any right now. Everything is surreal.

"So, Miss Fine, you looked like you saw a ghost when you walked in."

"Is this place known to be haunted? Maybe I did."

"No, not that I know of. Unless there are ghosts of ideas and dreams long forgotten."

"What does that even mean?"

"Oh, you know, I come here a lot to think. Sometimes I get an idea for a book or something and it doesn't always pan out. I haven't had a story stick, yet."

"What kinds of things do you write about?"

"You mean what kinds of ideas came here to die and haunt me forever?"

"Yes. Exactly."

He takes a moment before replying and I sense the hesitation. He takes a few more sips of his cocoa and then his whole body seems to relax as the warmth hits him.

"Love. Loss. Living in a different world at a different time in history. What that would look like. What life was like before we were given choices and what it must've felt like not knowing the future. Those kinds of things."

I shiver a little and Ethan notices and grabs a throw from the couch and wraps it around me. It's not the same throw from my dream—thank goodness—or else I may have fainted. "I've wondered about those things myself. But I've never even tried to write anything that wasn't needed for school. I don't know how hard it must be. You know, to sit at your typewriter and bleed." He smiles at my reference.

"Well, it's like spilling your soul and sealing your fate in ink."

"That's awful poetic of you, Mr. Ethan." He senses the sarcasm and responds in turn.

"It's true! There's a vulnerability to writing what your heart thinks."

"Oh, I can imagine. I haven't even written in a diary. For you though, the hard work must be worth it." "Oh, fair Miss Cassia, truer words have never been spoken. I'm a tortured artist and must remain so for the greater good of my work." Now we're both laughing. "So how about you? Are you set in stone on what you want your life to look like?" I feel his eyes on me and there's a sentiment of hope tied to that statement.

"I don't know anymore. I thought so. I thought I knew exactly what I wanted and where I wanted to be, but lately things keep making me wonder if I've been wrong all along . . ." I trail off and realize that's the first time I've said those thoughts out loud. I expected a weight to be lifted, but I was wrong. It's still there, pressing in on me slightly.

"Well, you know I told you I thought I had everything planned out until a few months ago, but I never told you why."

"No, you didn't. What happened?" He hesitates.

"It's hard to say. Something just didn't feel right anymore." There's something he's not telling me—his eyes say it all—but I don't expect him to. I know it's not a dream that caused the change, and it's not me that made him feel that way. I think that somehow makes me feel better, like I didn't have a hand in affecting him like he has me.

"Maybe everyone goes through that once they get closer to sealing their fate," I say.

"Maybe. Wouldn't be able to find out since no one remembers any details."

"I know! My mom wasn't much help either. I even tried scouring the library for research books on the subject to no avail."

"You did?" There's subtle teasing behind those words.

"Yes, of course, I did. I research everything."

"Did you research me?" My breath catches in my throat. Technically, I tried to look him up but didn't have any luck with that either.

"The only things I know about you are what you've told me." *How's that for truth?* "Did you look me up?" He looks directly into my eyes.

"Yes. I did. Or, tried to. Would you believe there are more than one Cassia in this town?" His cheeks turn a little pink.

"No, I didn't." He looks past me at the clock on the wall.

"It's getting pretty late already. Not ready to say goodnight, but I still have to look good for your parents." He helps me up and puts the fire out, and I fold the throw and place it back on the couch where it belongs. We drive back to my house, and there's a stillness in the air that permeates through the music. I'm happy and content, and not ready for the night to be over. As Ethan walks me to the door, the nervous feelings hit my stomach hard. It would be very inappropriate for a goodnight kiss, and I don't know how I feel about him as it is. He hugs me firmly, then pulls away and grabs my hand to kiss it. I feel my cheeks grow hot, and I'm thankful the light from the porch is too dim for him to notice.

"Goodnight, fair lady. Parting is such sweet sorrow. Until another day, perhaps?"

"I guess we'll just have to wait and see." Smiling, I back slowly away and walk up the steps and head inside. No one is downstairs, and it's dark and quiet. Odd. I was sure my mom or dad would have waited up for me. What a strange disappointment. As I walk into my bedroom, I hear my cell ringing. Perfect timing, Verity. She sounds both excited and sleepy, and she fills me in on everything that happened during the party and afterward. Jason introduced her to several people that will be going to the arts college, and even a couple of other fashion design majors. I haven't heard her talk so happily about future career prospects before. It's nice to hear her looking forward to something—rather than jumping around on ideas. My heart aches at the thought of losing her. I know she won't ever be gone from my life—and I've worked through these thoughts before—but her describing all the new people she met and the things they have in common that we don't pains me a little. She's going to leave here and start a new life and be a new person while I'm still in this town doing what I always had planned to do. It doesn't sound as appealing as it had before. While I crave stability, the last couple of days with Ethan has made me realize I also hunger for adventure. There is an internal struggle taking root within my mind and heart that leaves my body a battleground. What was once a given has turned into just a possibility. But is it? Am I strong enough to really make a choice? When push comes to shove, am I brave enough to pursue adventure? Or will I settle for what's comfortable? Can't I have both? An exciting life filled with love and passion and fulfillment?

The conversation turns in my direction, and Verity wants all the details of my time at the cabin with Ethan. Other than sitting in a chair by the fire and him drinking hot cocoa, there wasn't much to talk about. It wasn't like there were any juicy bits, and there wasn't anything romantic involved. Until that kiss on my hand, anyway. I fail to mention that detail. The lack of gossip loses her interest quickly, and I'm grateful because I'm tired and ready to get some rest. Tonight is the first time in a long time that I hope I don't dream. I don't want to live in a dreamlike world where my relationship with Ethan is much more involved. Now that I'm getting to know him in person, finding things out about him in a dream seems like cheating and wrong somehow. And only serves to further confuse me. My brain has been overloaded as it is, I need some simplicity infused back in. I lie down and stretch myself out and quickly doze off.

CHAPTER SIX

The past week has gone by so quickly that it feels like a blur. The dreams have since ceased and I'm grateful, as I no longer want any part of them. They're like an old friend I've moved on from, and details are getting a little fuzzy. I broke down and bought a journal and wrote everything I remember from the dreams, but I haven't cared to reread them. I've seen Ethan a couple of times when he was with Jason and I was with Verity, but we haven't spent any other time alone. There were occasions where I felt like I knew everything about him, and then almost like he was a stranger I was learning to unpack. He's let me through some of his walls, but I've decided to keep my distance from him emotionally. It only makes it harder for me to consider my feelings—and right now I don't want the complications. I've spent most of my time with Gunner and his friends, and we've fallen back into our relationship routine of predictability. Gunner is the least complicated person in my life, and right now that's what I need. I know that I care a lot about him—that hasn't changed. It's very easy to go back to him and know where my life is headed. Even if it isn't the right path for me.

Verity heads to the Trivium tomorrow, and I'm anxious for her. I want to know all about the experience, but of course, that won't be possible. She's spending her last day hanging out with Jason and going to an art gallery installation. I'm riding with her tomorrow to the building downtown that houses the Trivium for moral support, but she doesn't want me to wait afterward since her dad wants to pick her up. Gunner and I agree to see a movie and go out to eat. I imagine that being our typical date night, and the thought doesn't bother me—it's kind of nice. The want of adventure has died down somewhat, or else the embers are going cold without Ethan being there to fan the flames. I'm trying to focus on the upcoming college year and accumulating the supplies I might need. It gives me something to do even though I have until August to get things together. I should be spending my summer swimming and on a boat at the lake like everyone else my age— instead of in the library with the occasional date days.

I'm surprised when Gunner passes the restaurant we usually go to and heads in another direction. Where we're going is in the direction of the lake, not town.

"Where are we going?" I ask.

"To eat."

"Okay, but you passed the restaurant."

"We're not going to a restaurant." I see a smirk forming on the corner of his mouth. "Look, I know you don't like surprises, but you'll just have to wait and see."

I roll my eyes at him, but he's paying attention to the road and doesn't see me. We pull up to a camping area where there are multiple picnic tables, and he leads me to a tent at a campsite near the shore.

"Wait right here. Close your eyes."

Warily, I obey. It's not like to him to do something like this. Neither of us can be accused of spontaneity.

"Okay, now open them!" I open my eyes slowly, and before me, the tent flaps have been opened and pulled back. Inside there is a picnic basket on a large blanket with plates and cups already set out.

"Wow, Gunner. I think I'm speechless!"

"I know it's not the usual thing, but I thought since tomorrow was the first day one of us makes a choice for our future—and I know how worried you must be for Verity—I just thought a surprise was in order."

The thoughtfulness blindsides me, but in a good way. It's so unexpected and sweet. He leads me inside and we sit across from each other with legs crossed. He opens the basket, and I see he's packed an entire lunch consisting of sandwiches, fruit, and my favorite pastries from the café.

"I know I didn't technically make everything here, I ordered it from various places, but—" I cut him off as I lean over the basket and kiss him softly on the lips. "Well, I take it you like the idea." He beams at me.

"This is a sweet thing to do, I had no idea. It's just—wow. This is truly great, Gunner."

He serves the food onto the plates, gets out a couple bottles of water, and hands me one. He lifts his bottle up in the air in a mock toast of celebration.

"What are we celebrating exactly?" I ask him.

"To Verity: that she will choose correctly and love her life. And to you, that you will choose wisely next week. Which—if a choice includes me—you can't go wrong." He winks at me. "And to me, who knows what he wants from this life and is intent on loving every single second of it."

"Well, hear, hear!" We fake clink our plastic bottles and take a sip. Everything tastes delicious and the sound of the waves hitting the shore is relaxing. In the distance, I hear the hum of boats passing by on the lake. This is a pleasant surprise—I didn't know he had it in him to come up with such a romantic gesture. We leave the tent and hold hands as we walk along the beach. We're not talking, but it's nice to be together and listen to the sounds all around us—while enjoying the feeling of sand beneath our feet. I picture this life with him. It's easy. It's uncomplicated. I have a fondness for Gunner that I've never had with anyone else. I don't get nervous butterfly feelings around him—no pain in my gut or ache in my heart—and there's a sense of contentment. Maybe I don't need excitement in my life. Maybe I just need him.

I don't know where we parked when we came in, and I've lost track of where we're walking to. Neither of us comes out here enough to know the lake shoreline well, but we can always turn back and head the way we came. Before I know it, we're stumbling upon some quaint cabins in a secluded area and it hits me: one of those cabins is Ethan's. And then I spot it. I have been trying to keep Ethan off my mind, and for the most part, I've succeeded. Part of the reason I had stopped spending time with him was because I couldn't handle the thought that I was feeling something. It's not the same way I feel about Gunner. It's new and exciting, but painful and confusing. I don't care much for continuing to deal with those tumultuous emotions. I don't want to hurt Gunner either. I can't imagine how he'd feel if he knew how Ethan affects me.

We continue following the shoreline, and as I casually glance at Ethan's cabin, the memory of the fire gets mixed in with the dream. I catch myself wondering if he's there. I never saw the back side of the cabin, but I faintly see something white blowing in the wind. The closer we get the more the white thing is turning into the shape of a hammock, and my breath catches. It was easier believing that everything in the dream—except for Ethan himself—was imagined rather than real. I reach back behind my neck and rub the chip. I wonder if it's reading all these thoughts I'm having. Perhaps there's more to this chip than I ever thought before. Maybe it's malfunctioning. Mine could be the one chip with a huge glitch that somehow allows me to see another world where I'm with Ethan and we're in love. If that's possible. So, the hammock is real. I check that off my list of crazy things I've experienced in the past couple of months. I wonder if the gazebo is real, too. It's possible the gazebo is also near the cabin—even though I don't remember seeing a garden. Of course, it was also dark and rainy the night I came here. My thoughts are interrupted by that familiar voice that continually haunts me, no matter where I go.

"Cassia! Gunner! What are you guys doing here?" Ethan is sauntering up to us dressed in rumpled jeans and a white tee that's just tight enough to see a little muscle definition beneath it. I need to stop thinking about that.

"We were having a picnic lunch further down and decided on a walk. How are you?" Gunner is the epitome of politeness, but with an undercurrent of something malicious. He isn't normally like that. *Does he sense something about Ethan and me?* He has no idea how well I've gotten to know Ethan. *Is he angry or jealous?*

"I'm up here checking on my family's cabin. I figured it was a good day to get away for awhile." He glances at me, but I avert my eyes quickly. I feel awkward and not sure what to say. I want to ask if he has a garden, but that would be weird and I don't want to explain the curiosity. "Would you two want to come in and get something to drink?"

Gunner replies "sure" at the same time I reply, "no thanks," and they both look at me strangely. "I don't want to inconvenience you," I say, but Ethan doesn't seem convinced.

We follow him on the nicely kept path up to the cabin and go through the back door. I ask where the bathroom is—and as I'm walking down the hall—I hear both boys chatting about the lake, baseball, and college. I take my time perusing the photographs lining the walls of the hallway. Ethan when he was a baby, with his shock of dark hair and large eyes twinkling. A woman who must be Ethan's mother many years ago—sharing the same dark hair and smile—holding hands with a man that must be Ethan's father.

He's handsome and vibrant, and I see the similarities he shares with his son in his expression. There are wedding photos and various family pictures taken over the past eighteen years. Ethan playing soccer. Ethan holding a trophy for a spelling bee. It's only a small glimpse into his childhood and I yearn to find out more, but the pictures cease and the bathroom door is in front of me. When done, I walk back quickly and join them at the table in the kitchen. There's a bottle of water awaiting me, so I take it gladly and sit down. They're still talking about guy stuff, and I don't have anything to say about their chosen topics. I'm caught here between these two guys that I care about, and yet I feel like I'm intruding on their conversation. I would rather go exploring again, but that seems like inappropriate behavior.

"Cassia, you feeling okay? You're being fairly quiet, which is unusual." Gunner startles me. I hadn't been paying attention to them anymore. Sports to me is boring.

"Yes, I'm fine. I just don't have anything to interject into this manly conversation." Ethan suppresses a laugh and Gunner just smiles at me. "I'm getting kind of tired though, and I have to get up early tomorrow to get Verity. Gunner, think you're ready to walk back? It could take a while."

"Wait, *you're* driving? How?" Gunner looks surprised and laughs.

"I know *how* to drive, I've had my license since the day I qualified for it. Just because my parents can't afford to buy me wheels yet doesn't mean I'm not capable." I glare at him. "I'm borrowing my mom's car for the day. Which means I have to take her to work, get Verity, then come back later and get my mom."

Gunner raises his eyebrows. "Touchy, touchy." I continue glaring. Ethan clears his throat to break the silence.

"I have my car. Want me to drive you both back to the campsite?" Ethan is looking at me with an eyebrow raised. "It's no trouble, really."

Gunner is more than happy to avoid the long walk back and inevitable argument, so we pile into Ethan's car. We arrive at the campsite, and I walk to the driver side to say goodbye—catching him eyeing the tent suspiciously. He won't even look at me as if he's mad at me for something I'm not aware of. Ethan rolls his car window down and Gunner comes to join me, wrapping his arm around my waist. I move his hand away. I don't want him near me right now.

"It was good to see you again, Gunner. Cassia, a pleasure." He smiles insincerely and then drives off without another glance. We pack up the remains of our lunch as the sun is setting on the horizon. The sky becomes a sea of pink and purple flames, and we get everything back into the truck just in time before dark. The ride back to my house is quiet, and my mind is empty and free of thought. I watch the passing scenery out the passenger window with mild interest and revel in the silence. We say goodnight as we always do even though we didn't speak since we left Ethan's. This time my parents are sitting on the couch as I walk in.

"Hey honey, how was your day?" My mom is cuddled next to my dad on the couch, looking sleepy.

"It was okay."

"Are you ready for tomorrow?"

"Well, yeah. I mean, it's not me going."

"No, but it's a big deal. She's the first of the two of you to go. It's understandable to be nervous for her—since you don't know what all goes on—but I promise you she'll come out happy and things will go back to normal."

"I certainly hope so. I better get to bed." I give them both hugs and head upstairs. I'm barely under my covers and comfortable on my pillow before I drift off.

Morning comes before I'm ready for it. I'm groggy and I want to punch my alarm for going off so early on a summer day. My mom is already downstairs cooking breakfast, and the smell of bacon pervades the kitchen. We eat quickly and take off toward my mom's office. The entire car ride conversation is all about college and Verity—and it's a shallow attempt at small talk—but my mom is successful in keeping my mind off everything. Of course, it only lasts until she exits the car and walks into the office building, and then anxious thoughts creep back in. It's a short drive to Verity's house from here, and she's dressed up and waiting on her front porch when I arrive. The required clothing consists of a swim suit, swim cap, and sandals, but you can wear whatever you want over them. You're only allowed a small bag with necessities— and hers is slung over her shoulder. I expected nothing less than her looking fabulous even though it's not required.

"It feels a little weird that you're the one driving," she teases.

"Yeah, yeah, get in funny lady. I haven't had enough coffee for jokes."

"We have some time to stop and get some if you want to."

"Maybe later? When you're done? Think you'll be up for that?"

"Maybe. I honestly don't know. I wonder if I'll be a different person when it's over."

"I don't think it works that way."

"Yeah, probably not. Hope not anyway. I'll call you when I have my bearings. I think the recovery takes a little while. Or maybe you just get really sleepy and pass out for several hours."

"Sounds about right. At least from what I've heard. Are you ready?" She hesitates before responding.

"Yes. I've officially relinquished my fears and let go, and I'm ready to embrace whatever life is laid before me."

"You're quoting the Trivium pamphlet."

"I am but it's true." She giggles and any tension I was holding onto has gone away for now. "I'm not scared anymore, Cas. The past couple of weeks with Jason has showed me that anything can happen, and I should stop fighting destiny and go with it. I'm at peace." She sits back in the seat and stretches her legs out before her. "The passenger seat has its benefits."

"I need my own car. I would've thought I'd get one for graduation. Maybe since I'm staying local, they decided it wasn't necessary."

"Maybe they're trying to keep you trapped here."

"It's possible since dad expects me to take over the business one day."

"Is that what you want? To work with your dad? I know you want to be a doctor and all, but is staying here really and truly what you would choose?"

"I think so. I don't know. I guess I'll find out soon. Maybe when you get a chance to choose, you just know what's right."

"Just make sure that whatever you choose is for you and no one else."

We arrive at the Trivium drop-off lane and Verity looks peaceful—and perhaps a little excited.

"I love you, Verity. Please call me and tell me everything, okay?"

"Love you too, Cas. And I promise I will. Once I'm awake." She smiles and gets out of the car. "Don't worry about me. I'll be fine. Honest." She shuts the door, and I wait and watch her walk into the building. I don't know why, but my stomach aches. Must be nerves. If I hurt this badly and it's not even me walking into that building yet, I wonder how bad it will be when it's my turn.

I don't have anything else planned today, so I go back home. I'd rather sit in my room reading or sleeping, waiting on Verity to call, rather than chance missing her. It's nice to lay on my bed with nothing to do, nowhere to go until it's time to get my mom from work. The early rising takes its toll on me, and I swiftly drift off into a nap. I hear the cell ringing and it startles me, and I realize I've been out several hours. I was more tired than I thought.

"Hello?" I answer groggily.

"Cas, you ok?" It's Verity, and she sounds weary.

"Yes, yes, sorry, I was asleep. How are you?"

There's a slight pause, and the silence is confusing.

"I'm good actually. A little tired. I slept for a bit after I got home, but I'm okay now. It was fine, Cas. Nothing like I expected, but the crazy thing is I can't really remember the details."

"Oh, really?" Disappointment sets in. I had hoped she'd remember something, anything, about what happened there.

"I know, I know, I'm not going to be much help. But I can tell you there's nothing to be afraid of. There was a tank, a large one, and you float in it. I started to get a little groggy—I think they give you a pill to knock you out—but I do remember feeling like I was on air. Like I weighed nothing, and the world melted away and it was just me there—watching my life like it was a movie at the theater. I can't recall all of it though. I thought I'd remember more, maybe it was the medicine or something, but there's no chip anymore! It feels weird!"

"So, do you know what you chose?"

"I chose him, Cassia. I chose Jason. That much for sure, I know. He was there! He was in my future! And we looked happy, and we were creative, and I know I'll finish design school. I don't know all the details—they're fuzzy—but I know I chose him and I can't believe he was there!" Her excitement is apparent and I'm so happy for her. She gets a happy ending. We all do—if we're to believe the Trivium pamphlets—but to hear her talk about it with such enthusiasm is exciting. Maybe it's not such a hard choice after all.

"I'm so, so happy for you, Verity! I don't even know what to say."

"It's a huge relief to know that someone was in my future, and I'm doing something I love and with someone I love. I honestly didn't know anything like that was possible for me. It's so freeing, not feeling that chip in my neck anymore. Weird, but in a good way. Anyway, there wasn't anything to fear and I can't wait to tell Jason how I really feel about him. I can't believe I'm saying that! Me!" She starts laughing joyfully, and I'm so ecstatic that she feels this way that I join in too. I love hearing her sound so happy. I can't wait to feel that way. Soon, I tell myself.

We finish our conversation and hang up so she can get more rest. She's wanted to call Jason and plan a date or something, and it's fine because I have a lot to mull over like normal. If Verity can make many different choices in her life and ultimately find happiness, surely someone like myself that's been diligent in my choices can do the same thing. I look at the clock and notice my time alone is up. I leave to go get my mom and relay to her the happiness of Verity's call. Not that she's surprised by this revelation, as she's told me before everyone gets their happy ending—or something like that. Even still, she seems delighted that Verity has a great future ahead of her.

"You'll be acting the same way next week after you go. I just know it." She smiles at me and I try my best to put a return smile on my face though I'm hoping she's right. I only have days before I'll know what goes on, and then afterward I'm sure I won't know anything.

That night I lie on my bed wishing I had checked out *Slaughterhouse-Five* so I'd have something to read and zone out to. I'd like to get lost in someone else's world right about now. I scan my bookshelf to see if there's a book on there I haven't read a while No such luck. Instead, I grab a pen and a notebook and sit down on my bed and decide to make up my own story. It's a foreign concept to me to write instead of read. To decide what happens and who it happens to. I think about a girl who must make choices in life and what she would choose, and without even thinking, I put the pen to paper. After a while, I start yawning, and I realize how late it is. I had successfully zoned out into my own world for a couple of hours, and I'm just now realizing how much my hand is cramping up. I look down and notice I've written several pages. Amazing. I never thought I had something like that in me before, but it's exhilarating—and Ethan was right, it makes you vulnerable. There's freedom in letting go and seeing where the path takes you. If I don't feel like that in my real life, I can at least feel that through my characters. Maybe I should spend time writing more often, it will make a good outlet for my thoughts. Having safely deposited the notebook in the drawer on my nightstand, I stop fighting sleep and close my eyes.

I know within a second that I'm dreaming. There I am, curled up in a comfortable chair in a living room that is unfamiliar to me, and on my lap is a notebook. I'm writing. I glance around the room and I'm alone. There isn't much to look at except artwork on the walls, and none of it strikes a chord with me. Strange. My mood is serious, and I'm furiously scribbling with the pen as I let the ink bleed out from me. There's an emotional release that I feel coming on; it's invigorating and full of immense joy. I can't believe I have so much passion for writing. It's weird and new, but . . . nice. I look down to read what I've been writing, and before I make sense of the title, I wake up.

What horrible timing my dreams have. It's aggravating. I'm sure I only dreamed about writing because that's what I was doing before falling asleep, but the feelings I had were real. I feel a twinge of jealousy that Ethan gets to go to college and read literature and not scientific journals. It sounds heavenly. Still, ever since I was little, I liked to help my dad with bandages and watch him while he helped heal people. It's an admirable calling. Not sure I feel as thrilled handling his surgical instruments as I did that pen, but it's still my plan. I don't know if I can pull off the writing thing. For all I know, I'd be horrible.

I lazily get dressed and pull my hair back. I have no plans whatsoever today and it's freeing. It's nice outside, and the slight breeze keeps it from being too hot. I'd rather avoid the library, so I walk toward the park instead. The park is near a pond, and kids are swinging on the swing set and running around while their parents keep close nearby. I walk to the area near the pond where there are benches, and I sit and take in the birds and the surrounding sounds. Ducks are gliding on the surface of the water, creating tiny ripples, and I'm reminded of the butterfly effect and the theories on causation. If it's true that one small decision can ripple throughout your life and create different effects, I wonder how the Trivium takes that into account. I imagine a string following me everywhere I go, until there's a fork in a road, and it splits into two. A hologram version of me runs down one path with a string following behind while another string stays with the real me down the second the path. What would it look like to go down either road? That's something no one ever gets the chance to know. Not even us, this generation that knows so much about the future that we see three of those strings and follow them into infinity. I think back to the worlds of the books I've read and what it would've been like had Elizabeth Bennet known she would end up happy with Darcy. Perhaps there wouldn't have been as much drama and fighting. But without pride, there's no prejudice. And no story. I don't pay attention to contemporary fiction, I've always been infatuated with the classics, but I wonder how many of them have a lack of drama. If you don't know the pain and the hurt that goes with a lost love, or the loss of what you thought was love, how can you write about it? Fake it, I guess.

"Good morning. Interesting to run into you here. It's like the fates are toying with us." Ethan is dressed in khaki slacks and a polo, something I've never seen him wear. He walks up to me and joins me on the bench.

"I'm sorry, do I know you?" I reply, eyebrow raised.

"Oh, you cut me, right to my heart, fair lady. It is I, Mr. Darcy. The one and only." He clutches his hand over to his heart like I've wounded him physically. Who needs drama when you can have the dramatic?

"Oh, I don't think so, imposter. What have you done with the real Ethan? The Ethan I know would never dress like he's headed to play tennis at the country club." He cracks up laughing and looks down at what he's wearing and back up to me.

"Had to take family portraits. Not my idea. Although, I don't think it's that bad of a look."

"No, I guess not. Just not used to it." He jabs me in the shoulder playfully which makes me laugh. "What brings you to the park today? Or did you orchestrate this meeting as well?"

"No, no. That was a onetime thing. I'm here purely by coincidence. We just took pictures over by the gazebo. I decided to go for a walk."

I look around and don't see anyone resembling his family. That's disappointing.

"So where are they now?" I try to hide my curiosity.

"They took off. My little sister had piano practice. I told them I'd walk home or call a friend if I needed them. I didn't have plans today. And you?"

"You have a sister?" I flash back to various conversations, but I don't remember him mentioning her.

"Yeah, Hannah. She's ten. Have I not talked about her before?"

"I don't think so."

"Ah. Odd. I love that little kid. So, what are you doing here, or who are you escaping from?" It occurs to me that no family member is ever mentioned in my dreams, and he doesn't talk about his family when we're together. It stirs up more curiosity as to what they're like. Not that it matters. I don't need to know them. I barely know Gunner's family and we've been together quite some time. Thinking about it starts to bother me. I should probably know what family I'll be marrying into.

"I'm just here thinking. I didn't have anything to do today. Thought I'd go for a walk. So, have you heard from Jason?" I'm anxious to know what Jason's response to Verity choosing him was, but I was afraid to ask her directly.

"Yeah, late last night. Why?"

"Just wondering if he'd talked to Verity."

"Oh. Isn't she your best friend? You didn't just ask her?"

"I know it sounds weird, but I was afraid to ask her just in case things didn't go well."

"If by her telling him her feelings is what you're after, he's thrilled. He's been pretty stuck on her since they met."

"Oh good. Great." So, it worked out. Everything with them is going to be okay. I exhale a little too loudly.

"Were you that worried about her?" He has concern written all over his face. "Did you not think everything would go okay for her?"

"I had hoped so. I worry. It's less of a reflection on how I view her as a person, and more so my own shortcomings."

"You really are worried about choosing, aren't you? I thought you had it all planned out." His mouth is smiling but his eyes aren't.

"I'm out here thinking because it's all I can do anymore, and the more I think the worse it gets. I see these ripples on the water and I think things will be fine, but I also know if I choose wrong that those ripples will have lasting and possibly damaging effects to other people I care about—let alone what it would do to me." I sigh. "I wrote a story last night." There. I confessed.

"You wrote a story? About what?" He leans closer to me.

"Just about a girl making choices. It was weird of me to do, but I didn't have anything to read, and my mind was going nuts so I wrote. I thought it would help me relax."

"And?" he asks.

"It worked," I reply. He sits back against the bench and puts his hands behind his head with one leg crossed on top of the other. We say nothing to each other for a few minutes, but there's no rush to break the silence.

"Have you thought of actually becoming a writer?" He is still facing the pond and I can't see the emotions on his face, but I feel like this is a double-edged question.

"No. Not really. I'm probably awful."

"So, you are for sure stuck on being a doctor?"

"For right now, yes." This time the silence is deafening. He sits forward again, elbows on his knees with his head in his hands. Without thinking, I reach over and gently rub his back.

"Are you okay?" I ask. He nods, but he doesn't sit back up. I continue lightly stroking his back as if it's a completely natural thing for me to do. I feel his muscles through his shirt and the definition of his shoulders. For a writer, he's in great shape. I feel guilty for focusing on that. He *did* play soccer as a kid. Maybe he still does. I've never asked. Finally, he sits back up and I drop my hand, only for him to grab it and put my hand in his. I feel my pulse like a steady ticking clock coursing through my veins, and it's so loud in my mind that I'm fearful he'll feel it too.

"I get headaches sometimes. It's not serious, but it takes a minute to get over. Sorry to scare you, Cassia." He looks concerned for me, but I find that funny because he's the one that was just in pain.

"Headaches? Like migraines?" I ask.

"Somewhat, yeah. They're rare, but occasionally, I get caught off guard." He's still holding my hand, and I have no idea what to do. Do I take it away? Do I want to take it away? He looks down at my hand, and I can tell he's feeling better as his shoulders are no longer slumped as they were before. "Cassia, I know we haven't known each other that long. And I know you have your life planned out and you want to marry Gunner. Which, I get that, he's . . . something. I'm not sure anyone could compete with him. But have you ever wondered if there is a life out there you would rather live, one that doesn't include plans—or Gunner—would you honestly consider it?" He keeps staring down at his lap, refusing to meet my gaze.

"I don't know," I answer quietly. I have no idea how to formulate everything that's been going on in my mind the past few weeks into something reasonable. "Ethan, you don't even know me." Probably not the best response. This time, he looks up and stares directly into my eyes.

"Don't I though? Don't you *know* me?" His eyes are pleading for the truth, and I so want to confess it. Why is it so hard for me to be honest with myself and him?

"Yes. No. Maybe? Ethan, I'm not sure what you're getting at. We only met a few months ago . . ." He looks at me with a shocked expression, and I at once recognize my slip. "Weeks. Weeks ago." I pull my hand away quickly and start to stand. "I really should go." He stands up and grabs my hand again.

"So, it's true? It's all real? You dream about me?"

"Ethan, I can't do this now, I really need to go." I take my hand back and walk away abruptly, fighting back tears because he admitted that I wasn't alone in my dreams. They were real. I can't process any of this discovery and what the implications are. I hear his footsteps behind me, and then I'm being jerked back around—his hand on my shoulder. And before I can say another word in protest, he's embracing me fully—his right hand behind my head pulling me in closer. I don't object. There's a wild look in his eyes that I glimpse before his lips are pressed on mine, and I feel like the world is melting away in a soft blur. Nothing else exists except for us. I am keenly aware of the softness of his lips and the smells of a woody cologne. For the time being, I forget who we are and where we are, and I eagerly kiss him back. It feels like hours have gone by, though it is only mere minutes, before we part—both of us breathless. The park comes back into focus, and reality rushes back in so quickly I feel like fainting. Something inside me aches fiercely to grab him and kiss him again, but I know I must resist. My head tries to regain control of the rest of me, and the confusion of the situation creeps back in.

"Cassia, we need to talk about this." He's not smiling although his eyes are still on fire.

"Not right now, Ethan. I can't think straight. I need to go." This time he doesn't stop me as I walk away. I don't turn back.

CHAPTER SEVEN

"The oldest and strongest emotion of mankind is fear, and the oldest and strongest kind of fear is fear of the unknown."
—H. P. Lovecraft

I keep a hurried pace as I walk home, go straight upstairs to my room, and close the door. Throwing myself on the bed, I grab a pillow, bury my face in it, and scream. No longer fighting the emotions I've been repressing, I let go—and the release is a tidal wave of sobs. I stay like that for awhile—a mixture of screaming and crying—with my body shaking full of anger, confusion, and grief. Nothing makes sense anymore. I pinch myself to make sure I'm not stuck in one of my dreams, and the pain reminds me that I'm awake. How can it be real? After I calm down and my body stops heaving, I go to my sink and splash cold water on my face and stare at my reflection in the mirror. Who is she, this girl with the puffy red eyes and splotchy skin, who doesn't know anything about herself anymore? Am I still in there somewhere, the me who plans and maps out every decision and bases her life on facts? Is she in there battling a girl who insists on being unpredictable, creative, and passionate—and headed in a completely opposite direction?

There are two halves to my soul in direct competition with each other, and I don't know which half I want to win. Ethan has left me confused and bewildered, and I can't trust my own judgment right now. I make up my mind to call Verity. She picks up and instantly knows something is wrong. She agrees to come pick me up, and we sit silently in her car until we make it all the way to the lake and the camping area Gunner had taken me to. Sitting beside the water, staring into the vast blueness that knows no depths, she finally breaks the silence.

"Cassia, are you ready? To talk, I mean. You have me worried." I take in a deep breath and exhale slowly.

"Yes, I finally am. But please just listen to the whole story before commenting. I want to make sure I don't lose my train of thought." I hesitate at first, but then I start from the very beginning: the dreams. How the dreams became more frequent, and then one day I saw the boy in the diner. How that boy set up meeting me in the library. How we spent time together in the cabin from my dreams, and how in the end he let me know it was all real before he kissed me. She stays quiet. At first, she looks unhappy, then perplexed, and at times excited. I guess she is going through all the same emotions I did, but in a much shorter time frame.

"Cas, this is a lot to take in. I was a little upset that you've been keeping this from me, but I get it now. I don't think I would have handled it as well as you have, that's for sure. I knew there was something between the two of you, but I couldn't pinpoint it. It was obvious but didn't make sense. I guess my biggest question is this: how was it?"

"How was what?" I raise my eyebrow at her.

"The kiss. How was it?" I stop and think for a second about that kiss. It was unlike any I had ever had, and even though I hadn't dated much besides Gunner, it was a standout.

"It was everything." She looks at me and smiles. I didn't expect to say that.

"Then that's all you need to know." I sit there quietly for a minute thinking about that answer.

"That's not me, Verity. You know that."

"Maybe it should be you. Maybe these dreams are showing you a life you were born to live. Maybe they're to keep you from a making a mistake by choosing the wrong life." I think about that, but I can't reconcile my dreams and who I am in them with an entire lifetime devoted to being organized and methodical. It doesn't seem like both types of people can live in one body.

"What if I'm wrong? What if Ethan becomes a choice that I just can't choose?"

"You won't know until you get there, but if you rely on your gut instinct instead of trying to think your way out of it, you'll choose wisely. It's weird being on the giving end of the advice." She laughs, and it makes me laugh too.

"What about Gunner? I don't know if I can do that to him." Gunner has been on my mind all morning. He's been there by my side for so long that I don't know what I'd do without him in my life.

"I'm pretty sure—according to this whole parallel universe theory—that he'll choose you and you two will go off and live happily ever after in another life. You can't base a decision on whether you will hurt someone's feelings. This is the rest of your life you are talking about! You need to live it!"

"Easier said than done." I imagine myself living a different life in a different world. If Ethan is a choice, and I choose him, I may have to live in this world with Gunner's reaction. If I choose Gunner, then surely, I'd live my life knowing what Ethan thinks about it. Or maybe not. What if we become blind to other choices? Maybe right there in the Trivium our paths branch, and we can't look back and remember ever seeing the fork in the road. Verity, not knowing what other choices she had, would prove that idea. Maybe if I choose the one, I'll end up forgetting about the other. Would I forget every moment that happened before that?

"Ver, may I ask you something? Do you remember any boys you dated before Jason?" She eyes me thoughtfully.

"Hmmm." She rests her chin on the back of her hand, mimicking The Thinker. "That's so weird, Cassia. Did I date anyone else? Why are my memories fuzzy?"

"Are they? I was wondering if you'd forget everyone else after you chose."

"Maybe you do. It makes sense in a way. If you remember relationships and feelings about someone else, there's a chance you'll suffer regret—maybe just a small chance—and we're not taught anything about that happening. The point of the Trivium is to make an informed choice and not have regrets. Do *you* remember me dating anyone else?" I think back to a few months ago when Jason wasn't around, but no names come to mind. *How's that possible?*

"Come to think of it, I can't recall anyone besides Jason either. That's odd, right? So, either way, I may not even know what could have been, so maybe it won't be so hard." She leans over to me, wrapping her arms around me, and squeezes. Any choice, as long as it still includes Verity in my life, is a great one.

"Why worry about the path you left when you can make a new one? Leave the past at the fork."

"Evidently, the Trivium made you incredibly wise." She playfully punches my shoulder and laughs.

"I may not remember any boys in my life, but I most certainly remember all our times together. That's so clear to me when all the rest is hazy."

"Same. I'm so glad I have you. You could've treated me like I was completely crazy, with all my talk of dreams being real."

"Oh, I still think you're crazy." I return the punch. "Hey! You gotta admit, it's so strange, Cas. But like, romantic. I like both Gunner and Ethan, but hearing all of this makes me think there's really something to your dreams that you haven't considered."

"Oh yeah? Like what?"

"Like perhaps they aren't dreams, but visions. Don't give me that eye roll, Cas, it's not anything more perplexing than having shared dreams with someone you've never met."

"Touché."

"But seriously, think about it. I still think you're getting some kind of future vision of your life. Like you've torn through the fabric of time and saw what you weren't supposed to see. Wait, what if you two are—"

"What? What if we're what?"

"—soul mates!"

"Now I think you're the one talking crazy."

"I'm just saying, that would be pretty cool."

"I'm not entirely sure I believe in that concept."

"All I'm saying is, it's obvious you and Ethan have a strong connection. One that transcends reality even."

"You're getting awful sci-fi on me, you know that?" She giggles and hugs me.

"We're reversing roles you know. Me, all-knowing and wise and science-y. I guess that means you should start dressing better."

"Hey now! For one, science-y isn't a word. And two, my clothes aren't that bad!" We both laugh at that. I definitely do not have what it takes to work in fashion.

She drives me back to my house and I feel refreshed. I may not have all the answers, but my current decision is to not decide. Instead, I plan on acquiring facts. My time is coming up, and I want to make an informed decision. I know Verity wants me to go with my intuition, but I'm a rational person who lives a life of research and logic. The hardest part will be talking to Ethan and being completely open, vulnerable, and honest. I call him, and he sounds excited to hear my voice—which surprises me considering how poorly I left things between us. We make plans for dinner, and I make it very clear that this is not a date. He laughs like he doesn't believe me, but he agrees to it. I shower and wash off the roller-coaster of emotions I bathed in today. Since it's not a date, I don't wear anything fancy, but I do dress a little nicer than usual. Dress pants and a nice top with strappy sandals. I smooth my hair down and apply the faintest hint of makeup. Presentable, but businesslike.

I tell my mom that I'm going to dinner with a friend and that it's not a date, but she flitters about cleaning the house and getting dolled up anyway. A new boy in the mix has thrown her for a loop, but she doesn't ask me questions or make faces. She seems genuinely excited. Gunner doesn't spend much time here, so maybe she feels like she's missed out on my dating life. It's not his fault, he's usually at practice or we're in a hurry to leave—or my parents aren't home when he picks me up. It does seem odd that he's not really done the "meet the parents" thing in this manner. Sometimes they ask me if we're still dating since they rarely see him, but I thought it was always in jest.

Ethan arrives on time, dressed nicely in a sleek button down and jeans. It's a casually cool look that suits him, but I imagine it's not what he would wear on a date either. He got the memo. Good. He hands my mother a bouquet of flowers and makes it a point to tell me they are for her—not me—because this is not a date. Smooth. Of course, she delights in the gesture—why wouldn't she?

"It's so very nice to meet you, Mrs. Bellerose." He kisses my mom's hand and she blushes. I knew he'd pull something to impress my parents, but good grief. Sometimes I wonder if this man is for real.

"Very nice to meet you, Ethan. What exactly are your intentions with my daughter?" She eyes him coyly.

"Just dinner, ma'am. Cassia insists this is not a date, therefore I am obliging her request." He looks at me and grins.

"Well then, I guess we don't need to worry too much, do we?" She looks right at me. "No having-your-father-clean-his-gun-to-scare-boys, tactic?" I laugh. My father has never once owned a gun. We don't need them for self-defense anymore—as crime is nonexistent—and my dad doesn't hunt. We know all the old stories though about boys taking girls on dates and overbearing fathers.

"No ma'am," Ethan says. "I will have her back on time if not before, and there will be no impure intentions."

"Well, you two enjoy your dinner." My mom hugs me goodbye, whispers in my ear to not hurry back, and steps aside as we walk out the door. That's so unlike her that I laugh out loud, and Ethan eyes me curiously.

He opens the car door for me like a perfect gentleman, but I give him a look that clearly says this is not friendship behavior.

"It's just the polite thing to do, Cassia. And I do have manners. I'm very aware you can open your own door." I get in, but I keep my eyes on him.

We make small talk in the car ride to the restaurant, and it's all surface information. I know he's waiting for me to start a serious discussion. He takes me to a cool downtown pizza place I haven't been to where the ceiling and brick walls are covered in neat artwork. We're taken to a booth in the back, and it's perfect to have a conversation all to ourselves. We order, and after a few sips of my tea, I know it's time to begin.

"So, the reason I asked to meet you tonight was to talk about the dreams." His face brightens, and I know he has a lot to say on the subject. "Obviously, you have them. I have them. I'm here purely on a fact-finding mission, and I want to know your side of the story."

He sits up a little straighter and his demeanor is more serious. "Okay, Cassia. Where do you want me to begin?"

"From the beginning. You said you know me. I want to know how. When. Details. Everything." I sit back with my arms folded across my chest. Waiting.

He gives out a long exhale and then delves into his story. "It started a few months ago. I had a dream about this beautiful girl I had never met. It was both so real and fantastical that it took a while to figure out it was a dream. There was a boat, and we were on the lake. She was lying on the front deck, sunbathing, while I was steering. I didn't see her face, all I could see was her long blonde hair gleaming in the sun, whipping behind her with the wind. I stopped the boat and walked up to her—and then I woke up." I nod at him, remembering the dream but from my point of view. "There were several dreams over the next couple of weeks. We were in the garden and I was reading, and it started to rain so we ran to the cabin." I suck in my breath. That was the cabin? I had wondered, but couldn't be sure, since I never saw a garden. "We were lying in the hammock behind the cabin in another dream. It was dream after dream, and I didn't want to believe it was real. Well, I did and I didn't. I need to come clean with you though, the dreams were what made me break up with my girlfriend. I couldn't continue in a relationship that didn't feel as right as the one I was dreaming about. It may have been a crazy thing to do, hoping it was real, but I wanted that feeling with *someone*. Anyone. And I didn't have that with her." He pauses as if he's collecting his thoughts.

"I'm sorry to hear that," I say.

"I'm not sorry at all," he replies. My stomach knots up in response. "Anyway, I had given up on the girl being real, but then I went to lunch with a friend at the diner. And I saw you. I wanted to talk to you so badly, but I saw you were with another guy and I lost my nerve, so I took off as quick as I could. Then, when I saw you that day in the library—and you were alone—I had to at least know. I wanted to know if you recognized me. If you were as amazing in real life as you were in the imaginary. So, I bumped into you on purpose."

"Yeah, I still felt bad." He laughs, easing the growing tension.

"Well, I didn't. Anyway, all the feelings I had felt in those dreams came back to me, and I know they're real." He breaks off, looking away from me. The waitress brings us the pizza we ordered and we both dive in, shoving pizza into our mouths instead of talking. A couple of slices later, he looks back at me again. "Cassia, your turn. I want to hear your side of this incredible story."

I look down at my slice of pizza and take another large bite. He stares at me, waiting patiently. I swallow and take a sip of my soda to wash it down. "It's a lot like yours. Obviously, it's from my point of view, and I had no idea about the cabin or that it was yours. I recognized it when you took me there, but still didn't know about the garden."

"I took you there on purpose. To see your reaction." He grins at me.

"Yeah, well, I was definitely uncomfortable and caught off guard."

"I couldn't read you that night. Continue." He sits back against the booth, having eaten his half of the pizza.

"Well, I saw you in the diner and I froze. And here is where I come clean, I found out your first name, and I did try to look you up, but there were a lot of Ethans out there so that's as far as I got." He chuckles quietly to himself, shaking his head. "I about panicked in the library when it was you, but I did genuinely want to know who you were and maybe figure this whole thing out."

"And have you?"

"No. I have no idea what I'm doing." I take another bite of pizza and finish my drink. He leans forward against the table, closer to me.

"So, what exactly are you trying to accomplish with this meeting? I mean, clearly, I was wrong when I thought you felt the same way about me when we met. And that's okay, I'm not going to keep pressuring you. This hasn't been the easiest for me either. I guess I thought if I ever found out you were a real person, things would fall together perfectly—like fate." He sits straighter and gazes down at his lap.

"Look, this is all really complicated and neither of us understands any of it, but my life was great before you entered it and now I'm just trying to figure things out." I see him tense up at my words. "I just mean, I'm confused. I don't know what feelings I have for you, but I have a tough time thinking I should abandon everything I've ever wanted for someone I barely know. Maybe the universe is playing with us. Maybe it's a bizarre coincidence. I haven't figured that out yet, but I can't go scrap my plans on a whim. I invited you here to get the facts." He sighs and leans toward me again.

"And what are the facts, Cassia? Because none of this seems to be rooted in actual science."

"That it's true. That's as far as I have. I just wanted to corroborate our stories." He leans even closer across the table, and I'm drawn toward him as if pulled by an invisible thread.

"What if there's a chance of a future with us? What would you do?" he asks quietly. I feel his breath, and he's so close I could kiss him. The feeling is intoxicating.

"I haven't figured that out yet." He looks intently at me, and I feel his eyes searching mine for a hint of my true feelings. I guess he saw very little because he brusquely sits back against the booth again.

"Are you ready to go home? It's about that time. I promised to have you back early."

I'm startled by the abruptness, and I almost tell him my mom said not to hurry back, but instead, I nod silently. I'm on the verge of tears. We split the check for the pizza and head back to his car. This time he doesn't go to my door. His face is a mask, concealing all his thoughts and emotions except for one of disappointment. I hadn't realized he thought my call meant I reciprocated feelings.

The car ride home is quiet, except for the classical music he puts on. I know that means he wants time alone with his thoughts, so I don't press him. When we get to my house, he walks me to the door—appearing to be very stoic. We each say good night, and without thinking I hug him—my arms around his waist with my head leaning against his chest. I feel him soften, and he wraps his arms around my back, snugly.

"I have a tough time thinking I'm going to lose you when I just found you," he whispers quietly. "I don't know how to handle that."

"I wish I could give you some kind of reassurance, but it's too much right now. Give me some time to think about the consequences of any decision I make, okay?" I look up into his eyes, and I can tell he's also fighting back tears. "I could really hurt people depending on my choices, and I don't want that." He kisses my forehead gently, and I feel a lump in the back of my throat forming and moisture trying to push its way from behind my eyes. I fight the tears back forcefully and reluctantly let go. I watch as Ethan walks back down the steps and toward his car, a small wave, and a sad smile—and then he's gone.

I open the door and am greeted by both of my parents standing in the living room, looking at me strangely. My mom has a goofy grin on her face, and my dad looks like he got caught doing something wrong.

"What are you two up to?" I ask.

"Nothing. Nothing to see here." My mom is trying so hard to hold back laughter that now I'm curious.

"I'm not buying that at all. If this is about Ethan—" My mom interrupts me before I can finish.

"Oh no honey, not at all. That's your business, though I really like him. This has to do with your birthday in a few days." She eyes my dad, but his face is expressionless.

"Sweetheart, we wanted to wait and give you your birthday present *on* your birthday, but seeing as that's the Trivium day, we thought we'd give it to you early." Still no emotion on his face.

"Okay . . . again, what are you two up to?" I ask warily.

"Follow me to the garage," my dad answers. I feel my stomach tighten with anticipation, but I don't want to seem too eager. I'd hate to be disappointed. My dad points the way, and they choose to follow me there instead of lead. I hesitate before opening the door to the garage, and I look at my parents—both of them smiling and nodding to continue. It's dark, so I grasp the wall searching for the switch—and when I turn it on, I feel my breath catch in my chest. Sitting there staring back at me is a car. A blue, compact four-door vehicle, all nice and shiny with a big red bow on top. I'm speechless as I look wide-eyed from the car to my parents and back again. They're grinning from ear to ear, loving my reaction.

"Th-this is mi-mine?" I barely get the words out.

"Surprise! We knew you wanted a car. Is this one okay? Your mom picked it out." I turn around and embrace my dad with as much strength as I can muster and then do the same thing to my mom. I try to get the words of gratitude that are in my head to go out through my mouth, but I'm failing miserably.

"I can't—I love—you two. Thank you so much! It's perfect!" I never cared about what kind of car I wanted. I had no preference on make or style or color, I just wanted something to call my own. This tops anything I could've asked for.

"Go, have a closer look!" My dad is so excited for me that his face is lit up. He looks like a child who was taken to an ice cream store as a surprise. I walk over to the car slowly, admiring every inch of it, before finally opening the driver side door and peering in. Black leather seats. Brushed nickel lining the interior console. I sit down and put my hand on the wheel and take it all in. The smell of the new interior is so strong, it feels like I'm being embraced by a leather jacket. That smell awakens something in me, but I associate it with Ethan so I suppress it quickly.

"This is truly amazing. I don't even know what to say except, I love you both." Tears well up in my eyes and I don't fight them.

"Wanna take it for a spin?" My dad looks at me eagerly.

"Absolutely! Hop in!" I can't wait to see what it feels like knowing the car I'm in is completely mine.

"Well, I would love to, but I have a much better passenger for you on your first time out." I look at him confused, but then I see a wisp of red hair peeking out from behind him. I didn't notice Verity sneaking in.

"Surprise!" Verity bounces up and down and runs over to the passenger side. "Isn't it great?" She beams.

"You knew?"

"Of course, I knew. I was going to be the one to keep you out of the house before you decided to go out with Ethan. Which I need details about by the way. Are you ready to test this thing out?"

"Yes, yes, and more yes." I get back out quickly and hug both of my parents again before opening the garage door and gently easing the car back out. My dad must've had his car hidden somewhere else down the street to fit mine in. They wave goodbye, still glowing with happiness for me.

"So, what do you think?" Verity asks.

"I like it! I'm still in shock. I really had no idea. Honestly, I thought I'd get something old and cheap, which would have been completely fine, but this is overwhelming and amazing." We turn down my street, heading to the diner for some shakes.

"My treat tonight. Consider it an early birthday dessert." We head inside and slide into a booth at the back. "I'm not sure if I should admit this, but I've known they were doing it for awhile now. They swore me to secrecy. That was the hardest thing ever. I knew how sad you were after graduation."

"I'm impressed you could keep it in. I mean, I know you can keep my secrets, but to keep them *from* me? Incredible."

"Right? I don't want to do that again. I love telling you everything!" We both laugh and our milkshakes arrive. Her mouth completely full, she mumbles to me asking about my non-date date with Ethan earlier.

"Oh, we just talked. He confirmed we had all the same dreams. Only problem is, he's doesn't want a life without me. I don't know if I feel the same way."

"Well, you know how I feel. I think you should do what's best for you and not anyone else. Only you can know what that is though."

"I know. All I think about is who I'd be hurting. It feels so selfish to only think about what *I* want."

"It's your life to live though. They get their own choices. Maybe not in this world, but they're happy in another, you know?" I think about that, but all I picture is an intricate weaving of red strings. I'll never understand how it works. To me, they're still unhappy in this world. Maybe either guy will forget me if I choose the other.

Seems like the case since Verity can't remember. That's a nice thought, but I can't wrap my head around it. Putting boys aside, could I really choose between medicine and writing? For all I know I could end up with Gunner as an author, or Ethan as a doctor. Or neither.

"I went out for a fact-finding mission and I got my answers. Somewhat. I guess I need to see if Gunner is free tomorrow and compare. That just feels so wrong."

"Well, you never even know what the Trivium will do. I mean, you have three choices and only two boys so far, so you never know. Maybe you end up with neither or no one." She grins.

"That's not helpful!" I start giggling and she joins in. I'm going to miss these times with her. "Verity, we need to promise that no matter what happens, we'll always make time for each other. We can meet half way even. I don't want to lose this." My voice lowers, and I feel that familiar pang of sadness pushing its way into my chest and the back of my throat. *Get it together Cassia, it's not the time to be emotional yet. Save it for when she leaves.* I hate feeling like there is a goodbye on the horizon when there isn't. There can't be.

"I was going to say the same thing." Her face grows serious. "I am not letting anything happen to us, boys or no boys. *We're* soul mates and don't you forget that."

"Agreed. It's us, always." We continue our shakes and idle banter about summer plans before we both start yawning. It's dark outside, and the late-night crowd trickles in. Verity had hidden her car around the corner from my house, so I drop her off there and ease gently back into the garage. I guess my dad is willing to give up his space for tonight. The house is dark, so I know my parents are already asleep. I creep up the stairs to my room when I notice my cell lit up on my bed. There's a message from Gunner about plans tomorrow. It's like he read my mind. It's late, but I go ahead and message him back. Crawling into bed, I think about everything that's happened today. It's a lot to take in. I've experienced a roller coaster of emotions, and it's left me physically and mentally exhausted. Sleep comes very easy tonight.

The next morning, I see Gunner has messaged me back, saying he'd pick me up at eleven. I look at my clock while wiping the sleep from my eyes, and it's already ten thirty. Panicking, I hop out of bed and throw some clothes on, apply a little bit of mascara and concealer to hide the dark circles under my eyes, and then rush downstairs to grab an apple. Gunner shows up on time, ready to go, but he comes inside this morning and talks to my mom about school in the fall. *Odd.* As we get ready to walk out the door, my mom stops me and whispers in my ear, "You really can't go wrong with either, you know." I give her a surprised look, and she giggles and walks away. I don't need my mom's input on these matters right now. How *embarrassing*.

Gunner walks me to his truck, my arm in his, and opens the door for me before sliding into the driver's seat. "Are we going somewhere special today?" I ask.

"No, not really. Nothing like the surprise picnic. I just wanted to go get lunch at this neat little place I found downtown and maybe walk around and see what's going on. There are some art exhibits and outside activities. Does that sound okay?"

"Sounds like I don't know who you are and what happened to Gunner." He laughs.

"Just wanted to try something new. I know you like doing those kinds of things." I nod, still perplexed. The Gunner I know has never been into art, shopping, or museums. He'd rather go to the lake, watch sports, or go fishing. And there are times I go with him, but most of the time his friends go too and it gets a little crowded. We pull up to a quaint Italian restaurant downtown I've never seen before, and the inside is dim and dark, but cozy. The waiter brings us breadsticks and water and I look over the menu which looks mouthwatering.

"I'm not sure I can decide what to get. It all sounds delicious." The apple wasn't very filling, and I'm famished.

"Well, get whatever you want. I'm buying." He winks at me and I don't feel anymore comfortable with his behavior. It's out of left field. Not that he isn't romantic, but this is a different level. We order and he leans toward me, talking just above a whisper.

"I've missed you, Cassia. Where have you been hiding? I haven't heard much from you lately."

"I know, I'm sorry." I'm hoping he didn't catch that I was dodging his question. I don't want to get into where I've been and with whom. "My parents surprised me yesterday with a new car."

He raises his eyebrow. "Oh yeah? Wow. What did they get you?"

"A shiny, blue four-door compact. Me, as a car." He laughs.

"Guess you won't need me anymore. I may never see you again." He half-smiles, but there's a strange undercurrent of a different emotion beneath it. He's made jokes about me being independent before, and how I won't need him. This is just like that, except before, I didn't have any independence and now I do. I wonder if that bothers him. "Are you ready for the Trivium? Pretty confident in how everything will go?" His eyes lock with mine. I look away. It dawns on me that all of this is for show, to make sure I choose him. He's not so subtly trying to get me to pick him. If he only knew how hard that decision has become. I try to return a smile, but something isn't sitting right in my stomach.

"I don't know. Maybe. My mood changes on a day-to-day basis."

"Well, I'm sure you'll be fine. And I'll be waiting outside to pick you up when you're done." I mull that over. Before Ethan, we had talked about our Trivium day plans for each other. Now, I'm not so sure that I want him there.

"Well, about that. I know how Verity felt after. I think maybe I should ask my mom to pick me up. I know we made plans months ago, but I'll be tired and needing sleep. Would that be okay?" He looks somewhat angry but nods in agreement.

"Only if I get to come see you after you wake up." I'm not sure how to respond. I don't know how he'll factor into my future if I choose a life without him. He's already assuming my choice is made. That irks me though a month ago it wouldn't have.

"We'll see." He grimaces but quickly puts on a smile like someone puts on a mask.

We finish our lunch and spend the rest of the afternoon going to the local museum of art and seeing the vendors that line the streets. There's a festive atmosphere all around us, and it's energizing. I buy a leather-bound journal, something that will come in handy to jot my thoughts down on, and Gunner finds a small sculpture to put in his room. Even though he's being polite, I keep feeling like I'm walking on eggshells. He hasn't asked me anything else about the Trivium, but I can tell my responses still bother him. If I choose a life with Gunner in it, would we still spend days like this? Is this a onetime ploy to hook me, making it seem like he's willing to go to places like this in the future? We really don't have a lot in common, probably why people never saw us being a couple, but we enjoy each other's company. Or did. Today proved that at least he would take an interest in what I liked. I can't tell if he enjoys any of it, but he came. He puts his arm around my back, resting his hand on my waist, and pulls me in closer to him. As we turn a corner, I notice ahead of us is a familiar head of brown hair and my heart starts racing. Ethan turns around and sees me, waves hello, and then casually saunters off. I don't know if it's because he didn't come say hi to me, or because he didn't seem to react to seeing me there, but I feel a strange twinge of aggravation mixed with disappointment. I'm there with my boyfriend and yet, seeing Ethan affects me in a way no one else does. I look to see where he went, but I lose sight of him. I feel my cheeks getting hot. Why does he have to haunt me? My life was going splendidly until he showed up—and now it's chaos. How is that fair? What did I do to deserve it?

Gunner drives me back home and walks me to the porch. He leans in to kiss my cheek, but I lean forward and hug him the same way I did Ethan. I breathe him in, realizing for the first time that I never paid much attention to the cologne he wears. He smells of lemon and sandalwood, and I think about what it would be like to be forever engulfed in those scents. I look up and kiss him softly on the lips, my body relaxing instead of speeding up. I step back and he's grinning widely.

"Good night, Cas."

"Good night, Mr. Darcy." He looks at me strangely.

"Who?"

"Oh, it's from a book. I was being funny. Never mind. 'Night, Gunner." At that, he walks back to his truck and waves at me before driving away. I stand there for a bit, feeling foolish.

Lying on my bed, I decide to get out my new journal. I wonder if what's penned in ink stays written, or if time alters all things and the words disappear. It's a strange experiment I'm sure, but I write my thoughts about each boy down. If I choose, and it turns out it was the wrong choice, I want to remember what I'm missing. Assuming it works. I'm not so sure that you can't be wrong, that the Trivium really can decide what's best for you. Out of an infinite possibility of threads, it only gives you three. Seems like it's improbable that it knows your best options. Even with the D.B. chip taking everything into account. For once, I wish I could go back to before the dreams. Back to when my life was much simpler, and I knew exactly what I wanted out of it. When my life wasn't being consumed by my future husband and instead was focused on my career. Love triangles are for the birds. Can you really make the right choice for yourself based solely on feelings? Is compatibility already determined by the chip? It's a lot to worry about.

Fatigue sets upon me and my eyes are drooping so low I can barely see, so I put the journal away in my nightstand for another day. I never want to forget the words I've written, no matter what happens in a few days.

CHAPTER EIGHT

"Then took the other, as just as fair,
And having perhaps the better claim,
Because it was grassy and wanted wear;
Though as for that the passing there
Had worn them really about the same,
And both that morning equally lay
In leaves no step had trodden black.
Oh, I kept the first for another day!
Yet knowing how way leads on to way,
I doubted if I should ever come back."
—Robert Frost

It feels like the past few days have flown by so quickly, that when I wake up this morning to balloons covering the floor of my room, it takes me a minute to realize it's my birthday. My parents were very sneaky to manage such a feat without waking me up. I feel a mix of happiness and sadness balling up inside me. Today is the day I finally lay to rest all my confusion and doubts and move forward with my life. No more jotting down in my journal, no more lists, no more what-ifs. Today, I get to choose.

I made up my small bag last night so I could get ready quickly this morning. I pull on my swimsuit and then cover it with jeans and a T-shirt and slide into my flip-flops. My bag contains a swim cap, undergarments, and a hair dryer. The essentials. I'm sure Verity had taken makeup to put on before leaving, but I don't care how I look today. Smells of bacon waft up the stairs and under my door and my stomach growls in anticipation. My typical birthday breakfast has always consisted of bacon and pancakes, and I eagerly walk down the stairs. My mom is already sitting at the table with my dad, both with a cup of coffee in their hands. A plate of food has been set out for me, so I pour myself some coffee and join them. Even though they aren't saying much, I feel the change in the air between us. Today is a life-changing moment, and none of us know what it will be like afterward. I do know this is the last time I will wake up in this way on my birthday and have this breakfast with my parents. Even if I come home from college during the summer, it just won't feel the same.

My mom insisted that she be the one to take me this morning. I had shut myself in the past few days and didn't talk to anyone. I wanted to be alone, and thankfully both Gunner and Verity understood and didn't pressure me. Ethan also stepped aside, and I haven't heard from him either. In the car, my mom is merrily chatting about the weather and college, avoiding mentioning anything about the importance of today. I know she's trying to distract me, but I barely register what she's saying as I look out the window and tune the world out. I'm not thinking at all, just feeling numb as I watch the trees and buildings pass us by. I do my best to respond to her when there's silence, but she isn't fooled so she turns the radio on.

For some reason, the Trivium building looks much more intimidating today than it did last week. My mom leans over and gives me a kiss on the forehead, insisting it will all work out. She took the day off from work so she could pick me up later, and she's planned on taking a book to the café while waiting. I should only be here for a couple hours, and I can message her when done. I give her one last weak and nervous smile before getting out and walking toward the door. The large black doors feel oppressive, and the handles look menacing, like metal snakes waiting to strike. I enter the lobby, and it's pristine and feels clinical. There is a lounge area with a television playing movies for those that are waiting to be called. My mom could have waited here, but I look around and there are no parents to be found. I guess they choose not to. Perhaps it brings up strange memories for them. The receptionist smiles warmly and asks for my name and ID and then points to the waiting area to be called. I don't recognize any of the other kids, but there are many schools in this city. I do my best to listen to the comedy playing, thinking that laughing would help soothe the nerves that are rising to the surface. I scan the other kids, and their faces seem to be doing the same thing. One-by-one each is called by a different worker and shuttled into different rooms. After what feels like an hour, my name is called. I breathe in and try to exhale my fear.

The room I'm brought into is painted a calming shade of blue and the artwork is of oceans. There's only a white desk and two chairs, as this is where I get briefed on what is to come. I'm not entirely sure the attempt at a calming atmosphere is working for me. The blue room makes me feel like I'm being swallowed up by the ocean, rather than soothing me. It feels like drowning in a sea of blue.

"Cassia Bellerose, please sit." The worker, whose badge reads "Emma" pulls the chair out for me and goes to sit behind the desk. She opens a folder with my name in bold print and takes a minute to scan the information. I look around the room some more, trying to wait patiently. I have no idea how much information that folder contains. "It looks like everything is acceptable and you're qualified to begin."

"Qualified? I thought everyone came here." I eye her quizzically.

"Oh yes, but those that are currently ill or in poor health have to be rescheduled. It's very rare to do that, however. You are in excellent health." I let out a sigh of relief. I can't imagine having to summon the strength to come back to this place another day.

"You'll be entering Trivium Room Three. Have you read the pamphlet?" I nod. "Good. Today is a momentous day for you. I have a short video for you to watch first before going into more detail." Behind her, a screen lowers out of the ceiling, and somewhere behind me is a very well-hidden projector. She dims the lights, and music—that sounds like it could be decades old— starts playing. The video walks me through the sanitized version of the history of the Trivium—how after multiple wars ravaged the earth, scientists set out to learn more about future prediction. Though in rare sections of the world there are still violent factions that refuse peace, most of the world is now in harmony. People have no reason to be angry or discontent when they choose their fate. It talks about how there are still people who make poor decisions throughout their childhood—so things don't always appear so wonderful for them later, but that it's rare. Most people want a storybook ending, and will behave appropriately to get one. Everyone knows there are powerful consequences to their actions, it only makes sense to think things through. The D.B. chip is a reminder that out there somewhere, a computer is logging everything you do. I've never wondered if there are those that choose to behave out of fear of the chip, but it would make sense. The video shows pictures of what the tanks look like, explains a diagram of all the working pieces, and even has a model walk you through the steps of getting in and being hooked up to the wires that will read your chip. It seems easy enough. I wish there was more information as to what happens inside the tank, but I understand there isn't a way to show that with a video. The screen raises back into the ceiling, and Emma turns the lights back up. "Do you have any questions about the video?" I hesitate, wondering if my questions would be appropriate and if she'd be able to answer them.

"Well . . ." I know this is my last chance at answers. "Has anyone ever chosen wrong?" She looks shocked.

"Why no, I don't think that's possible."

"Well, will you remember what the other choices were?" Now a frown has set upon her once smiling face.

"Cassia, no you won't. The memories may be there at first, but they fade away into a haze before disappearing altogether. Let me reassure you that everything will work out just fine for you. Do you have anymore questions?" The sternness of her face is a sign to be quiet, so I shake my head. "Good. Let's walk into Room Three and I will show you how to get started."

I follow her into the hallway, and we stop at a very tall door with a numeral three on it. I giggle for a second and cup my hand over my mouth. Emma looks unhappily at me, but the gigantic size of the door makes me feel like a storybook character about to walk into the unknown. I keep thinking the oversized doorknob is going to tell me it's impassible, and the thought of being like Alice overtakes my senses. I regain control, and Emma pushes the door open like it weighs nothing.

I follow her inside and all the walls are a dark gray, reminding me of an impending storm. The tank looks like a giant gray space pod with a white lily painted on the side, sitting in the center of the room. The lid is raised open on hinges, and the water inside glows a calming tropical aqua. She motions for me to follow her to another door across the room, and it turns out to hold a shower and a space for changing clothes—as well as a makeup counter.

"Before we begin, I need you to go in here and remove everything but your swimsuit. Jewelry included. You can put everything in this locker, no one else will be in this room, and your items are very safe. Please rinse yourself off in the shower, apply your shower cap—and then when you are done, we will begin." She walks toward a giant control panel nearby, and her welcoming attitude is gone—replaced by a very detached one. I don't know if that's just her personality, or if my questions ruined it for me. I strip off my clothes and hang them up and wait for the steam to fill the shower before immersing myself under the rain-style shower head. I let the warmth surround me, hoping it will wash away my fears. I picture my doubts rinsing off me and into the drain. Not wanting to make her angry, I finish quickly with the shower cap and walk back into the larger room. She leads me to the pod—handing me earplugs—and instructs me to get in and lie down. There's so much salt in the tank that I float, and the temperature is adjusted to match my body. It's strange to be buoyant, and once the temperature adjusts, I no longer feel the water around me. It's like floating on air, much more relaxing than I had imagined. Emma leans over me as she places electrodes on my temples. She then feels behind my neck and attaches one there as well. After checking some things on her control panel, she gives me a thumbs-up and closes the lid. Everlasting darkness enshrouds me. Lying there, completely alone with my thoughts, my mind explodes into fear and excitement. I see nothing, hear nothing, and feel nothing. It's unnerving, and I make myself breathe through my nose and out my mouth to calm down. I know the sooner I relax, the quicker it will all be over. I shut out everything—including my thoughts—and let go. My mind goes blank, followed by a sensation of warmth and light. My temples tickle slightly, and nerves twitch in my legs. I was warned that could happen as my body tries to send sensory input to my limbs. I resist the urge to scratch and choose to ignore it.

An image appears before my eyes, very faint at first and growing sharper. I recognize the little girl as myself, about eight years old. I'm swinging at a park with my mom. I remember that day—later we went for ice cream, and my dad put a puzzle together with me. Puzzles were something only my dad and I did, and we could sit for hours piecing them together. One of my favorite things we ever had between us. I feel a pang of sadness because it's been a long time since we've sat across the card table quietly searching for the perfect piece. An image of red hair comes into focus, and it's the first time I met Verity. More images flashing before me, like a projection of my childhood blurring across my vision. My first kiss with Gunner. Graduation. But then new images beam in front of me that I don't recognize, and it hits me that this must be my first future. I'm not shocked to see Gunner beside me, holding my hand and walking through what looks like the local college commons area. Flash forward and we're eating at the diner, and I notice what appears to be a sparkly ring on my left hand. I feel a rush of excitement course through me. I had always believed we had a future together, but seeing it is something else entirely. I'm wearing a white coat and I'm in my father's office. So, I do become a doctor. As I had planned, I remind myself. A jump in time and my face has grown serious and lined. I'm helping what appears to be an accident victim and my heart aches. The victim is a child, and sorrow spreads through me like a flame. Deaths at an early age are extremely rare, so I have hope he will be okay, but the sudden realization that I would be front and center experiencing this amount of tragedy unnerves me. What was I thinking? I knew being a doctor would be difficult. It's not all colds and sore throats. The startling reality of it stands in sharp contrast to the practice of medicine I grew up around. I'm never near my dad when he performs an operation. Studying it and seeing it firsthand are vastly different experiences. A sick feeling creeps into my gut. Next, I'm walking through the park with Gunner holding my left hand and a small hand clutching my right. I don't see her face, but she must be my daughter. Her hair is the same color as mine. Everything goes dark again, and the blackness startles me. I'm consciously aware that I'm still floating in the tank. How long have I been in here? That future seemed perfect, albeit I don't know if I truly have the stomach to be a doctor. It seems like I do, but I can't ignore that stress obviously takes its toll on my face. There are sacrifices I'd have to make to live that life. I have a newfound respect for my father. No wonder he's learned to conceal his emotions.

I brush those visions aside and focus on seeing the next future. I take deep breaths and relax my muscles and the visions start again. There isn't any mention of my childhood this time though I assume that only happens once as the chip's being read. I have no idea what to expect, but I let out a gasp when I see Ethan's face. There we are, lying on the hammock, reading, just like in my dream. *Our* dream. This picture is not as clear and realistic, but it doesn't take much to bring back the senses I had when I was asleep. I feel the sunlight caressing my cheek and the slight breeze gently rocking us. There's serenity in this moment that I didn't fully appreciate when I was dreaming. Next, we're playing volleyball somewhere I don't recognize, and Ethan's playing against me. Red hair flashes next to me and Jason stands next to Ethan, and I know that I'm at the same college as them. *Interesting.* Images jump ahead. I'm tapping away on a tablet furiously. There are books stacked all around me and a mug on the table beside me. I recognize the couch from the one at Ethan's lake house, and he walks in carrying more books. I must be writing. Now I'm at a book signing in the local café, but it's my name and picture on the banner. *I wrote a book? Me?* I sit down at the table and there are people walking up to me, smiling enthusiastically and handing me open books to sign. *None of this makes any sense.* Ethan and I are on a tropical island sporting matching wedding bands, and we're laughing while walking down a deserted beach. Next, I'm in a hospital, and my dad is giving me some news. I'm crying, but I don't know what's going on. Ethan and I are taking turns playing ball with a brown-haired little boy that looks just like him. This time I have a son. Darkness arrives again and I'm left confused. What did I just see? Why was I sad? Why would I write a book? I looked incredibly happy, and my face was still youthful. Stress doesn't destroy me in this future. Now that the two hard choices are out of the way, I'm curious about the third.

Relaxing again, I breathe deeply, but nothing happens. I can't imagine at this point that there would be anything else, but everyone has three choices, right? A white light appears before me. Everything is a blank slate, and it's just me, sitting in a white room, at a white desk, with a blank piece of paper in front of me. I'm given a pen and left alone to write my own story. The image ends abruptly, and the lid opens so fast that I'm startled and start shaking at the sudden temperature change.

"Miss Bellerose, are you okay? What happened?" I'm blinking my eyes trying to adjust to the light and I don't know what she means so I look at her quizzically.

"Wh-what do you mean? I saw my choices."

"How many did you see?"

"Three . . ." She looks at me strangely. "Why, what's wrong?"

"Maybe nothing. Why don't you go shower and get dressed while I talk to my supervisor." She motions to get out quickly and I do so, but I watch her walk away sporting a mixture of shock and horror. I can't even begin to imagine what riled her up.

The hot water feels amazing though it takes some time to feel okay walking again. My muscles are relaxed, and I feel sleepy, and now I understand why everyone passes out for awhile afterward. I get dressed and dry my hair, just enough to pull it into a ponytail before walking back into the gray room. A stern, elderly, gray-haired man is eyeing the computer printouts, and Emma is frantically waving her hands around. I walk carefully in their direction, wondering when they'll notice me. Emma sees me first and stops talking to the man.

"Cassia, this is Professor Hawthorne. He needs to speak with you." She walks over to a chair and pushes it to me and points for me to sit. Professor Hawthorne grabs his own chair and slides it across from mine. He looks intently at my face like he's searching for clues.

"Miss Bellerose, I need to ask you some questions and I need you to answer honestly. Do you understand?" I'm sure the confusion has set on my face, but he seems to ignore it.

"I understand," I answer.

"When inside the Trivium flotation pod, how many choices did you see?"

"Three."

"I cannot legally ask you what each particular choice was, but only two were recorded into the system. As you know, once you make a choice your records are sealed from the public but are also held by the highest clearance in security. You say you saw three choices, do you remember the third one?"

"Yes. Well, kind of. It didn't really seem like much of a choice. There wasn't much to it." He looks warily at Emma and she returns the look.

"As it is, there are only two official choices for you to choose from. I don't know if there was an issue with the system or a glitch with the electrodes or chip, but this room will be closed while I investigate. I'm sorry to say, however, that you can only choose from the first two you were shown. I can reassure you that this has never happened since the inception of the Trivium, and you have my gravest apologies. Were either of the first two sufficient?" I'm taken aback by the situation, but at the same time, the third choice didn't make sense to me. Everything was blank. What does that even mean?

"Yes," I said.

Relief washes over him and he stands back up, so I stand as well. He offers my hand to shake and then tells me that Emma will take care of the rest. I follow her over to the control panel, and she points out that there are two buttons. The first button corresponds to my first choice. Likewise, with the second button corresponding to my second choice. A third button is not lit up like the other two. All I need to do is press one of those buttons and this is over. Emma will give me a pill to take, and I can let my mom know I'm done and go home. Emma acts like it's the easiest thing in the world, pressing one of those buttons. She keeps eyeing that third button but doesn't say anything about it. It makes me want to press it just to see what happens. She leaves me alone to pick, but I'm warned that there is a time limit, so the sooner the better. Nothing like being forced to choose your fate in a hurry.

I think about each life I would get to lead. Gunner or Ethan. Doctor or writer. Daughter or son. Stressed and tired looking, or youthful and radiant. But why didn't Gunner and I look happy? I recall the visions, and though he had smiled at me, that smile wasn't genuine. Like he had to force it. What is the cause of the stress? My work? What terrible thing happened in the hospital? And what is this about being an author? My silly little journaling can turn into a writing career? None of it seems remotely realistic. But Verity was there. She was never in my first vision, and even though that doesn't necessarily mean anything, she was definitely in my life in the second. A son that looks just like Ethan. So handsome, with eyes that twinkle when he's being charming or mischievous. I imagine he would have me wrapped around his finger. I looked happy. My heart sinks thinking that the perfect life I planned with Gunner may not be so perfect after all. There's a definite fault line in the relationship that's straining under the cracks.

I eye those buttons like they hold the key to life or death. Any mistake is mine to bear for eternity. Maybe I'm reading too much into things. I mean, I'm only getting a glimpse into what can happen or what will happen, not an entire movie reel's worth of information. Ethan scares me though. I would have to drop everything I've planned and move away from my parents to start a college life so foreign to me. Verity would be there; maybe we'd be roommates to soften the blow. What if we're not? What if she makes better friends with girls she has a lot in common with? I can't know everything, and I won't remember anything about this, but I settle the score for the last time. A lifetime with someone I've known many years, doing what I've planned on for the rest of my life, side-by-side with my dad—but obviously not as happy as I'd hoped to be. Or a relationship with someone I don't know very well, starting over in unfamiliar territory, and with a career that I don't understand—but very clearly in love throughout it all. Friendship versus passion. Familiar versus unfamiliar. Things going as planned versus something new and thrilling. Gunner is predictable. He's my friend. Ethan lights a fire inside me I never want to quench. I want somehow to have both in my life, and even though it wouldn't be in the same way, a part of me wishes I could write the future for myself. If only that third button worked. I pray that I won't remember anything having to do with this. I don't want to ever remember what could have been. I place my finger on the button of my choice, squeeze my eyes shut, and press it quickly.

CHAPTER NINE

I wasn't sure what I would feel afterward. Relief? Elation? Nothing at all? I don't feel different. I thought there would be more to the button-pushing ritual, but thinking balloons would drop down from the ceiling in celebration is ridiculous and silly. Emma walks back in pushing a wheelchair, with a forced smile on her face and a bottle of pills in hand.

"Well, Cassia, how are you feeling? Please take this." She hands me a small blue pill and walks to the sink and back with a plastic cup full of water. I take it quickly, showing her I swallowed it.

"I think I'm fine. That's it, though?" She eyes me, perplexed, then forces a smile.

"It doesn't seem like much after the push of the button, I know. It's not very climactic. The pill will make you drowsy and your memory will be hazy. From here on out, things start anew for you on the road you chose to be on. Everything will be fine. Go ahead and sit in this wheelchair and we'll call your mom to pick you up.

You won't remember this experience, but you should rest easy knowing you chose what your future will be."

I sit in the wheelchair as instructed and my eyelids feel heavy. I hear my mom's voice, but everything becomes a blur. No longer able to keep my thoughts, I drift off into the hazy dark.

"Cassia, honey, how are you feeling?" My mom hovers above me. It's bright, and I need a minute before my eyes adjust. I blink several times and try to sit up. My head is groggy. I'm in my bed, though I have no recollection how or when I got here. My dad sits at the edge of my bed, waiting patiently. My mom is still hovering—noticeably concerned.

"Mom, I'm fine. Sleepy, but fine." Why's she so worried? Isn't this experience normal?

"Cassia, we need to talk. The doctors said there was an issue with your chip and some glitches. They want you to come back in to get a checkup. I was so worried, I've never heard about issues before." She smiles wanly, pushing my hair back behind my ear.

"A glitch? What do you mean?" I don't remember anything from earlier.

"Well," She hesitates. "They didn't give me many details. It's classified, I guess. They did tell me they gave you a little more dosage of medication than normal, so you may have trouble with your memory beyond what's usual. Do you remember anything from this morning?" I shake my head. I can't remember anything at all. Not from this morning. Not even from yesterday. I furrow my brow as I rack my brain, trying desperately to remember any details, but I have no recollection of the past. Panic rises in my chest. "Sweetheart, you went to the Trivium today."

Trivium. I remember it. I haven't lost everything. I must've chosen today and something went wrong. But what? "Mom, do you remember your life from before you chose?" She cocks her head at me and there's noticeable tension in her face.

"Maybe you just need more rest. I'm sure once the medication wears off, you'll feel more like yourself and ready to move forward. Want me to have Verity come over? Would that help?" Hearing her name triggers something in my brain, and memories of her flood my consciousness. What a scary thought to think a pill could wipe my best friend from me in a single dose. Maybe my memory will come back faster than expected. I only need more triggers.

"Yeah. Maybe I have amnesia. Was that a side effect?" My dad clears his throat so loudly that I jump. I forgot he was still sitting there.

"It can happen honey, but in time everything will come back to you. Get some rest and we'll check on you in a bit. If you need anything, yell for us." He pats my back and saunters off into the hallway. My mom gives me a kiss on the forehead and follows him, closing the door behind her.

Verity arrives an hour later, plopping herself down on the bed beside me, looking extremely excited.

"So, how are you? Are you ok? Your mom said something about your memory being a little off. Did you forget me? How's that possible? What did you choose?"

"I don't really know. Things are hazy. I'm sure I'll be okay, but right now it's just weird. My chip had a glitch." She gasps, clearly shocked.

"How's that possible?"

"I don't know. I'm going back to the doctor soon. I'm sure it's nothing. Verity, can we go for a drive? Or a walk? I think my memory will kick back in if I see familiar things."

"Absolutely, let's go. I know just the place."

I had to convince my parents I was feeling better before they'd let me leave. There's a strange feeling in the air I can't put my finger on, but I sense things aren't what they seem. Maybe they're worried about me and don't want to let on too much. Maybe they know more than what they say they do. Either way, I can cut the sense of foreboding with a knife and I need to get away from it. Outside the sun is still shining, and I breathe in the fresh summer air. Verity drives us to the diner and we take a seat in the back. I'm glad to know I haven't lost my bearings on where I live and where I like to go. Just people are fuzzy. After we get our milkshakes and fries, Verity starts talking about her boyfriend Jason and college—and even though she's rambling on, I know she's doing it for my benefit. I remember Jason now. We went to the movies together and a graduation party. I close my eyes and picture those memories the best I can, but there's a shape just outside my reach.

"Verity, who went to the movies with us and Jason?" I blurt out while she is still mid-sentence.

"Your boyfriend, Gunner." She pauses. The silence allows me to picture Gunner, and he floods into my memories, but it doesn't feel right.

"Gunner? Oh, yeah. Gunner."

"Cassia, you remember!" She yells loudly, causing other diner patrons to stare at us. I should be excited too, but I'm not. Maybe it's more side effects of the pills, but this eerie sensation creeps up my spine. "We should go find him. Or are you ready to see him?"

"No, not yet. I'll call him later. I look like a mess. I'm just glad memories are coming back. Oh, my goodness! College! Medical school! I always wanted to be a doctor—" The reality of our college situation seeps in, saddening me. "Oh, Verity. I'm going to miss you. This sucks. It's really real that we're going to be apart now." Her smile fades.

"We'll be fine, Cas. I promise. Nothing with us will change. Ever." We switch the conversation to positive things we're looking forward to. She drops me off at home, and I head upstairs to my room. That short excursion drained me, so I lie back down and quickly drift off.

I wake up to my cell ringing, and I glance over and look at the display. *Gunner.* I grab the cell and roll back over and answer, my voice still groggy and hoarse with sleep.

"Hey, beautiful. How are you feeling?" His voice streams through the receiver, bringing back memories of our time together. Who else would I have chosen besides him? Except for Verity, Gunner has been my closest friend. We planned this.

"Hey, Gunner. I'm better." I sit up and wipe the sleep from my eyes.

"Are you feeling up for some company? I was thinking about coming by in a bit and taking you out."

"Sure. I need to get ready. See you soon." I get out of bed and head to my closet, searching for something decent to wear. I feel nervous, and the emotion bewilders me. I brush my hair and attempt to make it lie flat. In my typical, over-thinking manner, I ask myself what's different about this day and this time with Gunner. Why so nervous? It hits me like a slap to my cheek: I chose him. Today's different because there's no more uncertainty. It's set. There's no going back, even though I can't imagine what I'd go back to. In this life, this world, we're going to be together. There's security in that feeling, but at the same time, something feels off and I can't explain it. Everything from here on out is final. It's been written already, and I'm along for the ride. No more planning, no more worry about the Trivium, from now on it's us and the future I mapped out for myself.

It's not long before Gunner arrives and my parents greet him sweetly at the door. My dad is being friendlier than usual though he's always liked Gunner. There's an air that's different between them. They must realize they're greeting a future son-in-law. We're not engaged, but it's imminent. Choosing takes the surprise out of it. No surprises anymore. I may not know when he'll ask me to marry him, but I know he will. I've seen scraps of the future and I know we'll have a child and I'll be a doctor. That much has come back to me. Even though I don't know what lies ahead, as far as specifics, it seems wrong to have expectations. I've never liked surprises, so why does this upset me? I've always wanted everything in my life planned, and here I am being upset because it is? I'm such a paradox.

Gunner opens the truck door for me and flashes a toothy grin. There's a confident air about him—much more than usual—and I can only guess it's related to being chosen. Another me somewhere is probably excited that someone I loved chose me as well. I'll never know.

"I thought we'd get something to eat somewhere new, by the college. What do you think? Maybe go walk around there and acquaint ourselves with college life?"

"Sounds nice." I mean it sincerely, but it doesn't come out that way so I smile to reassure him. It works because he glances my direction and smiles back. I don't even know what to say to him, so I turn on the radio to his favorite station and we spend the time in silence.

He pulls up to an inconspicuous pizza place situated between two older dilapidated buildings, and I guess he notices my frown because he tells me it's supposed to be a good hole-in-the-wall place that students love. I just shrug my shoulders and follow him inside. It's dim, and the walls are covered in lyrics and words written by former patrons in permanent marker. There's an artsy atmosphere to the place. This has never been my "scene" before. We're led to a corner booth toward the back, and while waiting to order, I glance around and read the writings. Some thoughts are profound, some silly. Some are famous quotes, others are just signatures. One quote catches my eye: *You must allow me to tell you how ardently I admire and love you.* A weight presses against my chest and I can't breathe. I jump up quickly and make my way to the restroom, clutching my chest and telling myself to breathe. Luckily, it's a single room. I lock the door and lean against the cold tile wall. The area of my sternum is painful to the touch, and my constricted breathing is inciting the beginning of panic. I work through a mental checklist of cardiac conditions and their symptoms—but it doesn't add up.

There's a quiet tapping on the door and a muffled voice. "Just a sec!" I yell and lean over the sink. I close my eyes and focus on my breathing until the pain starts to subside. Why am I panicking like this? I've never had chest pains before, and it frightens me. The dizziness dissipates so I leave and join Gunner at the booth. His face is creased with concern.

"What just happened?" He asks just above a whisper.

"Gunner, I don't know. I'm sorry to scare you like that, but my chest hurt and I needed to get away. I panicked."

"Want to go see your dad? Is it serious?"

"No, it's okay. It stopped. I'll tell him about it tonight and see what he says. Can we go somewhere else? I need some air." I glance back at the wall toward the quote—but it's not there. My eyes dart around to the entire area encompassing our booth, but there's no quote about love anywhere to be found. I must be losing it. "On second thought, can you take me home? I think I need some rest. Maybe I wasn't ready to get out yet." His mouth turns downward at the corner and I know he's disappointed, but there is no way I can handle both chest pains and hallucinations right now. He sighs loudly but apologizes to the waitress that was heading our way and leads me back outside. The air smells sickeningly sweet, the sunlight makes me squint, and sounds are overwhelming. I cover my ears with my hands and quickly get inside the truck. My temples throb and it's hard to think. Gunner says nothing to me; the silence is deafening. His shoulders slouch forward with both hands on the wheel. He stares at the road, never turning his head. I can tell he's upset, but that makes me angry. After all, I'm the one that doesn't feel well and am seeing things. I don't mention that to him, I don't want to start a fight. He pulls up to my house and barely mumbles a goodbye. I'm in too much pain at this point to care so I say goodbye and rush inside.

The house is empty and quiet; precisely what I need right now. I don't even make it to my room upstairs. I crash on the couch instead—covering my face with a pillow to drown out the light. Colors swirl my vision, even though my eyes are shut tight, and the panic ebbs as I drift off into nothingness.

I'm back in the Trivium tank, and the colors swirling around take different shapes above me. I feel weightless, and I hear a voice and see a face that lies beyond my reach. I scream a name that comes out muffled, and the face rescinds back into the ether. I try to sit up and pound on the lid, water sloshing all around me while the salt is stinging my eyes. Someone is calling my name, and sunlight peeks through as the lid opens. The face is there, it was never really gone. Calmness rushes through my body, and I stop screaming and start crying. Strong arms lift me up out of the tank and wrap a towel around me, hugging me gently. I look up to see the face and before I can, I wake up.

My living room ceiling is above me, not the face I was desperately reaching out for. I'm tempted to analyze the dream, but at this point, I'll let the doctors figure it out tomorrow. Stupid side effects I'm sure.

My cell rings. It's Verity, so I go ahead and answer it. She's coy about asking me how I'm doing, but I have a hunch Gunner called her. Employ the best friend to get the scoop—very sneaky. I assure her I'm fine and I want to rest, and she begrudgingly lets me off the phone.

I don't want to think. I don't want to sleep and dream anymore. I want to cloud my thoughts with a book and coffee and stow away into some secret niche in a world of my own making. I grab my keys and make my way toward the only place I know where I can be alone in my thoughts while simultaneously drowning them out: the library.

It's fortunate that our library stays open late. I randomly choose a letter and walk down the fiction section surrounded by As. Gliding my fingers across the books, one catches my eye and I snatch it out without looking at it and walk toward an overstuffed chair nestled in a dim corner. Plopping down into the chair, I glance at the book cover. *Persuasion*. Another Jane Austen. Haven't I read this already? I'm too comfortable to get up and get another book, so I crack it open across my lap and begin to read, only to notice I hadn't grabbed *Persuasion* at all. I had actually picked *Cat's Cradle*. Vonnegut. Weird. I wasn't in the Vs. Maybe someone shelved it wrong? A woozy feeling hits me hard so unexpectedly that I grab my stomach with one hand and cover my mouth with the other—letting the book hit the floor. The white cover bleeds into a dark red and I see Jane Austen's name in bold right before everything goes black.

I awake to bright fluorescent lights and the incessant sounds of beeping, and I don't recognize the room. I lift my arm, and there are needles poking out of one side and tubes cross my body leading into the beeping machines. I try to sit up when my mom rushes to my side and stops me and gently pushes me back down.

"Cas, no. Lie down. You're in the hospital. You fainted at the library. Do you remember?" My mom speaks softly, but with a slight wavering undertone.

"I remember feeling dizzy and my book changed, and that's all I know." She smiles at me, but that smile is restrained and doesn't leave her lips.

"What do you mean the book changed? The one you were reading?"

"Yes. I could swear it changed into a different book."

She sighs and walks back to a chair I hadn't noticed before and fishes a red book out of her purse. "I don't know why I picked this up, but the librarian thought it best to stay with you in case you were here awhile. Have you read this one before?"

I nod my head and then shake it. "No. I think I did. I don't know. What's going on, mom? I was sitting there about to read this book when suddenly it was a different one, and then it switched back to this one and . . . I realize I sound crazy."

She lets out a tiny laugh and shakes her head. "No, honey. I don't think you're crazy. The doctor ran some tests and the Trivium doctors came and did some more. They're all trying to figure out what happened and why you're still sick. I don't think this has ever happened before because they're being very secretive. It worries me a bit. You need to rest." She pauses and looks away. "Do you want me to tell Verity and Gunner?"

"No. I don't want them to worry. We don't even know what to tell them anyway."

"I thought you had plans with Gunner tonight. Is everything okay there?" She turns back toward me and searches my eyes for answers. I can't hide my feelings, I don't even try.

"I don't know what to think right now. Something doesn't feel right. Maybe once I feel better things will go back to as planned, but right now it's all so strange and new and so . . . finite. Do you know what I mean?"

"Yes. And no. I mean, you know about things that will happen—if that's what you mean by *finite*. But you chose it. You made the right choice for you and what you wanted to do with your life—and who you wanted to be with. I thought choosing would appease the planning side of your personality."

I don't know how to respond to that. She's right. And yet she's wrong somehow as well. I should be celebrating that everything I had planned is going to happen. I should be embracing a future that I chose. The one I wanted. It's silly to not be completely overjoyed at this point.

"I'm sure once I rest, and they figure out what happened, I'll be fine." My mom smiles reassuringly and goes to tell the nurse that I'm awake.

There's a feeling at the back of my mind that things really won't be okay. That the glitch issue was more serious than the doctors may know. Is there something wrong with me? Has there always been something wrong? The doctor walks in with the nurse, and he's someone I've never seen before. The Trivium logo is embroidered prominently on his white jacket, and he smiles just enough to show teeth but is clearly uncomfortable with the emotion.

"Cassia, I'm Dr. Bachman. I'm one of the doctors working at the Trivium in the research department, and I've been looking over your file ever since you left. It says here that you fainted. Do you remember what led up to it?"

"I was reading a book at the library. The book changed colors—or I kept seeing the wrong book in my hands. My stomach started hurting and I felt sick, and that's all I remember before waking up here." He studies me intently like an ant under a child's magnifying glass. It's unnerving.

"So, the book you were looking at changed? Was everything else the same besides the book?"

"Yes, as far as I recall. You don't find that odd?"

"It's not what I would call a routine side effect of the procedure at the Trivium, no. Your vitals look good, so as far as your physical health, you're in great shape, young lady. As far as the hallucinations though, were there any others?" I hesitate to tell him about the restaurant with the words on the walls. Almost like an instinctual feeling in my gut says to hold back on that information, but I can't think of a good reason as to why. Relying on my intuition, I reply, "No, sir. That was the only time." The squinted eyes and creased forehead tells me he doesn't fully believe me. Why did I lie? What is it about the words that matter so much?

"We're going to keep you overnight under observation just to make sure nothing else happens. Will you alert the nurse if you experience another hallucination?" I wince at the word. Is that all this is? Just hallucinations? It felt so much more real than that. I nod and he walks away, leaving my mom alone with me in the room.

"Honey, can I get you anything? Food? Something from home?" She looks at me with a smile.

It comes to me so fast that without thinking I answer, "Yes. Please get me the book *Cat's Cradle* by Kurt Vonnegut." She looks at me curiously, but nods her head and walks quietly out the glass door. If I'm going to experience hallucinations about a book morphing from one into another, I need to know what that book is about and why it may be important.

A couple of hours later my mom returns, book in hand, and it's the exact copy I had seen. Same cover and everything. I reassure her I'll be fine for the night, so she agrees to let me stay alone in the hospital room—promising to return first thing in the morning. I roll my eyes and remind her I'd rather sleep in, and I manage to convince her I'll call when I'm awake. Finally alone after being checked on for the last time by my nurse, I crack open the book and begin reading. Nausea overcomes me and the room starts to spin.

"Do you believe in a karass, Cassia? Not a fictional one, but the actual idea that there are people out there that are in our lives for a reason? Cosmically connected?" His voice is deep and warm and at this moment, very broody.

"Maybe. I don't know. Perhaps there are reasons for everything, sure. How would we know the answer to that unless we had already lived our lives? That would mean everyone in our life was meant to be there. That's fate. But we don't live in a world dominated by fate and chance anymore because we get to choose."

"True. We can choose. But what if it's actually fate letting us think we have the choice? Does that mean we could never choose the wrong path?"

"You're being awfully pensive tonight. A part of me wants to believe that we have real choices. Real, concrete, unchangeable choices. That what we choose is completely up to us, and not something predestined. In that sense, we could choose wrong. Fate would mean that no matter what, we have no control. If we're unhappy with our lives, then it doesn't matter because we were meant to be unhappy. I want to believe that God really did give us free will. And even though we live in this world, where our singular choice seems finite, I want to believe that our choices are still choices. Sure, that means we could be wrong. Even with knowing what could happen, we could end up making the wrong choices. But at least we'd be responsible for that instead of being able to blame it on fate." He sighs and smiles warmly and then chuckles to himself. "Are you laughing at me or something?"

There's a glint in his eye and he's sporting a wry smile. "Cas, I love being able to talk so deeply with you and share my thoughts. No matter what the truth is, I do believe in a duprass. You and me, babe. We're a duprass."

"Oh yeah? If I died, you'd die too within a week?"

"No. Seconds." His hand reaches behind my head and pulls me in close. I feel his breath close to my cheek as he whispers in my ear, "You're my favorite."

I shake violently, my stomach convulsing. Everything I had managed to hold down comes up so quickly that I barely have time to lean over the bed and avoid soiling the sheets. I press the panic button between breaths before leaning over the bed again. The nurse races in, but she's composed and used to the rush. She helps me out of bed and into the bathroom, avoiding the mess I created for her to clean up. I feel guilty about it, but my head is spinning. It felt so real. The book triggered something in me. I finish emptying the contents of my stomach, and the nurse helps me back to bed. Within a few minutes, Dr. Bachman strolls in with a false casualness and pulls the chair closer to the bed.

"Did you experience another hallucination?" He stares at me intently, but there's curiosity behind his eyes.

"I don't know. I think I fell asleep and had a strange dream. I couldn't tell you."

"What were you doing before you got a sick feeling?"

"I was reading this book." I show him *Cat's Cradle,* and he takes it from me, leafing through the pages.

"I don't think I've read this one, though I did appreciate *Slaughterhouse-Five*. Cassia, all your vitals are still reading as normal, so I'm puzzled as to what's causing you to react this way. Neurologically, everything is sound. Blood pressure is within an acceptable healthy range. Nothing in your blood test seems to indicate any viral or bacterial issue. I'm going to check everything again in the morning, but I hope you do try to eat some crackers and drink some water and see if that calms your stomach. Anxiety has been known to increase psychosomatic symptoms. I can prescribe you something for anxiety and stress if you think that may be a contributing factor." He looks at me with genuine concern, but the idea that this is all in my head is unnerving.

"No, I don't think so. I'll let you know if I change my mind." He gently pats my hand and walks slowly out the door, glancing back at me one last time with a slight nod.

My body is tired, and my mind quickly catches up to the same level of fatigue. The thought of biting into the stale, dry crackers on the table beside me makes my stomach grumble negatively so I refrain—even though I know I need something to eat. I gulp down a few mouthfuls of water in the hopes that I keep from spitting it back up. My throat is sore from the stomach acid, and I'm in no mood to have more come up. I lie back against the pillow and lower the bed to a more comfortable position. All I can think about is that voice. His voice. One I know but don't know. I can't place it, but it's familiar. Like a long-lost friend getting back in touch. Beyond the nausea and vomiting, that voice affects me in a real tangible way, and I don't know why. I close my eyes and replay his words over and over in my head, *"You're my favorite,"* and drift off to sleep.

CHAPTER TEN

Morning comes quickly, and with it the return of my parents and Dr. Bachman. They have no new information about what's happening to me, so I'm left to handle the visions on my own. Though Dr. Bachman wants me to keep him updated on any other sickness or strange feelings, I have no desire to return to this hospital room—and especially do not want to see the Trivium lab again. So, life must go on as normal, and whatever happens, will happen.

My dad returns to his practice so my mom takes me home. I insist I don't need anymore rest and instead want to focus on my future. If getting back to life as normal will help me move past the last few days, then so be it. I have a list of books to buy and supplies I'll need for school, so I make that my mission for the day. I can't decide if I want to be alone today or if I'd rather have Verity with me, so I call her and get no response. I don't really want Gunner near right now even though that feeling surprises me. I should want to be with him, right? After all, we have a lifetime together and it could start right now. And yet, I'm hesitant. The sweet and smooth voice in my vision did not belong to Gunner. It felt like it belonged to a person who meant a lot to me. But I don't know him, and right now I don't want any boy on my mind. Even though I chose my future and it included a future husband, there is so much more to what I want for my life that isn't limited to my role in a family. Also, I have plenty of time. Medical school will take years, and it's still my plan to finish before starting anything else.

I drive to the local textbook store to see what kinds of items are on my supply list. There are so many books for diverse types of courses in there: history, government, literature, and biology are just a few, and the fact that I get to take a literature course excites me. Everything else? Not so much.

"Cassia?" Gunner startles me as I'm flipping through the index of the literary text.

"Oh hey, Gunner. I didn't know you'd be here."

"Yeah, I just thought you were going to call me so we could get supplies together." He's clearly upset with me, and it's not that I don't understand why, it's that I'm not bothered by it and I think I should be.

"Sorry. I just thought I'd be alone a bit. I didn't think much about it. But you're here, so do you want to finish up shopping with me?"

"Sure." He answers in a very blunt manner. I know he has things on his mind he wants to say to me, but I don't want to hear it. I continue talking about school to avoid a real conversation with him.

For the next hour, Gunner and I finish up all our shopping, and he helps me take the bags to my car. His mood has lightened slightly, but the edge on his voice remains.

"Cas, we need to talk." I brace myself for the onslaught of what's coming. I nod and wait for it. "I'm worried about you." My shoulders relax. That wasn't the response I was expecting.

"I'm sorry, Gunner. I haven't been feeling well is all." He reaches out to me and puts his hand around my waist, drawing me closer to him. His eyes are searching mine for truth he will never find, and he abruptly lets go of me and takes a step back.

"You're different, you know." The sadness in his eyes is unmistakable, and at once I feel ashamed and guilty that I've let him feel that way because of what, my own issues? I take a deep breath, gathering my thoughts and fighting the tears that are trying to form in my eyes.

"Maybe I am. But is that a bad thing? I'm still me, Gunner."

"You can say that Cassia, but I don't think even you believe it. I'm not sure what's happened to you, and you aren't letting me in to find out, but there is definitely something different. You act differently around me like you're uncomfortable. Like you don't know me. Did I do something to upset you?" The weight of that accusation hits me like bricks in the chest.

"No, no, no. No. You didn't do anything to me. Look, something happened to me in the Trivium, and no one can tell me what. I'm fine as far as I'm healthy and there isn't anything noticeably wrong, but I can't describe something I can't understand myself. This isn't about you. This is about me. And I know that's cliché, but I have no other way to say it. It doesn't matter though Gunner because it's you and me and our plans, and that's what I'm going to focus on—I just need a little time to sort that out."

He looks at me silently for several seconds and I try but I can't read his mind. "Okay, Cassia. Okay. Whatever you need. I'll be here if you need me." He bends over and kisses my cheek, squeezes my arm gently and then turns away to walk to his truck. He doesn't even look back.

I feel like I'm grieving, but I can't place what it is I've lost. I gained a future and insight into what my life holds for me, and yet I'm clearly in mourning. My heart hurts, a black hole has formed in my chest that is sucking life from me, and nothing I think about fills it back up. I know only one thing about what is going on, and that is I've lost a piece of myself that I never knew I could lose. I take my bags home and trudge up to my room and then lie on my bed and cry softly. Tears flow slowly down my cheeks, and the hole widens and swallows them up. I am broken. In an effort to complete my life by choosing my future, all I've managed to do is to lose something important to me that I never knew I had. There must be something out there that I'm missing. Something I was supposed to choose and didn't. A life I was meant to live that I shied away from. I can't imagine what that life would have looked like. If it had been so great why would I have chosen the life I did? What about it made it special? Was my chip so messed up that it altered my brain? There must be a way to fill the void. I should start by spending more time trying out the things I said I always wanted to do. Maybe if I submerge myself into the future I've chosen, I can find the one part of me I lost. And even if I can't, I can try to fill the hole with other wonderful things. Since I'm going to medical school, I may as well get a head start on training. And to do that, all I need to do is talk to my dad.

At dinner, my dad seems overly enthusiastic when I ask him if I can go with him to work the next day. I thought I would need to convince him to let me shadow him—or just be around to get him coffee—but at the very mention of me tagging along, he brightens up and starts chatting away about everything he can show me and things I can help with.

The next morning my alarm wakes me up early, and I'm jolted out of sleep. It takes me a moment to remember why I had set it, but when reality hits I pull myself out of bed and manage to get dressed in some scrubs my dad borrowed and pull my hair up into a ponytail. No need to be vain so I don't bother with makeup, and instead I brush my teeth and head downstairs to pour coffee in the hopes it will wake me up.

My mom gets to sleep in later than my dad, so it's still dark in the kitchen and there are no tantalizing smells of bacon wafting through the house like on a normal day. I throw a bagel in the toaster, slather on some cream cheese, and pour the coffee that was brewing thanks to the delay timer. Dad saunters in whistling and pours himself some coffee into a travel mug and then refills the carafe and gets it ready to brew more for my mom. That simple gesture gives me hope that Gunner and I will have that kind of marriage one day. Even though right now it seems odd, maybe after several years we'll somehow get to that point in our relationship.

"Ready to go, kiddo?" His smile is infectious, and it makes me happy to know that something so simple—me going to work with him—can make him smile like that. I nod with a mouthful of bagel and follow him out to his car in the garage. My car has been sentenced to the driveway.

The front desk receptionist greets me warmly and shows me where to check in and how to keep track of my time. I'm not actually getting paid, but my dad seems to think that this could qualify as an internship, and he wants detailed time sheets just in case I can use it for college credit. My first day is all about learning the structure of the paperwork system, as my dad wants me to experience not just being a physician, but also a secretary and even a custodian. I respect that he isn't above his employees in attitude, and I want to do an excellent job, so I don't complain—even when my day includes cleaning the bathrooms. I know it's just day one, but I've been promised that day two includes shadowing the staff, and I'm looking forward to it. After checking out for the day, dad and I head home. Verity and I made dinner plans, so my parents take that as a hint they need a dinner date alone. It's sweet and their dates usually last several hours, so I don't have a specific time to be home.

Verity picks me up and we decide that the local pancake house is where we want to go. It's not as busy in the evenings, but we love eating waffles and pancakes for dinner.

The coffee is roasted locally, and it's so freshly ground that the aroma permeates the entire restaurant. I breathe it in deeply when we walk in. I could douse myself in a perfume that smelled like coffee if they made such a thing. We order the house brew and a large carafe and two mugs are brought over.

"So, how was your first day working for your dad?" Verity sips her coffee slowly, blowing on it lightly to cool it off.

"Well, I don't really work for my dad. It's more of an internship. But it was okay. I didn't do much today though."

"So, no saving someone's life today?" She giggles. I roll my eyes in return.

"Yeah, no. But I saved someone from entering a dirty bathroom!" We both break out in a fit of laughter. It's been so long since we laughed like this, even though we both know we're laughing at something stupid. It feels good to feel normal, even for just a moment.

"Cas, are you ready for school yet? Miss planner? I bet you have everything already bought, huh?" She smiles and then winks at me.

"You know me too well. I bought everything for class. I bet you haven't even looked at the list, huh?" I respond, mocking her.

"You know, I did get a few things. Don't look at me like you're in shock, Cas. I'm not last minute on everything. Not this time anyway. Jason and I went together and got some supplies the other day." I had forgotten about Jason for a second and had to focus on his name to remember who he was.

"Gunner and I got a few things too . . ." I trail off, remembering how the day ended and not sure I want to talk about it.

"I'm going to check out my dorm room next week. Want to join me?"

"Um, only absolutely!" I could use some time away from home even though it's not too far of a drive. "Are you riding with Jason?"

"Yeah, I am, but you can ride with us." I go back and forth in my mind over whether I could handle being without my car now that I have my own sense of freedom. The ability to leave when I want sounds appealing, but my instinct says to ride with them. It would be more fun anyway.

"Okay, that sounds fun. I'll make sure taking the day off is cool with my dad, but I'm sure he won't mind. Not like I'm doing much to help, or getting paid."

"True." I want to talk to her about the fainting. I want so badly to have someone to confide in. Considering she's my best friend, I doubt she'd think I was crazy or blow me off. Now just doesn't feel like the right time. Perhaps if we can sneak away from Jason at the dorm, I can speak with her in private. I add that to my mental to-do list.

We finish our coffees and she catches me up on her plans, or lack thereof, for the rest of the summer. I know she's worried about leaving her dad and brother, but there's an excitement to her that screams freedom and it makes me happy to see that.

After she drops me off at home, I enter quietly just to realize that it's dark in the house and my parents must still be out enjoying their night. I smile to myself, thinking about how much they love each other, and then a pang of jealousy hits my gut and catches me off guard. I want that life. I want that relationship. I want to enjoy my days with my best friends, pursuing a career I find fulfilling while being married to someone I can spend my days with. Someone I look forward to seeing. If my parents taught me anything, it's that love doesn't always look like the passion and romances in the movies. Sometimes it looks like helping with house chores or remembering special days. Sometimes it's spontaneous date nights and deep conversations with a person that loves you—in spite of your beliefs and opinions—and sees past your flaws. Not everyone gets parents like mine that model such love. True, I've heard them argue over random things, but they always work it out. No matter the disagreement, they stick it out until they come to a compromise. And that's exactly the relationship I hope to have with Gunner. Getting to spend even more time with him this fall means we can really get to know each other more on a deeper level—away from the pressures of family and friends.

I lie on my bed, daydreaming about the future when I hear my parents walk in downstairs. They're trying hard to be quiet because I can hear one shushing the other, but they keep giggling all the way to their room. I smile to myself and feel warmth flow through me. I fall asleep dreaming of being wrapped in a love I long to have for myself.

The next week comes quickly, and Verity and Jason pick me up to head to their new university upstate. Gunner had no interest in going with us and made plans with his old baseball buddies. I was a little disappointed that after I tried to reach out to him and invite him along—with Jason's permission—he turned down the opportunity to spend the day with me. Jason and Verity must sense that I'm upset because they dial down the public affection between them. We alternate between chatting and listening to music, and the drive goes by quickly. Verity's dorm is on the opposite side of the campus from Jason's, so he takes us to hers first and drops us off. We make plans to meet up with him later for a tour, and Verity and I take a good look around. The campus is beautiful, riddled with purple pansies and peach begonias in neatly manicured flower beds. The buildings are all in the Gothic Revival style, lending a very cultured air to a sense of mystery and sophistication. It's a far cry from the more modern style of the university I'm going to. Something about it feels comfortable and interesting like I want to explore every crevice and learn its secrets.

We make our way into the dorm and the common area is littered with tables and chairs with a few well-worn sofas sprinkled throughout. At the far end of the long rectangular room is a large stone fireplace with accent chairs pointed toward it, and a couple of tufted ottomans in place of a coffee table. There are a few students living here in the summer, but only a couple are in the commons, reading what must be textbooks. While I was admiring the dark wood paneling and neat architectural features of the rooms, Verity was getting a key to her dorm room from the front desk. Since she can't move in officially for another couple of weeks, she won't get to keep the key, but at least they're letting us check it out early.

We make the way up the stairs, and it's lucky she's on the third floor since there are five stories. As it turns out, her dorm is co-ed, though boys live on alternate floors. I ask her why Jason is on the other side of the school, and she tells me that arts majors congregate together over there in an effort to keep the creative vibe flowing. I'm not sure how that works exactly, but I'm assuming it's a less studious and more open to an anything goes atmosphere.

Sounds much more fascinating than the strict rules and guidelines my dorm has posted. Though I haven't been there in several years, I did get to go visit a cousin once, and I remember it being a very sterile feeling sort of place. Which, it's mostly medical students, so it's appropriate, but it's very cold and isolating.

Her roommate isn't determined yet, but Verity does have to share. There are loft-style beds on either side of the room with the mattress on top and a desk below. Nothing adorns the walls so it's lacking character, but at least Verity gets her own closet even when she doesn't get much of her own space. The bathrooms are community style, something that would greatly bother me, but doesn't affect Verity in the slightest. Since I don't know yet what type of room I'll get, I have no way of knowing if I'm relegated to the same bathroom fate.

"Well, it's not much, but I can definitely work with this," Verity says, eyeing the lackluster décor and lack of square footage.

"I hope you really like your roommate, with you living in such a confined space together," I say.

"No kidding. I hope she's a free spirit, or at least like you." She winks at me but the words hit me hard. It feels wrong to not stay together and see each other every day. Living with her would be such a dream that someone else getting that privilege hurts a little. "Wouldn't this be great if that were your bed, Cas? I feel like we should be doing this whole growing-up-into-adults thing together, you know?"

I nod and swallow back the lump forming in my throat. I don't want to be tearing up right now. I close my eyes, and when I open them the room has changed. There are posters of different bands on the walls combined with black and white photos of people I don't recognize. Confused, I look around for Verity and I see her lying on the top bunk to my right, but there is bedding on the mattress and drawings of several styles of dresses pinned above her.

"Verity?" I manage to squeak her name, feeling light-headed.

"Cas, how was that writing class?" she asks.

"What writing class? What's going on?" I clutch my stomach and bend over slightly, taking in deep breaths. The bunk on my left is also decorated with lyrics, and the shelf is full of books— many of which I have at home. Verity sits up and looks at me quizzically.

"There's no way you forgot to go to class, Cas. What's up with you? Feeling okay?"

"No. A second ago none of this was here, and now I feel sick and I don't know what's happening to me." I sit down on the wood floor and put my head between my knees, breathing as deeply as possible in the hopes I won't throw up. Verity climbs down from her bed and I feel her hand resting on my back.

"Can I get you some water? Should I call your dad?"

"Water, yes. Dad, no." I hear her footsteps grow softer as she leaves the room to get a bottle of water downstairs. I feel like I can control the pangs in my stomach, so I stand up and focus on the walls to steady myself. The photos draw my eyes toward them, so I take slow steps in that direction—making sure I don't fall over. Some are people from the past as I recognize famous faces in what must be reproductions. I keep scanning the pictures and I stop when I see one containing the smiling faces of Verity and Jason in a mock pose to resemble the vintage photographs pinned next to them. It makes me laugh to see them like this, happy and silly all-in-one. My eyes drift to the next photo on the left, and it's Verity and me in a place I've never seen before. I have no recollection of this memory and it's jarring. Quickly looking at the wall, I notice more pictures of Verity and me in unfamiliar places, and my head starts to feel like it's spinning.

"Cas, I'm back with the water." Verity rushes over to me and I take a few sips, but once it hits my stomach the cramping pain comes back in full force. I bend over at the hips and continue breathing deeply, but the pain is getting worse and tears form in my eyes. A small scream erupts from my lips, and I crumple to the floor. Everything goes black.

I manage to open my eyes and I see Verity sitting above me, wiping tears from her cheeks.

"Are you okay?" She cries out, reaching her arms out to me to help me up. I shake my head and use her support to stand up.

"What happened to me, Verity? What did you see?"

"You suddenly bent over and started crying out, and then you just fell down! What's going on?" Panic is in her voice, and I know that nothing I say will calm her down, so I decide that it's time to tell her the truth of everything that's been happening to me lately. I take a deep breath before diving into my story about fainting in the library, the hospital visit, and that the doctors don't know what's going on. She sits in silence, processing everything I just told her. I sit in silence with her, instead of forcing the conversation further.

"So, that's odd." She stares blankly at the wall and then glances around the room. "So, what was on the walls again? Photographs?" I shake my head slightly and laugh to myself.

"Black and white photos. That's what you want to know? Out of everything I just told you?" She laughs and then puts her arm around my shoulder and pulls me closer.

"Honestly, I'm worried. I wish the doctors knew what was happening. You really freaked me out back there. I mean, you saw this room like it was ours, like you were lost in some kind of alternate universe or something. Which, it would be great if this were your room too, you know. I've always wanted that."

"I know. Me too." The air is thick with regret and lost lives and should-have-beens. What if she's right? What if I'm seeing into another world? Another future? Maybe the chip glitched in such a way that I can see what I didn't choose, a life I'm not living. The only question is, why didn't I choose this life, where Verity and I are together in college? What would I have been doing here anyway? Perhaps being a doctor meant more to me than whatever that life had to offer. Perhaps that life didn't involve Gunner. But if Gunner wasn't in it, who was?

We ease up off the floor and go back downstairs to the common room. Jason meets us there and we take a tour of the campus. I'm most excited to see the library, and Jason and Verity leave me to check it out on my own while they get their student I.D. cards made at the student union. The library is massive, with the musty-sweet smell of old books. Tables are lined up down the length of the main hall, individual study lamps on each one. The ceiling is reminiscent of a Gothic cathedral with ornate stained-glass windows throughout. Looking around, I feel so comfortable here, that I wish I could stay much longer. It's tempting to grab a book at random off a shelf and make myself at home at a desk. Jason and Verity find me and break my moment of reverie.

"Come on, daydream believer. We have to get going." Verity shows me her I.D. card, and I sense a pang of jealousy coming on. I like it here.

"Alright, if you insist. I could stay here all day," I sigh loudly.

"Sorry, sweetie. Maybe your alternate life self is going to school here." She winks at me.

"What?" Jason asks, eyeing us suspiciously.

"Oh, nothing. Inside joke." Verity smiles at him and slyly winks at me. She loops her arm under mine and we walk linked together back to Jason's car. I take one last look around, breathing in the atmosphere and storing the scenery like a picture in my heart before I get in the back seat. I wonder to myself if it's indeed too late to apply here, but I wipe that thought away. I mean, I chose my future. It's set from here on out. I'm certain changing anything is impossible, and extremely doubtful the Trivium would allow such a thing. Why am I even contemplating this? Of course, I'm not supposed to be here. Emotions are a fickle thing.

Verity and Jason are full of school talk and anticipation, so I tune them out and stare out the window.

"Are we boring you, Cas?" Verity turns around in her seat, looking at me with sympathy in her eyes.

"No, I just don't have anything to contribute to the conversation." That came out more harshly than I intended. "Sorry guys, I didn't mean it like that. I just really liked it there. But I'm sure I'll love my school too."

"Of course, you will," Verity chimes in, "I'll go with you on the campus tour if you want." She smiles wanly.

"I'd like that actually," I reply.

"Unless of course, Gunner wants to go alone or something."

"Oh, um, no it's fine. I don't really have plans with Gunner." I notice Jason looking at me sympathetically in the rear-view mirror, but he looks away immediately when he catches my eye. They must know more than what I told them, which wasn't much. I bet Gunner called them, and the thought he'd do that behind my back angers me. I don't like being blindsided by my own friends— especially since it's personal issues between the two of us. He won't open up to me, but he'll spill everything to my best friend?

"Cas, you okay back there? Your cheeks are turning pink."

I stare at Verity without blinking for several seconds till she looks away, clearly uncomfortable.

"What did Gunner tell you exactly? About him and me? And no holding back either. If he's going to tell you about our own personal stuff, I deserve to know the details."

Jason shifts uncomfortably in the driver's seat. Verity takes a deep breath and faces me again.

"Yes, Gunner called us. Well , . . . he called me. I don't want to get between you two and your personal issues, and I told Gunner to not talk to me anymore about you. I don't like keeping secrets." She sighs before continuing. "He thinks he's losing you and doesn't understand how that's possible. Is that true?"

I look down at my lap, thinking of the best way to respond. Can you lose someone who chose you? Can chosen paths diverge in a wood? I take a deep breath, realizing Verity never took her eyes off me. "I'm not sure how I feel right now, and Gunner can't understand either. These visions worry me, and I just need some time to either heal or accept my life and the possibility that I'll have these problems forever. It's just hard. I can't talk to him though, and now I'm not sure I want to."

Verity turns back around and doesn't respond. Jason avoids my eye contact in the mirror. They don't understand either. No one does. I've never felt truly alone before this moment and my chest starts hurting. My body is racked with dry sobs but my eyes refuse to water and that suits me just fine.

We pull up to my house and I get out without speaking. Their silence says more to me than any conversation would have. Verity gives me a small wave—which I return—before I walk inside. As soon as the door closes behind me, the tears pour like a cascading waterfall with no signs of receding. I mourn the change in my relationships and the loss of my unbridled optimism about life. It's time to admit to myself that everything has indeed changed. I've changed. My life has changed. There is something not quite right about the world I'm living in, and the Trivium was the beginning of this shift. The future I chose seems like it's been stolen from me. A self-awareness of the differences in what should have been and what things will be permeates my thoughts. I can't go back.

I dry my eyes and wipe my tear-stained cheeks and take several deep breaths, exhaling loudly. This may not be what I imagined my life resembling, but it's the hand I've been dealt. Time to pull myself up by my bootstraps and move forward. It's my life and all I can do is live it.

I spend the next several weeks at my dad's office learning the ins and outs of his practice. The work is monotonous and not exactly how I pictured it. A lot of general check-ups and routine procedures, combined with multiple sore throats and sniffly noses. Not exactly inspiring. I keep thinking that if I went into a different medical field that it'd be more interesting to me, but I know how much my dad wants me to join his practice after graduation. I spend all my free time at the library, perusing ancient texts and immersing myself into more adventurous and fantastical worlds than the one I live in.

One day, while I'm walking between aisles of books, an idea for a story comes to me quite suddenly. Fearing I'll lose the thought, I ask the librarian for some paper and begin jotting it all down. The words flow easily, and when I leave the writing trance I'm in and reread what I've written, I'm surprised at how good of a story it is. I share it with Verity that afternoon and receive positive feedback.

"Wow, Cas, you can write! You should send this to a short story contest!" Verity is clearly more emphatic about my storytelling skills than I am, but I glow at the thought. Is it good enough to get published? Gunner doesn't fawn over it the way Verity did—he doesn't have much interest in books—but he encourages me to submit it to a local publication, so I do. I wait for weeks to hear back before getting discouraged, and by then I give up any idea of writing another story. What's a future doctor doing writing fiction?

It's a few weeks later when my mom runs into my room flapping an envelope around in excitement.

"Cas! Open it! Open it! Open it!" She thrusts it at me so I eagerly take it from her. The return address is for the local magazine I sent my story to, and anxiety sets in. Is this a rejection in physical form? My mom is laser-focused on me, so I swallow my fear and tear into the envelope, finally unfolding the letter and reading it thoroughly.

"Well, what's it say? Don't leave me hanging like this!"

"Dear Cassia, thank you for submitting your short story for publication in our magazine. Our editor believes it will be a great fit for our upcoming issue. Enclosed is payment for the right to publish at our magazine exclusively. We appreciate your submission and encourage you to continue submitting more pieces. Sincerely, Amy Johnson, Submission Editor."

My mom squeals with excitement, breaking my incredulous stupor. Warmth spreads throughout my body and the shock starts to wear off.

"I'm published? I'm published!"

"You're like a professional writer now!"

"Well, mom, that's not true. It's one story." She beams at me.

"That's only because you only wrote one story. Imagine if you wrote more! And maybe a novel!"

"Are you even serious right now? I won't have time to write and go to medical school."

"But honey, do you really want to work with your dad? I've seen you up there. You don't seem happy. Not like this. Your face is glowing!"

"How can you ask me that?" Heat creeps up my neck and I feel my face flush. "I chose this life. That's it. You can only go to the Trivium once." Her eyes twinkle mischievously. "Mom, what are you thinking right now? What's that look for?" She looks around the room like she's paranoid someone is listening in. She leans in close to me, mouth right next to my ear.

"What if I told you the Trivium can be wrong? That you can still make your own choices?" She backs away from me, putting her index finger to her lips. She has me paranoid now too. What is she talking about? Has my mom lost it? "Hey Cas, want to take a walk with me? No cells, no electronics, okay?" She winks. "Just us two." I play along though I'm more confused than ever.

"Sure, mom. I guess I can do that." I follow her out of my room, leaving everything on my bed that had been in my pockets—cell included. I feel naked without it. We walk down the steps and she doesn't speak until we're about five houses away.

"Cas, I don't want you to repeat anything I say to anyone—Verity included. Understand?" An uneasy feeling takes root in my stomach, but I nod in agreement. Curiosity gets the best of me. "It sounds radical, but . . ." she pauses, "What if the Trivium is wrong? What if we can make choices even after our initial choosing?" We keep walking, and I notice we're headed to the park. I follow her to the swing set and sit on the swing beside her.

"Mom, why were you looking around my room? Like we were being watched?" She lets her feet dangle and then digs in and pushes off the ground, picking up speed and swinging higher. Clearly, I'm not getting an easy answer, so I push off also and propel myself higher till we're both swinging in sync. I keep eyeing her, but she just looks at me and smiles. With a childish laugh, she throws herself out of the swing and lands on her feet, hands up in the air like a gymnast who just stuck a perfect landing. I'm not as daring, so I put my feet down and try to stop myself, digging into the ground and dirtying up my shoes in the process. "Mom, would you please talk to me? You're acting childish and weird. What do you mean we can make our own choices?"

She turns toward me, the elation on her face turns to hardness—a serious and piercing look.

"Free will, Cas."

She turns away from me, saying nothing else and walks back to the house. I'm left there rooted in place like a statue, speechless.

CHAPTER ELEVEN

ETHAN

I blew it. I tried too hard and failed. I don't have much experience in the romance department, but clearly throwing every romantic gesture and quote I've ever read all together was not a failsafe way to get the girl. Movies and books lie. I should've known better. I think I did know better but ignored all the alarms going off in my head. It's amazing the things you'll say when you've experienced love the first time and are desperate to not lose it. But I did. In my moment of desperation, I have a great certainty that I lost the girl. When I saw Cassia in my dreams, I couldn't get over that feeling I had of being with her. Granted, I didn't know then that she was real and as wonderful in person. Even then, I had this feeling like my life could be so much better. That she would make me be a better person. But quoting *Pride and Prejudice*, who talks like that? Austen screws with the minds of girls, thinking men today are equally full of charm and integrity and wit as her love interests. I don't think they were really like that even back then. I tried to be witty. I tried to be sweet. It was over-the-top, but I was working on borrowed time. What choice did I have?

How far would you go and how dumb would you act to win the affection of a girl you only know in dreams? But they were real. I know they were, and she admitted as much. I don't know how it's possible. I'm not a scientist. And for a writer, you'd think I'd have the ability to come up with my own words, instead of relying on stealing someone else's. She didn't want me to contact her today. I can't stop pacing my room. I can't stop fidgeting. I'm torn between throwing something and screaming. I know that too much stress could trigger one of my headaches, but I'm not concerned about it. How can I feel so much for her?

Can I go to the Trivium in a few weeks and choose her myself if she didn't choose me? Is that possible? Would she be a choice? I was crazy enough to tout the s-word as a real possibility for us. It would explain our connection. My heart pounds quickly in my chest, and the light in my room seems to be brighter than before. I know this is the start of a migraine, so I need to calm down. I hear ringing behind me and know that sound signals Jason calling.

"Hey, Jason." I sit on the edge of my bed, still fidgety.

"Ethan, you okay? I thought I should check on you since . . . well . . . you know."

"I'm fine."

"You don't sound fine." I take in a deep breath and exhale quietly, trying to regain my composure.

"I'll be fine, Jason. Thanks for checking. Have you . . . ? Never mind."

"Have I heard about Cassia? No, not yet. And it's okay to ask, you know." He sighs loudly, clearly thinking I'm being ridiculous for skirting the question.

"Thanks for the update. Can you have Verity call me when she hears anything? If you're cool with that, that is."

"Ethan, I'm not worried whatsoever about you and Verity. Please, man. Get real. And yes, I'll ask her to call you if she hears anything new."

"Thanks, Jason. I wasn't insinuating anything about Verity. I just know it's an awkward situation with Gunner."

"Oh. To be completely honest, I don't think Verity likes Gunner that much anymore. She hasn't outright said anything, but she doesn't ever want him calling. Of course, he's usually calling to gripe about Cassia, and she hates that." I feel a pang in my abdomen. Is Gunner for real? He seemed nice enough at the cabin, but what does he have to complain about concerning Cassia?

"Interesting," I say.

"For a writer, you're a man of few words," he laughs.

"I know I need to stop borrowing words from other writers and start writing my own. But right now, there are no words."

"I think they're in a dictionary in case you want to find them."

"Shut up, Jason," I laugh. "I should write them down, instead of trying to speak them. I'd be better at it."

"Perhaps. Just don't go all Thoreau on me in that cabin, okay?" He tries hard to keep from cracking up at his own joke.

"Yeah, whatever. Although, going to the cabin doesn't sound like a bad idea. I'll probably do that. Check in with you later?"

"Yeah. And I'll forward your lovesick request to Verity."

"You're lucky you're not here or you'd pay for that."

"With what? Stab me with your pen?"

"The pen *is* mightier than the sword."

"Not in hand-to-hand combat."

"Ninja skills."

"Go to Walden Pond, Thoreau."

"Will do. And thanks for checking on me, Jason."

"No problem." He hangs up abruptly, and I look around my room for my notebook. It used to be in my nightstand, but I find it covered under other books and shirts on my dresser. Pen in hand, notebook under my arm, I'm ready to head out to the cabin. If I can't be with Cassia in person, I can at least write about the life we had together in our dreams.

I've spent much of my childhood in this place. Taken countless naps on the worn sofa in front of a raging fire. My mom continuously filling mugs full of hot cocoa while my dad would play music or sing. Hannah would be curled up by the fireplace with a book, not even minding how hot it was so close to the fire. She was too absorbed in her fairytales to notice. My parents have said that someday this cabin will be mine to do whatever I please. I've thought about living here full-time after college, or making it into a writer's retreat. With three bedrooms and two bathrooms, it's a decent size for a small family and has all the comforts of our house in the city.

Sitting on the couch this time feels different from all the times before. I vividly remember Cassia working in this exact spot. I don't believe they were dreams, all these experiences I've had with

Cassia. I believe them to be memories of what's yet to come. A portal into another life. The right life. The only one perfect for me.

The cabin feels empty and lonely without her presence. I always felt like there was a hole in my heart, a piece of me missing. I dismissed the first dream, blaming it on me having a wild imagination. The second dream I took notice of her, really trying to remember details. The third dream I realized that the hole was filling in. And meeting her was like finding that missing piece of the puzzle that is my life. *What are you choosing, Cassia? What have you seen?*

I want to write but the words do not come. I can't force them. When I'm lying in bed at night—when it's late and I'm supposed to be sleeping—that's the time that my brain goes haywire and starts writing stories. I see a story like a movie playing in my head. I picture the details and the characters. I hear the dialogue. And it's always when I should be sleeping that the words consume me, but it's too late at night to get back up and start writing. I leave that for the morning. The story sticks with me as if it won't let go of my soul until the words are written on paper. They flood my being until I release them, one drop of letters at a time. Though I may be drowning in anxiety, I'm unfortunately not swimming in prose. I look around the bookshelves on the chance there will be a book I haven't read yet, but I don't see anything new. My trip here to get my mind off Cassia is a bust. The stress has been eroding away my energy, so I lie down on the couch and cover myself with a blue throw. It's my favorite of all the throws my mother has knitted. She would sit in the rocking chair for hours, knitting away the time while the rest of us talked about books or music. She always listened more than she spoke, but you could see a hint of a smile creep on her face every once in a while. I miss those days. We used to come here together every weekend until the past few years. And now it's mostly just me that visits or stays. Hannah has my parents constantly busy as her chauffeur for all her various extra-curricular activities. She's a very talented girl, though I often wonder if she lets herself take on too much. My parents are saints for carpooling her all over town every weekend, and a few nights each week. I wonder if I'd be that kind of parent, or if I'd tell my kids they can try one thing at a time, but that's it. I like being home. Going out is tiring. But then again, if I had a child as talented as Hannah, maybe I *would* drop everything in my life to help her dream big. Let her explore life and her talents and pray one day she'd end up being very happy with her choices. This line of thinking does nothing to keep thoughts of Cassia at bay. Instead, I drift off into thoughts of what a family with her would look like. We both like books and writing. Neither of us is a fan of shallow conversation. I think of staying up late at night, having deep conversations about the world. Of travel and adventure and spontaneity. As free as we would allow ourselves to be.

My brain won't let me sleep. It won't let me write. I am doomed to play the past few months over and over in my head like a sports blooper reel. *Here's where Ethan made a pathetic joke from a book. Here's where Ethan acted like a complete idiot because he was hopelessly in love with a girl he barely knew.*

I sit up and look around the cabin, trying to recall family memories here instead of visions of Cassia. Mom and dad being ridiculous, dancing by the fireplace and making Hannah embarrassed. Hannah and I working on a puzzle with a thousand pieces at the small kitchen table. We couldn't eat at the table for months because it took that many weekends for us to finish putting together our masterpiece. Cassia sitting in the rocking chair, clearly uncomfortable but trying to act nonchalant about it. Stop it, Ethan.

There's no escape here. A jumble of happy memories, but they also include *her*. I've been here long enough and haven't accomplished anything but cause myself more pain. All those memories are in the past, with no hope of making more in the present. I stand up and grab my notebook, and my eyesight blurs suddenly. Panicking, I drop the notebook and rub my eyes, but when I open them again, I'm not at the cabin at all. I'm sitting in a booth at a restaurant. I close my eyes again, but when I open them I'm still sitting in a booth. Scanning the area, I realize I'm in the same pizza place I took Cassia to. There's a black permanent marker on the table, in case a patron wants to add to the artwork on the walls and ceiling. I don't know how I got here, or why I'm here. I look around at the people at the other tables and I don't recognize anyone. I look back down at the marker. I guess if I'm going to be stuck in some weird dream-slash-vision or whatever, I may as well do something fun. I think of the cheesiest line I can muster, one that would make Cassia laugh if she were to see it and then write it on the wall. "*You must allow me to tell you how ardently I admire and love you.*" I am no real Darcy. I mean the words, but curse myself for being so foolish around her. If the visions were real, she would have loved me for who I am, not who I was trying to be.

A girl's laugh carries through the hallway, and I turn to see Cassia walking toward me, taking a seat across from me. "I saw what you wrote, Ethan. Don't play coy." I'm in such shock that I stumble over my words, leading her to laugh again. "Speechless because you got caught?"

"What are you doing here?" I ask, almost breathless.

"What do you mean? We're here to eat pizza. Duh. Are you feeling okay?" Now she's shifted her smile into a frown, furrowing her brow in concern.

"One second ago I was in my cabin, and now I'm here with you. I guess I just don't understand. You were at the Trivium." She eyes me warily.

"Ethan, that was several weeks ago. Remember? We've spent almost every minute together like complete lovesick puppies, ever since I got back. What's happening?"

"Wait, you . . . ch-chose m-me?" She shakes her head at me, clearly bothered by my questions.

"Ethan, we did it. We chose *each other*. The Trivium people about flipped out on us, and we didn't know why. It was such a rare thing to happen. You're really scaring me." She gets up and joins me on my side of the booth, putting her arm around me and squeezing tightly. "Are you having a headache?"

I shake my head. "No, I don't think so. I just don't understand anything at all right now."

She puts her hand to my cheek, turning my face toward her. "Ethan, I love you. Whatever is going on, we'll figure it out, together." I feel hot tears lining my eyes, so I close them and put my head down on the table. Wherever I am, however I got here,

I'm fine with never leaving. Because Cassia loves me. *Loves.* She leans closer, kissing my cheek softly. "It's just you and me, and no one else. I'm right here. I'll always be right here. Remember? Wherever you are, there I'll be."

I lift my head back up and I'm staring straight at the fireplace in the cabin. My heart racing, I cry out for her, and when she doesn't answer and I can't get back to her, I scream. My cell rings, and I see it's Jason so I answer at once. "Jason, what have you heard?"

"Ethan, are you sitting down? Because you need to sit down."

"Why, what's going on?" I hear a woman's screams in the background, and I recognize it as Verity. Panic seeps through my chest. "Jason, what happened? What is it?"

"Ethan, I'm sorry. I'm so so sorry."

"Dang it, Jason, freaking tell me what happened!" There's a brief silence, and all I hear is Verity crying.

"She's gone, Ethan. Cassia's gone."

"What the heck does that mean, she's *gone?*"

"There was a glitch with Cassia's chip. And . . ."

"No!" I scream.

"She died, Ethan. Cassia's dead."

I drop my cell on the couch. Grief envelops me and I fall on my knees to the floor, violent sobs shaking my entire body. I know a headache could come at any moment, and I don't even care. This doesn't make sense. *I was just with her. We're supposed to be together. We did it. We chose each other.* How could this have happened? I scream some more, and I feel my body going numb. The waves of nausea pour over me, and the piercing sounds of a migraine flood my ears. I clutch my hands to my head and then crumple to the floor. Everything fades to black.

CHAPTER TWELVE

ETHAN

When I come to, I'm surrounded by darkness. Blinking rapidly, it dawns on me that it's nighttime. I slowly feel my way around the coffee table, grabbing the couch, and then following it around to the light switch. I find my cell still on the couch where I'd dropped it, and it's lit up with multiple missed calls and messages. I scroll through them, and the messages are surreal. Jason has tried calling me several times, and his messages are increasingly fraught with anxiety over my well-being. Our conversation earlier comes back to me with a vengeance, and the tears form again and fall slowly down my cheeks.

She's gone. Those were his words. Cassia died because of a glitch in her chip while she was at the Trivium. This can't be happening. This isn't real. It *can't* be real. I grab my notebook and rush out the door, racing to the only place I know to go: Cassia's house. I need validation. I need to see her parents.

There are several cars lining the street leading up to her house, and the whole house is lit up from the inside. I recognize Jason and Verity's vehicles, and a sinking feeling sets in. *No.* I walk up to the door and ring the doorbell. Verity answers, face red and splotchy from endless amounts of crying.

"Ethan, come in." She ushers me inside, shuts the door, and then wraps her arms tightly around me with her face buried in my chest. Her body is shaking, and I know she's crying again, so I embrace her back. Jason walks in and sees me and then comes up behind Verity and puts his arms around both of us. My chest has a weight crushing down upon it, the pressure making it hard to breathe. Tears form and fall in a stream that soaks my face and neck. I'm paralyzed, standing there trying to remember to breathe and feeling myself slip out of reality. Moments pass before Jason and Verity let me go, wiping their tear-stained faces with their sleeves and grabbing tissues from a box nearby. I join them, blowing my nose, but leaving the tears alone. I know that more will come even though I feel completely dry.

Verity leads me into the back den where a large group of people is standing around, and I see Cassia's parents in the middle. Her mom is silent, with anger covering her face instead of grief. Cassia's father is talking to some men in suits, fury and sadness mixed together in his eyes. Cassia's mom sees me and breaks away from the group and walks my way.

"Ethan, thank you for coming." She starts to shake my hand, but then pulls her hand away and wraps her arms around my neck, squeezing firmly. She breaks away after a few seconds, an embarrassed smile that quickly fades.

"Mrs. Bellerose, I'm so sorry."

"Ethan, I know without a doubt that you and Cassia had something indescribable. You could call your dinner date a non-date, but I know better. I know that look you both had in your eyes whether she wanted to admit it or not. This isn't right. It doesn't make sense. They've never had this happen before. She had a future. They don't even have any answers!" I feel the pain and fury she has radiating off her. Her eyes are lit up like fire.

"They just say there was an issue in the tank. That's it. A glitch. What does that even *mean*?" Verity starts sobbing again and walks away to grab another tissue.

"Have you seen her?" I ask.

"No. They won't even let us out of our house right now! They say she's still at the Trivium under observation, but they keep insisting she's dead. I don't believe anything they say until they'll let us go there!"

My heart pounds in my chest so loud I could swear everyone else hears it. Is it possible she's alive? That the Trivium officials lied? But why would they? What would they have to hide?

She turns toward one of the officials in a suit and loudly asks if she's allowed in her own backyard. Clearly flustered, he nods yes to her and takes a step back. She motions me to follow her outside. "So is it possible . . ." My voice catches in my throat.

"Ethan, I need to be real with you, because I think you can handle that. Do you see Gunner anywhere?" I look back at the house. "You won't find him in there. He's not here. He heard the news, apologized, and then said he needed space. Cassia dying apparently screwed up all the plans they had together, so I'm sure he's already trying to strategize his next move. As if life is a chess game! He's not a king. He's a pawn." The venom she spits out takes me aback. It seemed like Gunner really loved Cassia. How's it possible to show so much affection—which always made me uncomfortable—just to switch gears so that your future stays intact? How can anyone be so *calculating*?

"Mrs. Bellerose, I—"

"Ethan, call me Diana. Please."

"Yes, ma'am. Diana. What can I do?"

"Do you love my daughter, Ethan?" She stares intently, waiting for an answer. I swallow the lump that's formed in my throat.

"More than anything. But—"

"When do you go to the Trivium?"

"Two weeks. But what—"

"Listen closely, Ethan," she pauses and looks around the yard, searching for something I do not see. She moves closer to me. "Find her. Find my daughter. This is not her future. Find her, no matter what it takes. If she's not here, she's *somewhere*. Are you understanding what I'm saying?" I shake my head. I have no idea what she means. "She could be dead here. They could be telling the truth. But that doesn't mean anything anymore. When you go to the Trivium, see if you can choose her."

"But what if I can't? If she's really gone, wouldn't she be taken away as a choice?" I've gone from grieving to confused. *Is Cassia's mom crazy?*

"Maybe. Probably. I need to get back inside before they get suspicious, but if you truly love my daughter—and I feel like you do or I wouldn't risk saying this to you—then you need to do what it takes to find her and make this right. Her future isn't gone. I don't understand what's happening here, but it's not right. *Something* isn't right. Bring her back to me, in this life or another." She turns away from me, walking slowly back to the door.

"And what if I can't choose her? What happens if she's not one of my choices?" She stops, turns around to face me, and her entire demeanor goes rigid.

"Free will, Ethan." And with that, she walks back into the house.

I stand there, feeling like I'm going to fall over. Verity and Jason walk outside, no doubt curious about what just happened with Diana.

"Ethan, what did she say?" Verity asks.

"To be honest, I don't really understand her, Verity. She wants me to choose Cassia at the Trivium."

"But that wouldn't be possible, right?" Her eyes widen at the thought.

"I have no idea. I don't know how it would be possible at all."

"But then what happens if she's not a choice?" Jason asks.

"I guess I'll cross that bridge when I get to it. No matter what, she thinks I can find Cassia. Even if she's gone. Guys, I think she's just heartbroken and angry and confused. She wasn't making much sense. She did mention Gunner wasn't here."

"Yeah, that jerk showed his true colors." Verity scowls at me.

"Look, this day. I don't even know what to say. I think I need to go home."

"Want me to drive you?" Jason asks.

"No, it's fine. I can manage. Can we get together tomorrow? To talk some more about all this? Not Cassia supposedly being dead, but what her mom said to me?" They look at each other and Jason shrugs.

"Let's do that," Verity says. "Call me when you're ready." They both hug me again, only this time we're not in tears. The air feels different as if the tension has lifted and been replaced with electricity. I may not understand anything at all, but I feel that something big is coming.

* * *

I didn't sleep well last night. I dreamt of Cassia reaching out to me from somewhere in time and space, and I couldn't find her. I had a knife with me, and I was cutting away at time like it was nothing but fabric that could be easily ripped and torn. Across worlds, I searched for her, guided only by her voice. Every dimension I crossed, every universe I searched, her voice would grow louder. I thought I had finally found her when I woke up abruptly.

Groggy, I rub my eyes and stare at the ceiling. My face feels swollen from all the tears I shed yesterday. I can barely breathe through my nose, and my throat feels parched and dry. I pull myself out of bed, slip on a pair of sweatpants, and make my way to the kitchen for a glass of water. The house is quiet, and since I have no idea what day it is, I'm not even sure where anyone would be. Hannah could be out with friends. My parents are surely at work. Is it a weekend? I should find a calendar. And a clock.

I walk back upstairs and call Verity, and within an hour, she and Jason are at my doorstep. They make their way up to my room, and Verity makes herself comfy on my desk chair. I sit on the edge of my bed and Jason just stands there, ill at ease.

"Okay, Ethan. Walk us through exactly what Cassia's mom said. If you can remember it all." Verity's tone is serious and seeing her face lacking her usual spirit is unnerving. She's always had such a great, positive energy about her. I could understand immediately why Jason was drawn to her, and why she complements Cassia as her best friend.

"Well, for starters, she clearly does not like Gunner either." Verity sticks her tongue out in agreement. "I'm not sure how she knows how much I care about Cassia, but she does." Verity raises her eyebrow.

"It's pretty obvious, Ethan. We *all* know."

"Whatever. *Anyway*, she said she wants me to see if I can choose Cassia at the Trivium. And even though it may not be possible, she kept saying to find Cassia. To find her daughter. No matter where that may be. What does that even mean?" Jason walks to the bed and sits beside me.

"Honestly, Ethan. I don't know what that means," he says.

"What if—no—well—"

"What if what, Verity?" She bites her lower lip and looks away as if she can search for the answer amongst the mess in my room.

"What if Cassia is still alive somewhere else? In time?"

"What are you talking about?" Jason is now looking at Verity with the same amount of confusion on his face that mine must have.

"Well, if every time we make a choice, a new path diverges . . . then what if there are multiple universes where Cassia *didn't* die? And maybe she was able to choose something else? Maybe she even chose *you*?" My heart doesn't know whether to leap with joy at the possibility or burn with doubt.

"That's a great thought, Verity. But if that's true, I don't know how you'd cross into these parallel universes to find out. I mean, there's not a train to an alternate dimension. And not only that, what if she's happy in those worlds and has no idea who I am?"

"Ethan, do you still have the same dreams of her like she had of you?" My throat tightens. Of course, best friends talk, I just never know to what extent.

"I did yesterday."

"And?" She eyes me, thoughtfully.

"We were at the pizza place I took her to, but this time she said we had chosen each other. She had already made it past the Trivium. I had this vision right before—" I trail off, remembering exactly what happened after that vision and trying to fight back the tears.

"Then that means that that version of Cassia is out there. And she chose you and you chose her and you're supposed to be together." Her face brightens back up like a child at Christmas. "Ethan, that's the Cassia you need to find!" She squeals with excitement, catching Jason and me off guard so we jump.

"Verity, honey, that's a nice thought and all . . ."

"Oh, come *on*, Jason. I am nothing if not optimistic. And look, I realize I'm not a smarty pants scientist like Cassia, but there must be someone that will help us find out more info. It's got to be a possibility we can at least try, right?" Jason and I eye each other warily. I would hate for Verity to get her hopes up on a futile quest. We all want Cassia back, but at what cost to ourselves?

"If you can find out more info, Verity that would be great." I sigh loudly. I don't know whether to feel determined, relieved, or even more depressed.

"Was there anything else Diana said to you? Because you looked like you'd seen a ghost when she left." I hadn't forgotten what she said, I had just dismissed it as ranting from a grieving mom.

"Yeah, she said something about free will."

"Wait, what? Why?" Verity stands up quickly, knocking my chair over in the process. Embarrassed, she picks it back up gently. "Sorry."

"I don't know why, but I think there's more to Diana than meets the eye. Free will would be the ability to make a choice and not be stuck in what's chosen for us. Like it was in the past. But I didn't think it was still something that existed anymore."

"Wouldn't it cause the destruction of our world if we all went back to making choices? I mean, that's what caused the governments to create the science behind the Trivium in the first place." Jason is looking at Verity intently as if he's expecting her to know the answers.

"Jason, if being able to save Cas and her future means breaking some rules, no biggie, right?" She laughs, but Jason isn't amused.

"Verity, I have a feeling the Trivium authorities would flip out if they knew anything about this."

"Well, that's just paranoia, Jason. But we'd be super secretive about it. Like *spies*." She manages to make Jason crack a smile, obviously against his will. If a relationship like that could still happen for me, shouldn't I at least try? What do I have left to lose if I've lost her already?

"Let's not speak of this to anyone, okay? Verity, you do some library research and let me know if you find anything. Until then, I'll plan on going to the Trivium just to see what happens. And then we can go from there."

"I have a bad feeling about this," Jason says as he stands back up and heads to the door.

"Jason, I want both you *and* my best friend in my life. She was *in* my future when I chose. That tells me that, even with everything that's happened, she'll still end up with me. With us. And most importantly, with Ethan. I don't want to spend the rest of my life without my best friend." Verity walks over to Jason, putting her arms around him and leaning her head against his chest.

"Well, since we're going to be spies now, what should our code name be?" I wink at Jason, but Verity lets go of him quickly and beams at me.

"Team Free Will," she says.

CHAPTER THIRTEEN

ETHAN

Verity has probably spent more time at the library the past two weeks than she has her entire life. Desperately seeking answers, she's been reading every science book she can find. I'm proud of her and her dedication to getting Cassia back. I wish I could say she's found all the answers, but she's just opened up even more questions.

The Trivium finally allowed Cassia's parents to go see her, but they aren't allowed to speak a word of what they saw or confirm her death. I thought that detail would upset Verity even more than the original news, but she's laser-focused on finding out answers. Anything she can do to find Cassia again. My day to go to the Trivium is tomorrow, and my anxiety is at an all-time high. I know Cassia's mom—er, Diana—is counting on me to fix something I feel has been damaged beyond repair. Not only am I worried about my future now, I'm afraid of what could happen to me in there. If Cassia and I really do have such a strong connection—one that crosses time and space—what would the Trivium officials do to me if they knew? My life is about to change drastically, and I have no way of knowing whether it will be for better or worse.

My mom decided she would try her hand at cooking tonight, to make up for all the times I'm left eating alone. She isn't the best cook, but she's not the worst, either. I make my way downstairs to the kitchen, and my sister and dad are already seated at the table. I sit across from Hannah—my usual seat, even when they aren't here—and listen in on their conversation. Or try to, anyway. I'm not musical at all. I can't sing. I have no rhythm to be able to dance. I've always felt like the odd man out in this family. My brief foray into soccer didn't last long once the coach realized I wasn't very coordinated. I preferred to read from the bench. My parents eventually accepted the fact that I would not be their sports star, and I'm pretty sure they decided to hedge their bets on Hannah instead. Not that I blame them.

"Daydreaming as always?" My dad loves to pull me back into reality and out of my head.

"Always," I say.

"Ethan, aren't you excited about tomorrow?" Hannah is squirming in her chair, sporting a toothy grin.

"Sure, Hannah." I can't exactly unload all my insecurities on my baby sister. She's still at the age where the Trivium is a romantic and novel idea. I remember feeling that way once too. Back when I had never dreamed of a certain someone.

"Well, you don't seem so excited," she huffs.

"Hannah, leave your brother alone. It's not easy to walk into the unknown and make your future into something permanent."

My mom speaks gently to Hannah, but firm. A perfect line between teasing and seriousness.

"Hannah, I'm sure the day you go to the Trivium will be one of the most exciting days of your life. And on that day, you can tell me just how excited you are about it." I wink at her and she giggles.

"Dinner is ready! I hope it's edible." My mom makes a face, and even though she's teasing, the rest of us remember all her earlier inedible mishaps. My dad shudders. "Hey now, I was kidding! I did a taste test, and it's fine." My dad grumbles something under his breath, and my mom playfully swats at him before taking a seat.

I look around at these wonderful people in my life, and a pang of sorrow hits my chest. If something happened to me, what would happen to them? Could I live without them? I feel like not telling them what's happening is a form of betrayal, and it hurts me to be so deceitful. I've never kept anything so important from them. I mean, I even told them about the dreams and meeting Cassia. My mom was thrilled, convincing me that all would work out perfectly and not to worry. My dad was more passive, happy for me and all, but not greatly interested. He's never been comfortable with the idea of forming an attachment to someone unless it's an actual concrete choice. And I get that. He's such a soft-hearted man, he wouldn't be able to take all the loss.

"It's delicious, mom," I mumble with a stuffed mouth. And it is, which is delightfully shocking. Hannah and my dad mumble in agreement.

"Well, don't act too surprised, okay?"

"Honey, you did great." My dad leans across the table to give her a kiss. Hannah makes a barfing sound, to my mom's dismay.

"So, Ethan, now that the hot seat has been taken away from me, I'm giving it to you. What are your thoughts about tomorrow? How are you really feeling?" My mom smiles at me and winks.

"Nervous," I say.

"Care to elaborate?" my dad asks. I can't tell him about Cassia, and I can't talk about any plans I may have to investigate on my own.

"I don't know what to expect is all." I keep my eyes on my plate, munching silently.

"I bet it will be so awesome! I bet you get to see everything you've ever wanted, and then you just pick one! You can't go wrong!" Hannah's enthusiasm may be way off mark, but I fault that to age and innocence. At her age what they learn seems like magic. I don't believe in magic anymore. I believe in dreams and visions and . . . destiny? Choice? Fate? I'm not sure what to believe. Or even who to trust.

"Sweetie, you've had a great couple of months. What makes you nervous now?" I mull that question over. I'm nervous because she's gone. My choices are limited. They don't include her. And I can't tell you anything that's happened, or what I'm thinking.

"It's normal to be nervous, Calliope. We shouldn't forget how terrifying it can be to go it alone into the unknown."

"I'm sure that's it, dad. I'll be fine tomorrow after it's over." I've finished eating what's left on my plate, so I rinse my dish off and then hug each of them tightly before I tell them I want to go to bed early. My mom begrudgingly agrees to let me go but seems startled by the sudden affection. It's not that my family doesn't enjoy hugs, it's just that we haven't been in the same room together often enough.

"Get some rest, Ethan. I'll take you in the morning."

"Thanks, dad. I'll see you then."

I walk back upstairs to my room, but not before glancing back into the dining area to see Hannah giggling over something that happened at school, and my mom quietly listening and absorbing the conversation. I love them all. Do I have to choose between them and Cassia? I pray that I don't.

I flop onto my bed and stare aimlessly at my ceiling. My cell starts beeping, so I get back up and find it on my desk. I never remember where I put anything. The message is from Verity, and it just says, "Good luck." I need it. I turn my cell off and get ready for bed. I lay back down and watch the shadows on the walls and ceiling dance across my room before succumbing to sleepiness.

The next morning, I wake up to my dad calling for me. I didn't think to set my alarm on the bedside clock when I turned off my cell. I usually use it as an alarm instead, but I didn't want to risk being disturbed by cell calls or messages. I jump out of bed quickly, throw on my swim shorts and T-shirt, grab my sandals, and run downstairs. I had already packed a bag with extra clothes, and my mom smartly made me leave it in the entryway. Which comes in handy since I'm barely awake to remember to grab a protein bar for breakfast before running outside to get in my dad's car. Hannah and my mom stand at the front door and wave to me as we drive away. My mom almost seems sad. Perhaps she's secretly worried about me too. We pull up to the Trivium building, and my dad gives me a pep talk about my future. I know he's trying to help, but it doesn't settle the nerves building up inside me. He awkwardly pats my shoulder as I open the door as if he doesn't quite know how to handle this situation. I smile as normally as I can, tell him I'll see him in a while, and then grab my bag and shut the door.

The building doors are much larger than I thought they would be. Almost like entering a protected fortress. And perhaps in a way, it is. What secrets lie behind these doors? What are they keeping in? The receptionist smiles warmly and I sign in and then walk to the waiting area. It's stuffy inside, which seems counterintuitive as the ceilings in this part of the building are very tall. I'm alone in this room, which is disconcerting. Are there no others coming in today? The odds of that seem very low. I get up and pace around the room, paying attention to the artwork on the walls. I may not be an artist like Jason, but I can pick out curated artwork, and the Trivium has quite the unassuming collection.

"Ethan Rivers? We're ready for you." An older woman dressed in white scrubs is holding a clipboard in front of her and sporting a stern face. She looks scary. I walk to her quickly as she looks like someone you wouldn't want to trifle with. "Follow me."

She leads me into a room painted blue and motions me to sit. A few very uncomfortable moments later, a much younger woman walks in dressed nicely, with a much friendlier smile.

"Ethan Rivers, nice to meet you. Welcome to the Trivium. I'm Emma. I'll be going over your paperwork today." I breathe a sigh of relief. At least someone here seems relaxed. She pulls out a folder with my name on it and scans the contents. I wonder what's in there. Would it say anything about Cassia? "Your paperwork looks good to go and your health is great. I have a short video for you to watch, and then I'll talk you through the process." A screen pops out from the ceiling. I wonder if I can get one of those in my room. Doubtful.

The movie playing is all about Trivium history, and I'm so bored that I keep looking around for something more interesting to investigate. There are no files in here. Nothing I can tangibly get my hands on. I wish I knew what room they kept those folders in. I bet it's under a crazy amount of security. I'm not gifted when it comes to technology. What on earth did Verity think I could accomplish here? Emma walks back in and takes a seat behind the desk.

"Do you have any questions?" I shake my head. "Okay then, follow me. You will be in Trivium Room Four." I follow her down a hallway containing oversized doors. Why does everything have to be so *tall?* Inside the room is the tank, and I feel like I've entered a science-fiction movie. Emma leads me to a small area where the shower and toilet are. "I will need you to remove your clothing, except for your bathing suit, and stow all your items in this locker. Please rinse yourself off in the shower, apply your shower cap, and then when you are done, we will begin." She walks out to give me privacy and I take a look around before undressing.

I quickly get in and out of the shower in just a few minutes, grab a towel, and walk back to the main room. Emma stands near a display with many buttons. *This would be a great time to be a computer genius.* She walks over to me, handing me earplugs, and tells me to get into the tank. Apparently, serious Emma has replaced friendly Emma. I get in, and the water doesn't feel too bad. It's a little odd at first, getting used to the idea of floating. I'm not usually claustrophobic, but getting completely shut in here unnerves me. Emma attaches some wires to my face and the chip and then goes back to her control panel. I guess everything else is okay, because she walks back over, gives me a thumbs-up, and then closes me in.

My chest tightens as the darkness surrounds me. My heart beats loudly, and I try to focus on it to steady myself. The thought that Cassia went through this and didn't come back out makes my heart beat faster. *Calm down,* I tell myself. I take in a deep breath and exhale slowly. I'm used to being alone in my thoughts, but I've never felt this isolated and disconnected. Eyes closed or open doesn't matter, there is nothing to see. My nerves are lit up, and I feel little jolts of electrical currents flowing through my body. Floating in the tank gives the feeling of flying, so I imagine I'm an unknown superhero soaring above the city. The silliness of it works to steady my breathing and reduces the panic that is rising within me.

Just as I feel a wave of calm rush over me, visions start to play out above me like a movie projected on a big screen. A replay of my life thus far, I see myself as a young boy at the cabin with my parents. Hannah hasn't been born yet. My dad and I are on the lake in our small fishing boat, rod and reel in hand. I was notoriously bad at fishing. I never could catch anything. I enjoyed spending time alone with my dad, but I wasn't enthralled at the actual prospect of catching a fish. I didn't even like to touch the worms. At the hospital waiting on Hannah to be born, a bucket of nerves and excitement because I wasn't sure what to expect. My first date with Jane, which went horribly wrong. I was surprised she ever went on another date with me again after that. When I met Cassia at the library. Seeing her again makes me ache something fierce. I'm torn between sadness and anger. The first time I kissed her. The last time I saw her. The dreams are not included in my memory, which makes me think they weren't recorded on the chip.

The next few images that flash by are foreign to me. I don't know the people I'm seeing. I don't recognize the buildings or scenery. I'm surrounded by books, but I can't make sense of any of it. Who are these strangers? Where am I? Why would I even want to be here? It dawns on me that I'm at a book signing, and it's my image on a banner next to a book I apparently wrote. I feel selfish for getting excited about that possibility. Just because it's something that could happen in one future doesn't make it impossible in others. At least I hope not. I hone in on my hands, and there is no wedding band. Am I alone in this future?

The images shift so that the location is all new. It looks like my cabin, but it's been completely redone so that I barely recognize it. I don't care much for the look of the furniture, it's not *homey*. A woman is calling for me in the kitchen, but it isn't Cassia's voice. Jane flickers into my view and I feel like throwing up in the tank. *No.* The chip must be desperately searching for a future for me, because in no way would I be interested in being with her again. With Cassia out of the picture, my life is apparently doomed to be lonely or settling for someone I don't truly love. I wonder how many others had a similarly difficult choice. Could there be that many secretly unhappy people out there in the world? I want this vision to go away, so I close my eyes for a few seconds before reopening. I thankfully missed whatever else that future held for me.

The colors fade and all that's left is white. A plain white room with white chairs and a white desk. Confused, I keep waiting for something to show up. I take a seat on a chair and before me, a book appears. Leafing through the pages, I see a life full of the visions I'd experienced. Cassia and me in the hammock. At the cabin during the rainstorm. On a beach somewhere far away. It's a photo book of memories that haven't happened. I reach the end of the book and the pages are blank. What kind of cruel joke is this? As I stare at the blank pages in confusion, words slowly appear across the page, as if being handwritten by a ghost. *Choose this, Ethan. Choose me. Wherever you are, there I'll be.* Cassia? I hear my own voice reverberating through the tank though it's muffled because of the earplugs. A bright light hits my eyes and I scream out in agony.

"Ethan, it's over. It's just me. Go ahead and shower and get dressed and come see me." Emma looks worried. She helps me out of the tank, and when I start to fall, she grabs me and escorts me to the shower. There's a bench just inside, so she helps me sit down and I assure her I can take over from there. I let the warm water fall over me as I stand up, shaking and afraid. Somehow, Verity and Diana were right. I don't know how she did it, but Cassia sent me a message. I have a hard time believing the chip could reveal that to me. The question is, now what?

I dry off and change clothes before walking back into the room. Emma looks very displeased as she hovers over the control panel.

"Ethan, I don't know why this happened, but the recording here only shows two choices. It seems there was a glitch—" I wince at the word and she notices. "—but it's nothing major or any cause to be concerned. I will be reporting this to the officials, and they may be contacting you to do a follow-up. How are you feeling?"

"Fine." Why doesn't she know I saw three things? I don't trust her enough to tell her.

"Great. Well here are the three buttons, but you'll be pushing only button one or button two. The first button corresponds to your first choice. Likewise, the second button to the second choice." I look down at the control panel and only those first two buttons are lit up. "Don't take too long choosing, I'll be back with a pill for you in just a few minutes." She forces a smile and then walks out the door.

I look down at the buttons and wonder what would happen to me if I didn't choose anything. Would they force me to? Would they choose for me? Either button isn't an option for me. I remember the handwriting on the pages of the book. *Choose this, Ethan. Choose me.* I eye that third button again. Without caring what happens to me—as a life without love isn't a life worth living—I press the third button.

CHAPTER FOURTEEN

CASSIA

"If you want to make enemies, try to change something."
—Woodrow Wilson

Two little words were all she gave me. *Free will.* No explanation. She won't even broach the subject. Anytime I approach her, she rebuffs me. I've accepted the fact that I can't crack her, no matter what I try. For whatever reason, she doesn't want to let me in on any other secrets she may be hiding. It feels unfair. And a little maddening. I've known her my whole life—but do I really know her? Can we really know anyone?

All the scouring for keywords I've done at the library has left me empty-handed. Other than vague references to free will and the ability to choose everything in history texts, there is nothing current that covers the topic. I haven't wanted to bring Verity in on this investigation—thinking it was futile—but I'm thinking she can help me work it out. I call her up to ask if she'll come over so we can talk, and she arrives in less than an hour. With all the preparation for college lately, I'm lucky she can fit me in at all. She's been hard to reach.

"Is this boy stuff you want to talk about?" She flops on my bed and crosses her legs, hands on her knees—waiting for details.

"Actually, no. It's about my mom. Something kind of weird happened recently. At first, I dismissed it, but now I want your opinion."

"Shoot."

"Okay, well . . . have you ever thought about the concept of free will?" She stares at me quizzically.

"Like, in the past? With choosing every decision?"

"Yeah. Basically."

"Other than memorizing what I needed for a test, no. Why?" She leans toward me, expecting me to whisper. I'm not paranoid like my mom so I don't.

"My mom thinks I'm unhappy with the choice I made, and she mentioned free will. And I'm stuck because I don't know what she means and she won't elaborate on the subject." Verity sighs loudly and then sits back.

"Wow, Cas. I guess the more important question is this: *are* you happy?" The question takes me aback.

"W-well of course, I am. Why wouldn't I be?" *I chose this life.*

"Cas, you may be fantastic about lying to yourself, but you can't lie to me. I know you too well. And you can keep saying that over and over like a mantra, but that won't make it true. So be real. *Are you happy?*" I mull the question over and I don't like where my thoughts lead me. I haven't even started medical school yet, and I already dislike working with my dad at the office. Gunner is distant—and while I fully take responsibility for my actions in driving him away, we really don't have anything in common. I had never noticed that before, being so caught up in his charm and statuesque good looks. I *should* want a guy like him. Athletic, funny, and sweet. I didn't just get a guy, I got *the* guy. But lately, that bronze shine has been slowly forming a patina, and the formerly flawless face has shown cracks and scarring. I should love a guy like him. I should love *him.* And yet I cannot fully let myself for reasons unknown even unto me. I take a deep breath and let it go.

"No." A weight lifts off my shoulders, having finally admitted something wasn't right. "I don't think Gunner and I are really compatible. We lead two separate lives. He tried to join my world but was so miserable that it just upset me more. And I don't like sports. Not enough to watch every game. And Verity, my dad's office. Oh my goodness, I don't like going! It's not at all what I thought it would be. I keep daydreaming while there because I'm just not interested. The paperwork, and the blood, and ugh it's just so . . . different from what I expected."

"And?"

"And what?"

"And what would you rather be doing? What are you daydreaming about?"

"Writing. And going to college with you and Jason. And going to theatre productions, and art galleries. Just . . . not this life. I keep going back to the life I saw in your dorm room. And thinking that maybe—just maybe—that was where I was supposed to be.

Where I *am* supposed to be. Is that completely crazy?" She bursts out in laughter, shocking me so I jump.

"Cas, it sounds perfect. So how do we make this happen?"

"Wait, what? I'm pretty sure since I already went to the Trivium, that I can't change anything. But it feels great to admit that out loud." She frowns at me.

"Unacceptable answer."

"Well, what do you think I can actually do about it?" My pulse quickens. Can there really be free will? "Verity, this—even talking about this—could get us in a lot of trouble. I'm pretty sure we're not allowed to actually change our course."

"Pish posh. I think your mom knows exactly what she's talking about. And it could be very dangerous, but Cas, think of the adventure! And going to college with me! Although, what does that mean for Gunner?"

"I have no idea. I hate the idea of hurting him. I mean, how do you take back a choice? I *chose* him, Verity. And I still care about him. I mean, why didn't I choose something else if there had been better options? It means I made the right choice at the time, right?"

"You had a glitch. I guess it messed with your head." She giggles at herself. "I really wish we knew what else there was for you to choose from. Hey, do you still keep a notebook in your nightstand? We can make a plan."

"What kind of crazy idea are you concocting? And yes, I think so. I haven't needed one since I came back." Verity crawls on the bed over to the nightstand, pulling out my notebook. It's not the one I was thinking of, so I'm a little surprised to see it. She opens it up to find a blank page, but the look on her face changes to confusion.

"Ver, what's wrong?" She keeps scanning the pages, leafing through them furiously.

"Cas, who's Ethan?" She looks up from the notebook, with terror lining her face. I search my memory for that name, but I can't think of who it would be.

"I don't think I know an Ethan, Ver. Why?"

"Apparently, you did. And I did. And Jason did. But we don't anymore." She thrusts the notebook at me violently, looking like she's about to cry. I take it from her and start reading. This is my own handwriting, but I don't remember writing anything at all. Stories of an Ethan Rivers that I have strange dreams of. Of meeting him in the library. *What is this?*

"I have no idea what this is!" Verity sits next to me and pats my back gently.

"Cas, I don't know how anything like this from your past could make it into the present. Not after you chose at the Trivium, but it did. And it sounds like this guy was the right one." I put my face in my hands and muffle a scream.

"I don't understand any of this. If he was really that great why didn't I choose him?" She reads the next couple of pages over my shoulder as I flip through them.

"Fear," she says.

"Fear of what? Why would I fear this life?" The stories I've written don't jog anything from my memory.

"Of the unknown, honey. Of going against what's comfortable. Of putting yourself out there and being who you were meant to be, and not who or what you thought you should be. You know I love you, but you weren't put on this earth to follow in your dad's footsteps." I let her words sink in. Is she right? Have I only chosen the life I'm living because of false expectations I had of what others wanted me to be? Is this the life I wanted or the one I created?

"But if all my planning was for someone else, then who am I? My entire identity has been wrapped up in my plans. If I don't have that, what do I have?"

"Choice. Look, I've seen you light up over writing. You don't act like that after leaving your dad's office. And that choice is great for your dad, but maybe it's not so great for you."

"I hate admitting this, but I think you're right." I lean my head on her shoulder and she hugs me. "What have I done, Verity? I've lied to myself. I've lied to Gunner. What now?"

"Be honest with Gunner. He can find his own way. He still has a Trivium trip. You two aren't soul mates in this world. Maybe you are in another." I think about that for a minute. Would Gunner be able to go and choose me, but it be a different me? That is such a weird concept. Quantum physics isn't one of my strengths. *Ethan, if you are out there, where are you? Who are you—to me?*

"I think it's time I talked to my parents."

"What are you going to say?"

"Well for starters, how about a change in college?" Verity squeals so loud that I cover my ears with my hands. I may have no idea what I'm doing, but at least she'll be with me.

That evening, I sit down at the dinner table and have a serious discussion with my parents. My dad is of course, very confused, but my mom is delighted. There's a twinkle in her eye now that wasn't there before. She convinces my dad all will be well and fine, and he is shockingly at peace with it. For all he knows, this would've happened in my future anyway, so he doesn't see a need to fight it. Or be worried. My mom pulls me aside after dinner and gives me a strong hug. Knowing she put me on this path and supports me no matter what brings a tear to my eye.

"Mom, thank you."

"For what, honey?"

"For making me realize what I truly wanted."

"Cassia, you were born with talents. Why you chose to ignore them all these years is beyond me. All a mother wants is for her child to be happy. And I'll do whatever it takes to help you." She kisses my forehead and then puts her hands on the side of my head. "Whatever it takes, Cassia. Remember that." I know when there are double meanings hidden between the lines being spoken. I don't doubt at all what my mother just said, and it makes me shudder. *Whatever it takes.*

That night I lie awake and think of all the things that could go wrong. I open my notebook again, and I see a pro and con list of Ethan and Gunner. I think to myself how many more items I could add to Gunner's con list. I guess it's true what they say: love is blind. Or in my case, blinded by a person whose flaws I refused to see. *Con: is not loved by me.* Somewhere out there is a guy named Ethan that I used to care a lot about. Maybe even loved. Do I know what love is? I thought I loved Gunner, but I didn't. That's very clear to me now. Caring for someone and loving them is a different emotion entirely. Perhaps I do love Ethan, and I can find him somewhere out there in this great expanse of universe. Until then, I need to find myself. And maybe in the process, I'll find him too.

CHAPTER FIFTEEN

"Deep into that darkness peering, long I stood there, wondering, fearing, doubting, dreaming dreams no mortal ever dared to dream before . . ."
—Edgar Allan Poe

Saying goodbye is hard. When I called Gunner on the phone, he seemed so excited to hear from me that it hurt my stomach to feign the same level of excitement. I have to tell him it's over. And I'm scared because I don't know how he'll react.

I have him meet me at the diner instead of letting him pick me up. I knew I wouldn't want to deal with the awkward silence of him taking me home—or the possibility he'd storm off and I'd have to find a ride back. He sees me in the booth by the window—where we've sat many times before—and gives me a quick kiss on the cheek before he sits down across from me. I'm fidgeting nervously, wringing my hands beneath the table. I must be emanating nervous energy because he suddenly has concern spread across his face.

"What's going on, Cassia? I thought we were getting together to get back on track with our futures. Why am I really here?" I can't even look him in the eyes. *Such a coward.*

"Gunner, I asked you here because I needed to talk to you." I clear my throat and take a drink of the glass of water the waiter brought to the table. I feel his eyes boring into mine with high intensity.

"Just say it, Cas." He speaks with so much iciness that I almost feel heat leave my body. I feel frozen, a deer in headlights about to be overcome by an oversized truck. I knew this wouldn't be easy, but I didn't realize just how hard it would really be.

"Gunner . . . this just isn't working anymore." I take a deep breath and glance at him. He's completely rigid, all feeling has dissipated off his face.

"You know Cas, you're right. You are so freaking right about that. Because the girl I dated and was counting on has gone off her rocker. She's flown off the deep end. I thought I was dating this girl with ambition to be a doctor, not someone who *writes.*" He accents the word "writes" as if it leaves a terrible taste in his mouth. What does writing have to do with this?

"I'm sorry, Gunner. I really am. I just don't think a doctor is something I want to be anymore." I choke back tears and focus on my breathing. Steady and calm.

"Cassia, I don't know what happened in the Trivium, or what caused this change in you, but you aren't who I thought you were. I thought I would be marrying a successful doctor. I don't even know what you plan on doing with your future, but you're right in that I don't want to be a part of it." The words sting. Is that all I was to him? Someone to hitch a ride on the coattails of?

"I know you have time to decide whatever you want at the Trivium, so I hope you find happiness there." I am losing my calmness. I feel the heat rising back up inside me like I'm lit up from within. What kind of future did he truly envision? Did he think he could just attach himself to me and then do nothing? The gall of that revelation incites fury. Gone is the feeling of sadness for him, it's been replaced by disgust.

"I can't believe I wasted all this time with you. My chances of getting what I want at the Trivium are probably slim now. Thanks for nothing, Cassia." The bitterness in his voice doesn't do anything but anger me more.

"Good luck, Gunner. I would say I wish you the best, but clearly, you were only with me because of what you thought you could get out of this relationship." I stand up abruptly and grab my purse. "So instead of good luck, screw off!" I walk away quickly, shove the restaurant door open, and get in my car. I don't look back at him. I don't care what emotion he may have left. I had never once thought he was using me. All this time, he was buttering me up to choose him so he could have a specific future. Past conversations come to mind about our futures together, and it dawns on me that he never showed any concern for his own career. I don't think he ever thought much about it. He would go to college with me, but then what? Probably nothing. I pull up into the driveway, put the car in park, and scream as loud as I can manage. All the fear I had about hurting him dissipates the louder I get. I look up and see my mom standing outside my car door, not sure whether she should laugh at my antics or be concerned. I get out and she puts her arms out for me, so I move closer to her until she wraps me up in them.

"I take it things with Gunner didn't go so well?" I start laughing so uncontrollably that my stomach cramps up.

"No, not really," I say.

"Why are you laughing?" She stands back and looks me up and down. "What happened?"

"Well, for starters, he was only with me because of what prestige he thought I would bring to the relationship." I start giggling again. I can't help it.

"Oh, honey. No. I'm so sorry." She hugs me again.

"It's fine, mom. Really. I'm better off without him. Apparently writing is a four-letter word to him." I start laughing again.

"You're taking this awfully well, kiddo."

"Yeah, well, he made it very easy for me. Mom, I need to show you something." I lead her upstairs to my room, and she sits beside me on the bed. I pull out the notebook. "Verity found this in my nightstand, and for some reason, it made it past the Trivium." I flip it open to a part where I wrote about a dream I had with Ethan in it.

"What's this?" She eyes me curiously.

"Before the Trivium, there was apparently a guy in my life named Ethan. Do you remember anything about him?" She looks at me and shakes her head. "Isn't that odd, mom? How can they completely wipe away your past, but also memories you share with others?"

"I wish I knew."

"Well according to this, Ethan was a big part of my life. And I think he may be in my future. But I don't know how to find him."

"Serendipity, sweetheart."

"What?"

"If it's meant to be, you'll find him when you aren't looking. Serendipity."

"I don't understand how that works." She laughs.

"You don't have to. Just know that things always work out, even when you don't expect them to. You have a lot to focus on, with transferring schools and whatnot. Don't worry about looking for Ethan right now, I'm sure he'll turn up." I hope she's right. I can't exactly find a guy when I don't even know what he looks like. "You're going with Verity to the college tomorrow, right?" I nod. "I'm excited for you, baby."

"I'm so nervous! I don't think it's quite sunk in yet, you know? We're going to ask about room assignments. I hope it's not too late to room together."

"Have faith. And call me tomorrow after you find out all the info." She leans over to me and kisses my forehead before walking out of my room. I look back down at the notebook and flip back to the beginning of the journal. I had written about dreams I was experiencing, and it's weird to read my words but not remember it happening. It's like these are someone else's memories in a diary not meant to be read by me. As if I'm intruding on my own past. Who is this girl, this Cassia that dreams of a man she doesn't know? I can only handle this info in doses, so I put the notebook away for now.

The next day I ride with Verity to the college, and the entire time we're giddy and nervous, but excited. This was always a dream of ours, and I can't believe it's getting to be a reality. She leaves to talk to her advisor while I go to Admissions. With my grades, I knew I wouldn't have much of an issue getting in, but with so few spots every year, I wasn't sure if I made it in time. I get admitted and head to the advisor's office in the Arts College. My advisor is young and full of energy, and very passionate about her job. She sets me up on the track for a creative writing degree, and I get my schedule for the fall. Surreal doesn't quite capture the emotions I'm experiencing. Disbelief. Anxiety. Excitement. My classes cover some of the basics every college person must have, but I get to take a course in literature and that makes me happy.

I meet Verity at the dorm to speak with the person in charge of room assignments. While we wait, we show each other our schedules, and it turns out that we have a history class together. Of all the odds. She gets to take an introduction to fashion class, which sounds fun for her. The Residence Instructor finally meets with us, and we go over the dorm assignments. Much to my complete surprise, no one else was assigned to the room Verity was in yet.

"Roomies!" Verity shrieks, making both the Residence Instructor and me cringe. We get the keys and head up to our room. *Our.* How awesome and strange that sounds. I remember the last time I was in this room with her, back when I was jealous of the life she was getting to lead. And now I'm joining her and it's so unreal to me. "Cas, can you *believe* it? This is so exciting!"

"Everything seems to be working out a little too easily." I look around the room in awe. We'll get to move our things in next week, and I can't wait to see how it all comes together.

"More like, it's working out how it should've always been."

"That too."

We drive back home, and when she pulls up to my house, some cars are parked out front that I don't recognize. Black sedans with tinted windows. I get an ominous feeling in the pit of my stomach.

"Cas, are those Trivium officials? Do you know what's going on?"

"I think so, and no I have no idea."

"Want me to walk in with you?" She eyes me nervously.

"No, I'm sure it's just a follow-up. I'll be okay. I'll call you later."

"You better. Good luck."

I walk inside and toward the back den, and there are a couple of government-looking men in suits seated on the sofa. My parents don't seem to be worried, so the tension loosens a bit on my shoulders.

"Hello, Cassia. You do remember Dr. Bachman?" The official in the dark gray suit smiles warmly, but I don't recall meeting him before. I look at the other man and I do recognize the doctor.

"Yes. Hello, Dr. Bachman." I shake his hand and he motions for me to take a seat, so I sit on the chair opposite the sofa.

"Dr. Bachman is here to ask you how you're doing," my mom says.

"Fine? I haven't had any more headaches or visions if that's what you're concerned about."

"Oh, good to hear. Yes, I wanted to ask about that. And ask you about your Trivium results. It says here that you are going to medical school, but we received word today that you've transferred colleges to pursue writing." I feel my stomach knotting up. He's holding the file with my name on it from the Trivium.

"I did enroll today, yes. Is something wrong?" He opens my file and scans through it, with a look of confusion swarming over him.

"W-well n-no apparently not. Your file says you are to enroll in the creative writing degree program. I could swear earlier it said medical school . . ." He keeps scanning through my file, getting red in the face each time he reads it. How is it that my file changed as I changed?

"Cassia has always wanted to room with her best friend in college, Dr. Bachman. That has never changed. Are you sure you didn't have someone else's file confused with hers?" My mom winks at me. The poor doctor is still flustered and doesn't even look up from the papers to notice.

"Sir, is there anything else we can help you with?" my father asks. He isn't remotely interested in this man taking up more of his time and makes that point clear in his tone.

"I-I'm sorry to bother you all. I guess I did misread this information. Thank you for your time today. And Cassia, if you have any more headaches or health concerns, please let me know." He gets up and his companion follows him to the door, never speaking a word.

"I will, doctor, and thank you." I walk him out, smile and wave, and watch as the cars leave. Closing the door, I take a deep breath. My nerves start to settle and I feel much calmer.

"Well, that was fun." My mom comes up behind me, making me jump.

"How did my file change?" I turn around and face her, and she seems very amused.

"Who knows? Does it matter? How was your day? Tell me all about it." She walks with me back into the den.

"Mom, do you know something? Should I be worried about the Trivium officials?" She smiles and shakes her head, but offers no more information. I don't like feeling as if she's hiding things from me, but I let it go. "Okay, well today was great! Verity and I got our dorm room keys and schedules. We have a class together, albeit history, which is whatever. I get to take a literature class though. I'm so excited, mom!" She beams at me.

"So, when can you move in?"

"Next week."

"Oh! That doesn't leave much time! We need to go shopping for your dorm!"

"Well, I really didn't expect to take much. And I figure the supplies I bought can carry over to most of my new classes."

"Sure, but I want to go get you some stuff to decorate with! And new bedding! Do you have time now?" I instinctively look to see what time it is even though I don't have any plans.

"Yep."

"Let's go then."

We spend several hours visiting multiple stores because my mom insists it all needs to be perfect. We make it back by dinnertime, and my dad is surprised to see we brought pizza back with us. My mom not cooking is such a rare thing, but we're both tired and decided a treat was in order.

I lie awake that night thinking of the dreams I no longer have. I try to remember what the dorm room looked like in the vision, and details slowly pop back in. The walls covered in Verity's sketches. Black and white photos pinned at random. Faces and places I don't know. Is this supposed to be a true vision of my future? Or a coincidence?

The next week Verity and I drive up to campus to unpack our things. My mom and dad had a lot of work to catch up on so they couldn't come too, but my mom promised to come up for coffee next week to see the place. We decide to stay for a few days and then go back home for the weekend. Verity's dad was taking her leaving pretty hard, and her little brother wasn't coping that well either. I know it's tearing her up to leave them, so they all decide to spend a couple days together as a family. We'll get our first dose of campus life tonight and tomorrow night, and then we'll be back at home. It makes saying goodbye much easier since the drive isn't as long and terrible as I had thought it would be. If our weekends aren't full of studying, we should be able to make it home often. In the meantime, Verity focuses on the present and is full of her normal amounts of energy. She's already made up her bed and unpacked her clothes, while I'm lost in my thoughts doing nothing. I start with my bed first, and as I put the new bedding on, it hits me that this is the same bedding I saw in my vision. Of course, there won't be any photos anytime soon, but it makes me wonder what's in store. Could everything in that vision come true?

We finish putting up our things—which isn't much considering the small space—and agree to walk to the café near campus for something to eat. It's such a cool, artistic-feeling space. I imagine lots of time being spent here, sipping coffee, and studying. *Or writing.* There's a tiny stage at the back with a microphone stand, and I see flyers posted that they have open mic nights and poetry slams.

"Maybe you'll read your short stories or poetry here some night," Verity muses.

"I'm not sure that poetry is my thing, Ver. But I'd love to come listen sometime." I hear the high-pitched noise of an amp and grab my ears and shut my eyes. When I open them, there are more people sitting in the café, and Jason is at the table with us. Shocked, I look at Verity and she's not eating a sandwich anymore, but a pastry with a coffee. I feel a wave of nausea forming over me, and I know now I'm stuck in another vision. *Why? What about this do I need to know?* People start cheering as a guy appears on stage, seemingly out of nowhere. He seems to be in shock. He looks around the room, but it's dark now except for the stage, and the spotlights seem to be blinding him.

"What are you waiting for?" someone from the audience yells at him. Several people laugh. Another guy jumps on the stage and grabs the mic.

"Welcome to another fantastic poetry night at the Campus Café! Give it up for—" He whispers to the guy on the stage. "Ethan!" My stomach clenches tightly. *It can't be.*

He clears his throat, obviously nervous. "Thank you, everyone. I actually didn't prepare anything. I must be on this stage for a reason though, so here's my poor stab at a poem." He's almost shaking, and it's endearing how anxious he is. Why am I seeing this? *Is it really him?*

"Haunted dreams of passing strangers . . . sharing words and love at night. S-searching for her through the dangers . . . fading beauty at dawn's light. Memories like visions in books, reaching out through . . . time and space. Cassia . . . your truth, through time she looks, to once again see your face. Don't give up on us my darling . . . you will find us if you look. Diana misses her starling . . . king at F7 . . . H rook." He stops and peers out into the audience but doesn't see me. I'm so startled I can't speak. People around me slow clap and he walks off the stage. The high-pitched squeal comes back at full force, and I grab my ears again and scream.

"Cassia! What's going on?" Verity is reaching across the small table to me. "Was this another vision?"

"Yes, and this time Ethan was there. Here. He was *here*. In this café. In another time. When is the next poetry night?" She gets up and takes a flyer off the wall.

"Tonight. Why?"

"We need to come back later. I'll explain on the way back to the dorm." We finish our lunch and I tell her everything I just saw. Somehow Ethan is still connected to me, and I think he's trying to send me a message. That doesn't make sense, but right now nothing about these visions do. I write down what he said to me, as much as I remember, and Verity and I look over the words.

"What does this mean about a rook?" She peers over my shoulder at the poem. "Also, that's terrible poetry." That makes me laugh.

"I don't think it was meant to be good. I think it was meant to say something. To me. Like a clue."

"Whoa, Cas. Dream guy from the notebook is reaching out to find you? Was he at least good looking?" I find myself blushing. "I take that as a yes." She laughs.

"A rook is a chess piece." I take out my school-issued tablet and run a search on a rook and seventh rank. "The only thing I can find is that—if you have the rook in the seventh rank, and you're left with your king—you can take the opponent's king. Checkmate. Or something like that."

"Basically, he's telling you that you can actually take over? If you make a move, he can too? And you can both win? I don't understand chess."

"That's a smarter surmise than what I was thinking. I believe you're on to something. Also, he said 'your truth.' Verity, your name means truth. Does that mean you're in another world helping him look for me? How weird would that be?"

"Pretty weird. Not as much as him mentioning your mom by name, Cas."

"Yeah, that would imply they know each other. And why wouldn't I be there with her? None of this makes any sense. These aren't the kinds of puzzles I like."

"We'll go tonight then and see if he's there."

That night we get a table near the stage, and I keep my eye out for Ethan, but he never comes. Many students get on the stage and share their words, but none are him. Disappointment sets in. Verity seems to echo my sentiment, and neither of us says much on the way back.

When we reach our room, the dry erase board on the door has been written on. Since we haven't met anyone yet, neither of us expected messages anytime soon. Verity walks up to it first and puts her key in the lock. She freezes.

"Cas, it's for you." I walk up to the door and look at the board. I see my name written in black marker. I read the message and start shaking. I feel tears forming and I struggle to swallow. How's it possible? How is any of this possible?

"Cassia, you will find us if you look. Ethan."

CHAPTER SIXTEEN

He's out there somewhere, in another world, another life. Searching for me. In a way, it seems he's found me, but he has no way of reaching me completely. It's a strange feeling, knowing there is someone out there who loves me so much he's willing to do what it takes to find me. Am I the person he thinks I am? Am I the person I want to be? I feel like I'm on the right path for once. I'm experiencing a part of life that I thought was no longer an option for me. I am free. Free of the constraints I put on myself to be someone who would make my father proud. Free of the pressures to be the perfect girlfriend to a boy that did not love me. Free to follow my heart, my instincts, and my passions. Free to live by my own rules. I can make it up as I go. Would Ethan be able to handle this part of me? Would he support my ambitions? I had gone back home like I'd planned and reread the notebook countless times. The girl in those dreams, I don't know if she is who I will become or who I left behind. Is she someone I truly want to be? Is she the person Ethan fell in love with? Is she me?

Verity and I had gone over the poem, and the only thing we could agree on was that it meant more visions are imminent. In another life, Ethan is breaking through barriers to reach me and give me messages, though I wish he'd known that I was terrible at logic problems and puzzles needing clues. I wish I understood more, but knowing Verity and my mom are a part of his attempts to contact me, it must mean they support him and us being together. There is great solace in that.

Verity called me yesterday and filled me in on her family time. Her dad and brother have accepted that she will be gone, but she's made plenty of promises to come back on weekends. She even managed to talk her dad into hiring a housekeeper, if anything so the boys aren't completely on their own. She takes such great care of them that I know one day she'll make a wonderful mother. It seems odd that there are new phases in our lives, marriage and children being one of them. So many adventures to have with each other. So many adventures yet to come.

I pack up the rest of what I'm taking to school, knowing I will be back in this room in just a few short months for the holidays. Still, an end of an era is upon me, so I take a few deep breaths and quietly say goodbye to my room. Will it ever feel like mine again? I have grown up and changed while this room remained the same. There may be more lines on the door frame from where I've charted my growth since I was a toddler, but the room was never altered much over the years. I've never been one for design, so I left it pretty much bare and intact. Verity tried convincing me to paint it once, and I had my parent's approval to change it as I wished, but I never could decide on a color. They all felt wrong somehow.

It stayed a neutral cream, plain and boring. But it suited me. We can't paint the walls of our dorm room, but I know Verity will find a way to give it character and personality. And hopefully littered with black and white photographs of a life I get to look forward to.

My dad helps me pack the rest of my things into the trunk of my car and then hugs me so tightly I can barely breathe. He kisses my forehead before letting me go, tears forming in the corners of his eyes.

"I'm going to miss seeing you every day, Cassia. I know being a doctor is not in the cards for you, but I did love having you in the office with me."

"I'll be back before you know it. And you never know, I could graduate and end up right back at home." I wink at him and he laughs.

"Oh, no. I think once you move forward in life, you should keep moving forward. But I do look *forward* to having you *back* again. It's going to be much quieter around here."

"Maybe you should get a dog." He laughs and puts his arm on my shoulder.

"I'm not sure I'm that desperate yet for noise. I'll keep that in mind though." My mom comes out the front door carrying a tray of food wrapped in cellophane.

"I can't send you to college without some treats for the drive." She puts the tray on the front seat of my car and then closes the door. "Helping you get a head start on the Freshman Fifteen."

"Oh, geez. Thanks, but no thanks on that one, mom." We all laugh and it's nice, but laced with sadness.

"I'll be up there in a couple days and we'll go on that coffee date, okay?"

"Sounds like a plan." I give them both one last hug and say goodbye before making the trek back to the campus. I make it back before Verity, so I spend my time rearranging my closet and going over my supplies list. I made sure to bring the notebook with me so I can jot down every vision that happens, and I get it out of my suitcase and put it on my desk. I get bored, so I go for a walk around the dorm common room, but I don't know a single person and it's intimidating. It's not that I'm shy, it's just that I prefer small groups of people I know. I do not like talking to strangers. It's awkward, and I'm always afraid I'll say something wrong. It's hard for me to make friends, which is why I cherish Verity's friendship so much. She has never once made me feel terrible about myself, or ever hurt me. And she always makes me feel included. I'm not looking forward to all these classes I have by myself, but I'm excited about the opportunity to make more friends. I don't feel like watching television, and I left most of my books at home, so I go back to the room and climb on my bed to do nothing but think about the clues. *Does every word mean something, or did you just try to rhyme on the fly?* I'm so frustrated. I want more answers.

Verity walks in carrying another bag of her things and unpacks while telling me about her trip home. I've already heard most of it, but she neglected to mention that the housekeeper was single and pretty, and was hoping something would happen between her and her dad. She was also widowed so that part of her future is over. It's pretty sneaky, and I give her props for that—while also reminding her to not get her hopes up. She shrugs and finishes putting away her things. Fall semester starts next Monday, so there's plenty of time to scope out the campus and find where our classes will be. We've set aside time tomorrow to meet up with Jason and all go together. This is the first time I'll be an official third wheel, and it's a little strange. I'm happy for Verity and Jason, but I'm not jealous like I thought I would be. Instead, I'm excited. I have no one to please but myself, and I'm perfectly okay with that.

The next day, while we take a campus self-guided tour, Verity and I tell Jason about the latest visions and what we know about Ethan. At one point he gets mad, smacking himself in the forehead because he feels like there's a memory he can't get to. Ethan's name rings a bell, but he can't figure out why and it frustrates him. I know the feeling.

I'm not too confident about making it to all my classes on time, once I realize how far apart some of these buildings are. We joke about getting scooters, but I'm thinking that may be more realistic than running across campus, books in hand. Jason walks us back to our room, and I show him the notebook and the poem. He doesn't understand it any more than we did. As far as the clues go, we've hit a dead end.

The next day my mom makes good on her promise to meet over coffee. Besides the café, there's a local coffeehouse within walking distance that I can't wait to try. We find a small table at the back of the shop and slowly sip our lattes. Pretty certain I found my new favorite place near campus. Better coffee than at the café, which I didn't think possible. My mom puts her mug down and straightens herself in her chair.

"Cassia, there's an important reason I came here today. It wasn't just to see your room—though it's quaint and I bet you'll love it. I came here, to be honest with you about my past." I stiffen instantly. "I came here to warn you."

"Warn me about what?"

"Can I tell you a story?" I lean my head to the side and nod. She hasn't opened up before, and I'm secretly afraid of what she has to say. "I know I haven't been forthright about my past, and I'm sorry. But I'm afraid that my choices then may be impacting yours now."

"Is this about the Trivium?" She eyes me warily.

"In a way, yes. But it's much deeper than that. You see, what's happening to you now is my fault. The visions are because of what I did." I feel my heart thudding loudly and my muscles tense up.

"Mom, what did you do?"

"I ripped a hole in the so-called fabric of time. I know that's not the real definition of it, but it's the best way to describe it." She takes another sip of coffee. "I didn't choose your dad at the Trivium, sweetheart. He wasn't a choice. I chose a completely different life."

"What . . . life?" She goes on to explain that she grew up as a gymnast. She was passionate about gymnastics and wanted the rest of her life to involve training, competing, and eventually teaching. So, when the Trivium offered her that life, she took it. She only gave the other choices a passing glance. The great part of the future she chose, is that it took her to several national titles. She was a rising star in the sport and was dedicated to it. But that also meant sacrificing relationships. She lost friends because she was always away traveling. She didn't have a marriage in her future. At the time, she didn't care. The Trivium had shown her a life of gold medals and trophies, and she felt like her dreams would come true. And in a way, they did. She had everything she aspired to. But she felt something missing. One night, she was at a theatre production supporting an acquaintance in the show, when she bumped into my dad.

"For me, that was when my life was over. I met your dad, and he made me realize that I was fine with certain aspects of my life, but I was lonely. Inconsolably lonely. I don't know then what made me think of changing course, but perhaps love does crazy things to you. I changed my mind, I wanted to get to know him better. And I fell in love. And that single decision, where I altered my future, caused a rift."

This woman in front of me, I don't know her. That hits me hard, and I'm fighting the urge to be angry. "You're telling me that *you* made your own choice and caused a rift? What does that even mean?"

"It means that there are consequences for altering your path, and at the time I didn't care. However, when you showed me your notebook, I . . . I started thinking about what all this could mean. For you. And I felt like it was time to be honest because I wouldn't forgive myself if something bad happened—" She fights back tears, and my anger subsides a little.

"But you encouraged me to change my fate. Why would you do that?"

"Because I saw myself in you. And I didn't want you to end up down the road living a life that made you unhappy. I couldn't bear it. I just didn't realize that in doing so, it would make the rift larger."

"This rift, what is it exactly?" She sighs.

"The best way I can describe it is it's like a wormhole. It's a window into the alternate universe. Or one of them. These visions you have, they aren't just dreams or daydreams or whatever—they're windows into the other world."

"So, I'm seeing another version of my life?"

"Basically, yes. And in that life, someone like me is out there looking for you. Someone who also chose to disregard all conventions to go after what he wants. The life he wants. The one with you in it."

"This is a lot to take in." She sets her empty mug down and smiles.

"It's kind of romantic though." This makes me crack a smile against my wishes. It's a crazy notion, this guy eschewing all tradition in favor of the unknown. Kind of like what I've been doing. Ugh.

"But what is the problem? If a rift has been there all these years, why worry now?"

"Back when I married your dad, Trivium officials came and talked to me. They had noticed I'd change my plan, and they didn't understand how I could do that. They are the ones that found out about the rift and told me there could be unknown consequences. I first suspected you were affected when you ended up in the hospital. The officials knew about me and wanted to know more about you. I had a feeling they were watching me closely, to see if things got worse. Cassia, that rift is going to get larger and larger as time goes by."

"Okay, then how do you close it?"

"We're still working on the details."

"We?" She leans back against her chair, rubbing her hands on her temples.

"Trivium officials and myself. *We* are monitoring the situation and trying to understand what impact it will have. But I don't want you to base any decision from here on out on what could happen with this thing. I want you to continue pursuing your dreams. Can you at least promise me that much?" I think to myself about how each decision I make can cause more problems for others. Without knowing the extent of the damage my mom caused by creating the rift in the first place, I don't know how bad it will get with each passing choice I make. Can I be that selfish? Does this impact anyone else besides myself? "Cassia, promise me you will keep moving forward. That you won't let knowing this information stop you." I nod slowly, not sure what I'm agreeing to exactly. "Good. Sweetheart, I told you I'd do anything for you to be happy. That will never change." She reaches across the table and rests her hands on mine, squeezing gently. She's my mom, but she's also a stranger. A contradiction of great proportions.

That night, I fill Verity in on the meeting with my mom. She's as speechless as I was at first. I try not to dwell on all the things that could go wrong, but it's hard to ignore my mom's warning. Choices have consequences. Will my choices affect those I care about? Have they already?

Verity and I get ready for bed, and as I'm about to crawl up the small ladder, the onset of a vision headache takes over and I sit down quickly. Verity rushes to my side to hold me up and then everything around me is gone. I'm no longer at the dorm. I'm sitting at a small rectangular table across from Verity and Jason, and we're playing cards. I look around and I don't recognize the house we're in, but it's cozy and charming. There's a fire glowing in the living room, and the smells of pine permeate the air. I like this place already though I don't have a clue where it may be. A figure to my right comes walking in, holding a couple mugs. He sets one down in front of me before kissing my cheek, and I know this is Ethan, but I'm also in shock.

"Cas, your deal." Jason is pushing the deck of cards in my direction. I feel frozen here, not knowing how long I'll stay in this place and if I should reveal how lost I am.

"Cas, you didn't forget how to shuffle already, did you?" Verity is grinning widely at me and then winks as if there's a secret between us. I have no idea how to shuffle cards. I never really learned. I was always so bad at it that my dad would give up waiting and take them from me.

"Cassia, you need anything?" I look over at him, and I can't help but smile. This guy, this crazy fool of a man, has been sending me messages to another time and place. Is this my future I'm seeing? Or what it's supposed to be? Can I still have it? I realize I'm staring at him intensely, and it causes me to blush.

"No, but I don't know how to shuffle cards." They all laugh at me like I just told the funniest joke.

"Funny, Cassia. We're waiting." Ethan leans over to me and kisses my cheek again. It tingles in the spot where his lips touched me, and I feel the shocks trickle down my face and through the rest of my body. This feeling is new. And terrifying.

"Cassia, where did you go?" I open my eyes and I'm back at the dorm, Verity hovering over me with concern.

"Ver, we were with Jason and Ethan, playing cards. And I was supposed to shuffle—"

"—but you don't know how to shuffle—"

"—I know! But you all acted like I did know. And Ethan . . ." That warm feeling engulfs me and I feel my cheeks getting hot.

"Cas, spill. Ethan what?"

"He kissed my cheek!" She bursts out in giggles. "Why is that funny?"

"Because this poor guy has been searching for you, leaving you messages from another dimension, and when you're there he kisses your *cheek*?" Now she's on the floor, rolling side to side, clenching her stomach.

"Well, I'm glad you're amused by this." She sits back up and tries to keep composure, but she's on the verge of losing it again.

"Okay, I'm done. So, we were playing cards, and in this life, you know how to shuffle, and the great love of your life kisses your cheek. Got it. Anything else?" I see her eyes glossing over, so I playfully punch her arm.

"It's not funny! I was happy, Verity. *We* were happy. All four of us. No matter what the consequences of choosing this life are, it all seems to be worth it." She straightens herself up, seriousness taking over her face.

"Then let's find that life, Cas. For all of us. Let's go find Ethan."

CHAPTER SEVENTEEN

ETHAN

I stand alone frozen in place and time. No alarms were sounded. The silence echoes off the walls and I keep waiting on edge as if I'm about to get a verbal lashing for pushing a button that wasn't an option. Emma walks back in, without a look of concern on her face, and hands me a pill and a cup of water.

"Take this. It will make you a little sleepy, but then you'll be fine." I eye that pill warily, knowing it will erase parts of my memory. I don't want to risk losing my memories of Cassia. I still don't know exactly what I chose, either. I push the pill up inside a part of my cheek next to my back teeth and take a sip of water. I open my mouth and show under my tongue, and she seems satisfied with that. I ask to go to the bathroom and she nods, so I make a quick show of it and flush the pill down the toilet. I'm guessing no one has ever tried to avoid the pill, so they aren't suspicious. Knowing it's supposed to make me hazy, I feign being tired by yawning. Emma instructs me to sit in a wheelchair and I oblige, continuing my yawning charade. I close my eyes and she wheels me into the lobby. My dad is already there waiting for me, and I let them lift me into the car, acting like I'm out of it.

"Mr. Rivers, I'm Dr. Bachman. May I speak with you just a moment?" I don't dare open my eyes, but I focus on their voices as much as possible. My dad moves away from the car but thankfully doesn't close the door yet. "We were a little concerned with Ethan's options today. For some reason, he was only given two choices. We'd like you to keep an eye on him to see if he feels alright once he's lucid, which should be in a few hours. Will you contact me if there is any cause for concern?" I don't hear my dad reply so I assume he nodded. "I'll be personally looking over his file this afternoon. We'll be in touch." My dad closes the car door, gets in on his side, and takes me home. My mom helps him get me into bed, and I'm grateful that they leave so I can stop pretending to be asleep. What will my file say? Will they know what I did? Tension takes over my gut, and I worry that I'll be in a lot of trouble when they find out I didn't make one of the two choices. And I certainly didn't take their pill. I wonder if I'm the only person to avoid a memory wipe. Cassia somehow sent me a message, but does she even remember who I am? Is it really her trying to contact me, or am I dreaming up what I want to see?

I lie in bed for several hours, pondering what my next steps are. When I feel it's safe to come out, I make sure and walk downstairs while rubbing my eyes for full effect. My dad is sitting on the sofa reading a newspaper. He looks up and sees me standing there so he folds it and sets it beside him.

"How are you feeling?"

"Good. I'm fine. How long have I been out?"

"A few hours. They said you'd need some time to rest. Anything I can get for you?"

"No, I'm okay. I think I may go see some friends. Would that be alright?" He cocks his head to the side.

"Sure you feel fine for that? A doctor at the Trivium said there were some complications with your results. They'll be checking in with you later. They didn't say when." I try to keep calm and not show worry on my face.

"I bet it's nothing. Really, I feel fine and rested. If someone comes by, call me and I'll come back home."

"Okay then." He reaches beside him for the paper and opens it up, fluffing it in the process. I head outside and call Verity, and we agree to meet at the diner.

"So, what happened? Can you remember anything? I don't remember anything from when I went." She's so bouncy and full of energy that I wonder how Jason handles it. He's so laid back though, I guess it doesn't affect him. I lean closer to her so I can whisper.

"I didn't take the pill." I lean back and she puts her hand over her mouth and gasps. I look around to make sure no one noticed, but there are only a few others in here and none of them seem interested in our conversation. I can relax at least a little.

"How's that possible?" She tries to talk quietly, but even her whispering is loud. I chuckle to myself.

"I hid the pill in my mouth and then flushed it. I remember everything I saw in the tank." She squeals with excitement.

"What did you see? Did you see Cas?"

"Kind of. Not directly, no." She frowns, disappointment setting in. "It's okay though, Verity. She's still there, somewhere." I explain to her each of my choices and relay everything that's happened since. She sits back against the booth, clearly conflicted. I see the gears turning behind her eyes, so I allow the silence to settle between us. Several minutes pass before she leans forward and clasps her hands on top of the table.

"Well, now what?"

"I guess we wait."

"That's not a good enough answer."

"I don't know a better one." She sighs loudly. "I don't know what to say, Verity. I don't even know the repercussions yet for choosing a button that wasn't supposed to work. If that button means I can make it up as I go, then that's what I'll do. I'll work on finding ways to talk to her. For now, everything needs to seem normal. We're all going off to college anyway, and Jason and I planned to get a room together. So, let's focus on moving forward and starting college, and who knows? Maybe we'll find her, or find a way to talk to her."

"Hurry up and wait it is then," she huffs. I echo her frustration. Now that the Trivium is over, I need to make sure all my college aspirations are still intact. My one small act of rebellion has the potential to ripple into tidal waves, and I'm not sure how safe I am away from the shore.

Life must go on while we wait. I hope that wherever Cassia is, she's pursuing her dreams. I hope in that world she's not trying to be something she's not. Maybe she's over there writing the next big novel. Maybe she's enjoying getting ready for college. Whatever she's doing, wherever she is, I hope she's happy. Well, not *too* happy. I mean, she's not with *us* so it can't all be perfect.

The next day when I wake up, I'm greeted by Trivium officials in my living room. My parents are ill at ease on the couch, my mom's wringing her hands.

"Ethan, I'm Dr. Bachman. I'd like to ask you a few questions if that's alright." He smiles, but his overall face is stern.

"Okay." Do I have a choice?

"Yesterday we were aware that there was an issue with your experience in the Trivium tank. First, I'd like to apologize for that because it's not a usual occurrence. Second, I wanted to go over your file with you, because we had some peculiar issues with it and your results were unclear. Please, have a seat." He motions for me to sit in the chair next to him so I oblige. He opens my file and I can barely make out the words on the page. "It says here that you were given two choices, but it's not clear which one you chose. I know you can't tell us what your options were, but I wanted to make sure you were satisfied with what you were given."

"Yes, I was." Not really, no.

"Good. Also, it was recorded that you would be going to college upstate, as a creative writing major. Is that correct?" I think about that for a second. How would it show that in my file?

"Yes. I have a dorm ready to move into next week." *Of course, I haven't verified the details yet.*

"Good, good. Have you experienced any headaches, dizziness, or nausea since you returned home?"

"No." *Does he know about the visions?* "Does that file show every single part of my future?"

"Not necessarily. Sometimes there are only snippets of major life events recorded in the file. Yours, however—as strange as this may sound—is mostly blank."

"Doctor, does that mean he doesn't have a future?" My mom is sitting perched on the edge of the sofa, looking on the verge of tears.

"No, no, Mrs. Rivers. I'm sure that's not the problem. It could be that with the issues we had, not everything was recorded. Ethan should know parts of what he saw for the future he chose, so it should all be okay." She breathes a deep sigh of relief. "We'll continue to monitor the situation from our end." He stands up and motions for the other officials to stand as well. "We'll leave you be, but Ethan, call us if you have any problems." He hands me his business card.

"Thanks," I say. He shakes my hand and then also shakes my parents' hands before leading the men outside.

"Ethan, should we be worried right now?" The doctor's lack of concern apparently didn't sway my mom.

"Mom, you heard what he said. I'm sure everything is okay."

"If something bad happened there, you would tell us, wouldn't you?" I look her in the eyes and smile.

"Mom, if something bad had happened, I would've told you. But nothing happened. There were just some issues is all. I'm okay.

No headaches. I'll tell you first thing if I don't feel well." She relaxes and then gives me a soft hug.

"You do that." She walks into the kitchen with my dad, and I'm left wondering what else to do with my day. I don't need much for school, but I go ahead and grab a few things for my dorm room. I call the college, and sure enough, they have Jason and me together in a room with my enrollment completed. All that's left is moving in and meeting with my advisor. Jason and I plan on driving up Monday so we'll have enough time to get acquainted with the campus. Verity wants us to go on a self-guided tour with her, so we give in and say yes. It's interesting that she was never assigned a roommate. Especially for freshmen in college that doesn't usually happen. She's not in a single room, it's just that no one was assigned. It's like Cassia is supposed to be there too, and the universe is keeping the possibility open. That would make Verity's day.

Over the weekend we have a family game night—something we haven't done in ages. Cards, board games, and even charades. We all laugh so hard our stomachs hurt, and it pains me to think of what I'll be missing out on. Granted, it's been a long time since we've done this together, but not getting to see them every day is going to be hard. Hannah will probably grow up so fast I won't recognize her when I come back to visit. And it doesn't matter if I try to come back each weekend, they're usually gone. There is so much in their lives that happen that doesn't include me that it hurts a little feeling left out. I didn't realize how much I missed us as a family until. Not separate and individual pieces, but together.

Leaving on Monday morning is tough. I say my goodbyes and pack up my car. My room looks empty and sad without all my books and clothes strung about. My mom is probably thrilled that at least the room will stay clean. I follow Jason to the college, and we get our keys and start unpacking. A new chapter is starting in my life, but the pages are still blank.

Verity meets up with us and we indulge her whims with the tour and then stop at the local café to eat. It's an interesting place, and I notice there's a stage at the back. Oh, no. They do slam poetry and readings here. I am terrible at poetry. A short story reading, maybe. Poetry? Never. I shudder at the thought. The coffee and sandwiches are good, so at least I'll eat about as decently as I do at home.

"Okay Ethan, we're here. We need to get to work on contacting Cas." I about choke on my coffee.

"Verity, how do you propose doing such a thing? Because I might read a lot of science fiction, but I can't exactly use their methods to just walk into a parallel universe to talk to the girl I love." Jason almost spits out his coffee from laughing and then starts coughing enough that he needs to get up and walk to the bathroom.

"I'm being serious. You two jokers can laugh and make fun, but I want my best friend back. Jason might be the love of my life, but Cassia is my soul mate. I'm not me without her." I'm not sure what's worse, the fear that I may never find Cassia and I'll end up alone, or disappointing Diana and Verity if I don't bring her back. *Cassia, if you only knew how loved you are over here.*

"I thought Cassia was *my* soul mate. What gives?" She winks at me but offers no witty retort. Jason returns to the table, red-faced from the coughing, but otherwise okay.

"What did I miss?"

"You missed nothing, Jason. Just Ethan trying to be his normal witty and sarcastic self."

"So, basically all is as it should be."

"No, that's not true. Verity was talking about soul mates." Jason starts coughing again. "Not *you*. Cassia."

"Oh, well that's okay then." He cries out in pain, and I assume Verity kicked him under the table. "Verity, I'm kidding! I'm kidding!" His face grows an even brighter shade of red.

"Back to the topic at hand, gentlemen. Ethan, are you still having dreams and visions?"

"I haven't, no. Not since the Trivium." She bites her lower lip and scrunches up her face like she's trying to solve a puzzle. Or a case. *Detective Verity* sounds fitting. I need to stay focused.

"Well, I'm sure you will again. And when that happens, do whatever you can to get a message across."

"And what would I say?"

"That we miss her and we're looking for her. Or that she needs to come find us. Anything that could help her. Please, Ethan." She's pleading with me now, and I feel a great responsibility on my chest. I nod and drink more coffee. The air has shifted with our moods.

That night, Jason and I get ready for bed, and it's eerily silent in our hall. We technically drove up early, so there aren't many other students checked in yet. Neither of us has the energy to hang out in the common area, so we get in our beds instead.

"This whole Cassia thing has Verity torn up something awful." Jason sits up and turns toward me. I guess neither of us can sleep.

"I don't want to let her down, but I don't know what to do either."

"I know." He lays back down. I sit up, and as I do so my head aches and I feel sick to my stomach. Thinking I'm about to throw up, I quickly jump down from the loft bed and feel around the dark for my trash can. "Ethan, you okay down there?"

"I feel sick."

"A vision?"

"N-no I-I—" and then I'm on a stage at the café from earlier and no longer in my dorm room. *Why am I on the stage?* I peer out into the crowd, thinking perhaps Cassia is here, but I can't see anyone. All the faces look dark and I can't make out facial features. Someone announces a poetry reading, and I freeze. *Oh no. Oh no, no, no. No. This can't be happening.* I feel like I'm about to black out from fear, but Verity's words ring in my head. *Get a message across.* But poetry? Of all the terrible situations to put me in, this would be at the top of my list. Above paper-cut torture. The guy with the mic asks me my name. I'm glad I remember it. The next few seconds are a barrage of verbal vomit with some rhyming words mixed in. And then it's over. And I'm gone. And the light in the dorm room is on and Jason is staring at me.

"What did you see?" He's curious, but worried—and perhaps a little excited. He hovers over me like a dog waiting for a bone to be thrown. I explain to him what happened and what I said, and he bursts out laughing so hard that if the room next door had occupants, they'd probably be mad at us.

"So that's it. A bad poem I can barely remember that's basically a bunch of gibberish and rhyming words."

"That describes a lot of poetry." He can't help himself at this point. I think he's cracked up so much that it doesn't take anything at all to push him back over the edge.

"I'm glad you're getting joy from this."

"Dude. Ethan, if this girl doesn't love you already, I'm pretty sure all chances would be lost after that." I give up. All I can do is sigh and not partake in his ridiculousness.

"I'm going to try to get some sleep." I climb back up to my bed and Jason thankfully turns the light off before getting into his.

"You need to tell Verity what happened tomorrow."

"I will," I reply.

The next morning, Jason and I walk over to Verity's dorm. It's different in atmosphere from ours—more studious, perhaps. I fill her in on everything that happened last night, and to my surprise, she doesn't make fun of me. All I've done is strengthen her resolve.

"This is fantastic news!" She jumps up and down in excitement. I'm glad to see the old Verity peeking through. Too much seriousness doesn't suit her. "Let me know when it happens again!" I promise her that I will, and I tell them I have an appointment with my advisor to go over my class schedule. They have their own plans, so they follow me out the door and Verity locks it. I notice that the dry erase board on her door is blank. I stare at it and think of Cassia, and then my head hurts again. Why does it have to hurt so much?

I'm still standing in the hallway of Verity's dorm, but she and Jason aren't here beside me. I know this must be a vision, because the pain and nausea sets in, and there's no way Jason and Verity disappeared on me. I look again at the blank board and get an idea. Sure, the poem was stupid. But it was something she would know was from me if she ever heard it the first time. I grab the marker that hangs on a string beside the board and write a line I remember from the poem. *I hope you get this, Cassia.* And I'm back again, like being sucked through a vacuum into a black hole.

"I left a message on your dry erase board for Cassia." Verity turns toward me quickly with a look of surprise. She glances at the blank board and then back at me.

"Another vision already?"

"You didn't know?" She and Jason shake their heads in tandem. "I was still here, but there. You both were gone. I took a chance and left a message."

"Ethan that would've happened in a split second, because we just walked out here and I was locking the door."

"It felt longer. That's weird." I look around and there is still a blank board in front of me.

"There's no way to know if she's in the same room over there. Or even here at this college."

"I have to believe she is. And that's why I ended up at the café. It's like I'm thrust into another life each time. She must be here. *Has* to be, or else it wouldn't make sense for me to see a vision of your door."

"I don't think these are visions, Ethan. I think they're windows." Verity is staring at me wide-eyed.

"Windows? What kind of science fiction or fantasy have you been reading, Verity?" Jason doesn't even chuckle at my joke. The mood is serious.

"I think she's right, Ethan. Maybe it's possible outside the realms of science fiction."

"Are you both serious?" I look at them incredulously.

"Absolutely. Ethan, maybe we don't need to find her across many planes or worlds. Maybe we just need to find her in that *one*. We might be able to find her. If you left a message on this door in another world, she must be on the other side of it."

"I certainly hope you're right, Verity."

"I know I am. We'll find our girl."

CHAPTER EIGHTEEN

CASSIA

I'm officially a college freshman. I survived my first week of classes, organized every single syllabus in a binder by day and time of class, and spent the rest of my time in the library looking for answers on how to find the wormhole. I wish I could say that the library was a wealth of knowledge, I need only to search for it—but in the case of actual science and not the fiction version, the library has left me hollow.

Verity joined me a couple of times this week to help me look but she came up empty like I did. She and Jason have been busy with their class schedules as well, so I don't fault her for being gone so much this week. One of her fashion classes requires a rather large project, and she's already started pinning sketches to the walls. It makes me smile to see them, knowing I've seen many just like them before. I was assigned several large novels over the semester for one class, so I spend a lot of my time in bed reading. At least Verity and I get to connect with each other at night and talk about our day.

It's been weeks since I've had any visions, and even though they're painful at first, I miss the world that they show me. And strangely enough, I miss seeing glimpses of Ethan. How can you get to know someone better when they don't exist where you are?

The days mesh together and Verity and I live life in a rhythm. We know each other's schedules by heart, and each day is an ebb and flow of activities, assignments, and projects. We buy a wall calendar so we can keep track of due dates and tests. I've only been home once for a weekend since school started. It pains me, and I know my parents are disappointed too, but there's so much to do here that it's been hard getting away.

Fall on campus is stunning. The grounds are aflame in bright reds and oranges. The cool, crisp air has a bite to it, but it's decent enough outside that it doesn't require wearing layers. Jason's been so inspired by the foliage that his room is covered in canvases mimicking the hues outside. There's something about fall that makes me feel warm inside when the outside temperatures drop. Hot cider, the smells of cinnamon and cloves, and the ever-increasing temptation to eat everything created with pumpkin. It's also a time when couples seem to start hibernation behaviors, and Verity and Jason are not immune. The way they look at each other, I want that for myself. They're best friends in a way Verity and I can never be. It's not that I wish to fill the lack of romance in my life right now, but it's so intriguing watching their love unfold and deepen. And here I am, with a great romance just a lifetime away in another world. A world I cannot reach and a man I cannot find. But he's out there. I know that for certain, and as long as I hold on to that, I have hope.

I've been writing in what little spare time I have. Mostly short stories. I started outlining a novel idea I had, but I haven't finished it. My thoughts often drift to Ethan. Is he also in college right now? Is he making the most of his life while he keeps looking for me? *Is he still looking for me?*

Friday after my last class, Verity and I make plans to see a movie. Just us. Jason has other things to do. We choose a noir classic detective film, at Verity's behest. A break from action films is much welcomed, but I'm surprised that she picks a very old movie instead of a new one.

The theater is relatively empty, save for a few older patrons that must be waxing nostalgic. Verity sits next to me holding a giant tub of popcorn she's slathered butter all over. I don't usually add butter, but I don't protest either. The cranky detective on the big screen plays coy with the wealthy socialite who hired him. I feel like I've seen this film before, but I push the thought away. I try to not laugh at inappropriate times, but the helpless damsel in distress versus the femme fatale gets me every time. I don't want to ever live my life as a cliché.

After the movie's over we drive back to campus, ditch the car, and then walk to the coffeehouse. I've spent more time here than in the common room at the dorm, and the staff knows my order before I even utter a word. I very rarely deviate from my favorite type of coffee. Verity is highly animated as she talks about the movie. Her arms flail about excitedly, and at times I'm afraid she'll end up accidentally hitting me. Or my coffee, which is worse.

"I can't decide if I like the detective. He was so stern and machismo. And not macho in a respectable way but a very patronizing, patriarchal way." Verity realizes she's talking with her hands and decides to fold them together on top of the table.

"I'm sure a lot of that had to do with when it was made. Society was very different back then."

"Can you just imagine though? Being a woman back then? I don't think I could handle all the fake fainting and fawning over me and that nonsense."

"Verity, something tells me you would be a femme fatale. You'd just do what you wanted. And the rest of that I bet is just movie fluff, not reality."

"Yeah, maybe. I like living in an age where I can choose what career I'm best suited for. A femme fatale is so often cold and calculating, at least in these movies. I don't think I'd like that either."

"You are exactly who you should be." And she is. It's admirable how self-assured she is.

"And are *you* who *you* should be?" She winks at me, but there's seriousness in her undertones.

"I'm working on it," I say.

"Any luck on the wormhole search?" She and I both laugh at the mention of a wormhole. It's such an unpleasant sounding concept. I picture a worm the size of a galaxy eating its way through universes like a giant apple. It's an image I can't get out of my mind.

"No. No luck finding the wormhole or gigantic worm that created it." That makes us both laugh again.

"So, your mom has no idea where this window is? I figured she'd share more details since she's working on it and all." Truth is, my mom hasn't shared much of anything with me concerning the window. She keeps reassuring me they can fix the mess she caused, but so far nothing.

"Nope. I think it would be nearby though. I just can't pin down an area. But you know what? I'm a little apprehensive about finding it. We find it and then what? I don't want to lose a part of myself."

"You know, Cas, I don't think you'd lose a part of yourself, I think you'd find it. I don't lose who I am because I chose to be with Jason. I chose him because he feels like another part of me. If Ethan complements you in the same way Jason does me, then you'll be finding a piece of yourself you didn't even know was lost. That's how relationships should be." It stings a little to hear her say this.

"I guess I feel like I was sacrificing a lot for a life with Gunner, and of course, I know he wasn't truly accepting of who I was and what I wanted to be. I don't want to have these high expectations of Ethan, just to find out he's another guy that wants something from me that I'm not willing to give." I think of the words Gunner said when he left. That he was with me because of the life he thought I was choosing. It didn't matter to him that I was happy, it mattered that I had status or money. I don't want to be loved because of what I do for a living, but for who I am.

"Cas, something tells me Ethan is about you. Just *you*. Who you are and what you stand for. I don't see him making all this effort just to be with someone for superficial reasons." She finishes her coffee and walks up to the bar to get a refill. I mull over what she's saying. It's easy to say that, but I don't know him. Not anymore. I wish I did. I close my eyes and imagine what my life would look like if it included Ethan. I think about him being a wonderful addition to my life, instead of subtracting away my time and energy. In another life, he and Jason were best friends, so I know they could be again. That makes me sad thinking about it. How cruel this world is if one single choice can eradicate those we care about from our lives. Who else have we forgotten? Who has forgotten us?

"Cassia, what are you daydreaming about?" His voice startles me, and I open my eyes to see Ethan across the table from me, sitting where Verity had just left. I look around the coffeehouse, and there's no sign of Verity anywhere. *A vision, that's what this is.* But there were no signs this was going to happen.

"Ethan, how are you here?" A look of confusion washes over his face.

"We came here together a few minutes ago. To study for finals. What do you mean?" I laugh to myself. Pretending I belong in this moment won't change anything. Not pretending apparently doesn't change anything either.

"Well, here is what I know. We're not really here together, because you're in another universe and I'm in this one, and you're just a vision that seeps through sometimes as if I'm dreaming, because of a wormhole my mom caused that tore the fabric of time." He whistles through his teeth.

"Whatever you say, Cassia." He goes back to drinking his coffee and then opens a textbook.

"If this is real, riddle me this: why do you like me?" He almost chokes on his coffee and starts coughing violently. A few seconds later he's able to get a drink of water and return to his seat.

"Well, that's one way to get my attention." He smiles at me weakly, red in the face.

"I'm serious. Why do you like me? What is it about me?" I sit back in my seat and fold my arms, waiting patiently for him to respond.

"I like your strong interrogation skills? And your tactful use of intimidation?" He winks at me, and when I don't show any emotion on my face or say anything, he continues. "Cassia, I like you because of what you stand for. You're loyal to those you care about, and you'll never back down when it comes to protecting them. I like you because you're witty and charming—except for right now because you're a little frightening." He chuckles to himself and I force myself to not smile. "I like you because we can talk—really talk—about hard things. History, politics, religion, the future—you don't hold back in deep discussions. You challenge me. You inspire me. You motivate me to do and be better. We want similar things in life. We have similar goals." He leans closer to me, his eyes intense and fiery. "And if the universes collided, and our worlds melted away, you'd be the one I'd want to spend my last moments with before oblivion." Heat rises through my heart and up my neck until I feel my face flush. Even though this is a vision—and I'm painfully aware the moment won't last—I know he's telling the truth. Ethan doesn't want something from me, he just wants *me*. He moves to the chair beside me, and I feel my pulse quicken. I'm afraid of the power this man has over my emotions, but my heart aches for all of this to be true. This notion of having love and a life that are not in conflict with one another. A life where we dream together. He puts his hand on my cheek and gently turns my head to face him. I have never been looked at the way he is looking at me. As if he's able to see past all pretenses and right into my very being. "You are my adventure, Cassia. If I have you with me, I have everything."

He kisses me gently. I don't want to move, I want to live in this moment. I fight back the tears forming, but I lose the battle. I feel a droplet making its way down my cheek.

"Cas, are you crying?" I wipe the tear away and force myself to open my eyes. He's gone. I knew he couldn't stay with me, but how I wish he was still here. Verity sits in the seat Ethan sat just moments ago, refilled coffee in hand.

"I had a vision." I reach for a napkin to blow my nose and wipe my eyes again. Verity reaches across the table and grabs my right hand.

"Did something bad happen?" I shake my head and blow my nose again.

"You were right, Verity, about Ethan. We were together, right here. Supposed to be studying for a test in a class we have together. I asked him why he liked me, and . . ." I trail off, not able to make myself repeat his words. They are too personal, and I'm too emotionally raw. I take a minute to breathe deeply and calm myself down. She patiently waits for me to speak. "It's like you said, someone who complements you. He does. I know that now. I know I won't be giving up the life I want, but getting to experience it with him beside me." She smiles a big, toothy smile and shakes her head at me.

"That's all I want for you, Cas. Someone that loves you and sees you the way I do. I sincerely hope we can find him." I've searched for answers, but only half-heartedly. My desire to make sense of this world has been renewed. Where before I felt fear about the unknown, now I feel determined to journey headfirst into it. I won't lose anything by finding Ethan, but I'll gain another best friend. And more than that, I'll gain a partner I can do life with. One who dreams beside me, isn't threatened by my passions, and who fits in with my friends. I don't have to lose it all, I just have to find it.

CHAPTER NINETEEN

ETHAN

All this time I've been living my life in pieces through a window. Not dreaming or imagining a vision, but seeing my life—the correct life—through a lens of unquantifiable proportions. All this time the answers were right in front of me. I can see into the other world though I know not how nor why. I have been impossibly connected to another person that no longer exists in my plane. A small invisible thread binds us together like stretched gold. Or two points of a compass. If I search far and wide, will she remain centered? Or will she lean toward me the further away I go? If all this can be explained by a window that allows me to peer into the unknown, where I can find it? Can I travel through it?

I finally have my first weekend I can spend at home, and I plan on using it to further my investigation. I'm hoping I'll find out more info, but I don't know where to look. As I pull up to my parents' house, I notice black government standard-issue cars in the driveway and know the Trivium officials are back. No surprise there. I walk in and set my overnight bag down in the entry and am greeted by squeals and a huge hug from Hannah. I missed her so much more than I thought possible. The officials are waiting in the living room again like last time, and it's the same doctor that greets me.

"Ethan, your parents informed us you would be home today. May we have a minute of your time?" I nod and follow him back to the couch. I can't imagine what else they need to know.

"What can I do for you?"

"We just wanted to check in with you, a routine follow-up per se, and make sure all is well."

"I appreciate that, but I'm fine." He peers down at the same manila file folder.

"I'd like to show you something." He opens the folder and points to some pages covered in text. "Do you see this page right here?" I nod. "Last time we were here this was blank. I know it was. I documented it both on the computer and a recorded file." He flips the page over. "This here was also blank. And now there is text indicating some parts of your future. Can you look this over for me? Maybe you can explain what has happened." He hands me the file, and I cautiously read the words.

The first page lists the same information as last time: college upstate, roommates with Jason, creative writing. At the bottom, there is new text. I'm almost afraid of what it will say and I hesitate to read it.

"I've read it, it's nothing bad, I promise." He smiles reassuringly. He must have noticed my hesitation.

My throat is dry and I try to swallow before continuing. I take a precursory glance and a name pops off the page: Cassia. I close my eyes and breathe slowly before opening them and reading. Cassia is tied to my future. She's with me in college, we're both writing, and she rooms with Verity. *Does this mean we really do find her?* I look back up and see that Dr. Bachman has been watching me very closely.

"Can you explain how Cassia Bellerose is a part of your future?" His eyes are focused on me intently, and I know instantly he could tell if I lied.

"Not really, no." He keeps his eyes on me like a hawk watching a field mouse. I fidget in my seat and tell myself to stop being nervous.

"Ethan, let me be frank with you. I'm greatly concerned about the presence of Cassia Bellerose in your file. To be blunt, she shouldn't be able to be in your future. Now, I don't know how anything included here is possible when these pages were blank, and I know no one added to them since they've been in my personal vault. Only I can get into it. It went straight from your house at our last visit into the vault, and I only opened it up yesterday to check on it. That's when I noticed this and called your parents to see when you'd be home." I look around and don't see my parents anywhere. Hannah had gone back upstairs, but where are my mom and dad? Dr. Bachman sees me scanning the house and tells me my parents are also upstairs. He had asked them to speak with me in private.

"Sir, I don't know what's in my future." The truth flies out so quickly I don't think about the consequences of revealing that information before it's too late.

"Ethan, I had a feeling you didn't. Or I should say, I had a feeling you were on a different path than we expected. Can you and I take a walk?" He motions for the door and tells the other men to stay at the house. Fear grips me and panic sets in.

I follow him out the door and walk beside him on the sidewalk. His pace is slow, and I pay close attention to make myself slow down to match him. It's a very awkward pace. I'm too scared to speak, worried I will give away more than I should. More than I already have. After a few minutes and several houses past, he stops and faces me.

"Ethan, here is where I trust you with complete honesty. And I expect absolute confidentiality. Can you do that?" I nod in reply. "Good. I have a feeling you can. Many years ago, we had a young person alter her timeline, and it caused a potentially dangerous situation for her daughter—and quite possibly you, too. We've already seen repercussions from that decision, which you are not supposed to remember, but clearly, you do—since you didn't forget who Cassia was." *Oh no, I shouldn't have remembered Cassia at all!*

"I-I'm—"

"No need to apologize. I had already assumed as such because of the strangeness of the file. I gather you didn't take the pill given to you?" I avert my eyes and shake my head. "Very well. Thank you for your honesty. In a way, it's probably better that you didn't take it." I look back up in surprise.

"Why is that?"

"Because of what's happening with our world and another. Ethan, when this woman made the choice to go off the beaten path, she caused changes in our little part of the world. While we are not sure the exact extent of the damages—and whether it affects anyone else besides those around her—we do know that the rift she created is getting larger. Ethan, that woman was Cassia's mother, Diana." I gasp and step away from him.

"How? You mean, Diana did all this?" Diana, who has been pushing me to find Cassia, is the reason we lost her? How can that be?

"In a way, yes. Diana was the catalyst for the rift that occurred, but it wasn't intentional. There are serious consequences that can happen when you choose to go a different way after you've already chosen at the Trivium. Diana is the first, however, to cross that line. We are still investigating the fallout from that decision all these years later. I feel it very well could have led to Cassia's unfortunate death."

"Why are you being so candid with me?"

"Because Cassia's name being in your file is a warning sign, I believe. It means that you are writing your own future, and you're able to bring her back. I came here to warn you, Ethan. Bringing Cassia back somehow can have dire consequences for you both. What they are, I don't know. We do believe that the rift needs to close, and we're monitoring it very carefully."

"Wait, you know where it is?"

"We do. That's classified. If in the future we need to tell you, we will. Right now, we're going to keep an eye on you and your file." I nod in understanding. He knows where this window is. I need to know where it is. He isn't going to tell me. Diana wasn't completely honest about her past—not that I blame her. I can't imagine the guilt she must be dealing with, knowing her decision could've cost her Cassia's future. At least in this world. *No wonder she wants her back.* I need to speak with Diana before I go back to school. I promised confidentiality to Dr. Bachman, but I wonder how much I can safely repeat to Verity. Would he know?

We walk back to the house in silence, and they all leave without much else to say. My parents are relieved to find them gone when they finally emerge from their room, and we spend the weekend enjoying time together. I leave early on Sunday so I can catch Diana before driving back to school, and lucky for me, she's home. She opens the door and her face is full of surprise and excitement.

"Come in! Ethan, it's so great to see you!" She pulls me inside and leads me to the back den. "What's new?" I sit on the chair opposite her and think through how much I should reveal. I need info, and she's the only other person who would have it.

"The Trivium officials know I didn't take the pill. They're watching me. A doctor there swore me to secrecy about a few things, but he also told me an interesting story about a rift and a young girl that caused it." She sighs and looks defeated. Her shoulders seem to collapse.

"I had hoped you wouldn't know that story. But I'm not surprised he told it. All of this is my fault. Everything that's happened since the day I met Cassia's father, it's all been such a mess." Her eyes gloss over and she grabs a tissue and dabs at the corners.

"So, this is because you met Cassia's dad? You changed everything, for him?" She nods and rubs her fingers on her temples as if she's massaging a headache.

"I chose a career over everything else offered. And I don't regret that whatsoever. I went after my passions, and I was successful. And then one day I met Cassia's father and everything changed. I changed. And somehow I managed to alter fate to be with him and the whole rift thing happened in return." My initial anger toward her softens as I hear her recount her story. I can't be as upset as I want to be because I've gone and done the exact same thing. I've decided to write my own story, instead of letting fate plug me into a future I don't want. And I can't hate her for that. I can't say I wouldn't have made the same mistake because I did. I took fate in my hands and crushed it.

"This rift, Dr. Bachman warned me it could get larger and have terrible consequences. Do you know what that could be?" She shakes her head.

"Not yet, no. But I'm trying to zero in on it. I'm working *with* them, Ethan. With Dr. Bachman."

"So, do you know where the rift is?"

"No. They won't tell me. I think they're afraid I'll go after Cassia myself. They're not entirely wrong."

"If you find out more info, will you tell me? I can come by on a weekend or you can call my cell." I stand up to leave and she walks over to me and gives me a hug.

"If I find out how you can get to her, I will let you know. Immediately. Until then, sit tight. Don't say anything to Verity or Jason about this."

"I won't." And I know that I can't. I have enough eyes on me right now that dragging Verity into this part of the search could be dangerous for her. We say our goodbyes and I make the long drive back.

That night I grab a pen and my notebook and begin to write a story. A story about a boy who has dreams about a girl. And how he meets her and falls in love and loses her. The story isn't near done yet, it is only beginning. But I want to be the one to write it. If I can control my future, then I need only to start with a single blank page.

* * *

The months pass by without a word from Dr. Bachman. I guess my file hasn't changed anymore, so there is no reason to contact me. I spend the holidays at home with my family, and in my free time, I work on my manuscript. Verity has never given up looking for answers, but she knows I'm holding back something from her. I've tried telling her that I don't know any more than she does, but she doesn't believe me. You cannot lie to someone named for truth.

Spring comes and with it a new outlook on life. The glimpses into the world I share with Cassia still come and go but each time they are echoes of a life we have never lived, and not a future where we are together. It does not matter what I say to her in those moments, she won't remember them later. Faint ripples lying outside the center, spreading further and further away, and leading me no closer to her. I don't want to live in an echo. I'd rather fly into the eye of the hurricane.

While I enjoy all my classes, I'm never fully present in them. It's hard for me to want to make new friends when I don't know what's in store for my future. If Diana had known she would lose her daughter as a consequence of choosing her husband, would she have strayed from the path she originally chose? Does loving him undo the pain losing her has caused?

I blink and my first year of college is over. It's time to pack up our rooms as if we never lived here and venture back home for a few months. When you leave home, you don't think about coming back. The idea of leaving Jason and Verity and our life we've cultivated here is just as difficult as it was to leave my parents. We've had a wonderful time here, the three of us. With Jason's art and Verity's designs, and occasionally my short stories, we've become a regular trio of creatives. It's only a couple of months, but it feels like ages.

"I'll be seeing you next weekend, right?" Jason asks as he packs the last bag in his car.

"That's still the plan. Ver going?" He shakes his head. "No, her dad made plans for a family thing."

"Is that code for 'she's still mad at me?'"

"Ha! No. Not a code. She really did say she had plans. If she keeps having plans every day, then it's probably the code." Verity was not happy with me when I said I was tired of chasing Cassia's ghost. She thought I was giving up, which isn't true. Couldn't be further from the truth. But I know that I need to create a life worth bringing Cassia back to. I still need to fulfill my own dreams while I wait. Every time I get a chance to see her, even though it's only temporary, it's like finding a beautiful oasis and then realizing it's a mirage. It's not real. It's beautiful and glorious and what you need, but it isn't real. And I know Verity gets a little jealous that I can peek into a life where Cassia is alive. I'm not unsympathetic. I'm just not sure what's worse: not ever seeing her, or seeing her every once in a while, for a few fleeting moments.

"Alright, well drive safe. I'll see you soon."

"You too, man." I offered to be the one to turn in our summer contact info and keys, so I'll be leaving in a few hours. I'm ready to be back to see Hannah, but I'm also worried what surprises may await me there.

That night, once I'm reacquainted with the bedroom I grew up in, I lie in bed and think about the story I'm writing. I've reached a crucial point where the main protagonist goes in search of his true love. It sounds cheesy, and I'm doing my best to avoid that, but I also cannot work out the best way for him to go. What kind of journey does he go on? Does he rebel against the government and destroy their entire system? Would it free everyone to make their own choices? What would happen if they did? Wars, poverty, crimes? There's a good chance that could all come back. In this world, the one that's fictional, I can't decide the best way for him to find her. It's art imitating life because I can't find the best way to reach Cassia either. Diana hasn't been forthcoming with any more info like she promised, so I'm hoping that means she doesn't have anything to share. My brain tries to work through my plot dilemma, but to no avail. I may have to actually find Cassia in order to finish the story I'm writing.

I think about the Trivium and the blank pages at the end of the memory book. They were blank because I hadn't written them yet. And no one else would get to write them but me. If my life were a story, how would I write it? I envision those blank pages again, and the words come alive on the page. I know how the story should end. I know how I want it to end. I pick up my pen and start writing.

CHAPTER TWENTY

CASSIA

"Fill your paper with the breathings of your heart."
—William Wordsworth

It's amazing how quickly time can pass when you're busy standing still. I've been rooted in place, while the world changed colors and the leaves fell, and fresh buds reappeared. Every minute of every day I am closer to finding him, but I also feel as if I'm only a hamster on a wheel to nowhere, but running as fast as I can go. With every hint of him, every scent that seems familiar, every voice I think I know, I strengthen my will to live two lives at once. I am a student with a career path, but also a girl falling in love with a boy I cannot see or touch. Spring is full of newness, freshness, and hope. The world has been bathed in a clean slate and rejoices with multitudes of blooms. Love is in the air, and it's beautiful and tragic. It's hard to be surrounded by couples, but it's also a cause to spend more time alone and write.

I wrote more stories and submitted them to the college paper and other local publications. My one published byline turned out to be an immense help for my portfolio and has even led to more opportunities to share my words. I know that I can be overly ambitious, but why wait until graduation to start honing my craft? There have been several rejections, as I knew there would be, but it only fuels my fire to write more and better. I write about what love must feel like. It's hard to reconcile how something that feels so wonderful can also cause so much pain. There is no greater force of inspiration and destruction than love.

Unbeknownst to Verity, I follow her and Jason's story closely, gleaning pieces of information I can use in my writing. I watch how they communicate with each other, how they handle conflict, or how they compromise. It's a fascinating character study to see two people in the throes of a passionate relationship work together to maintain harmony. Two very similar people in talents, but very different in character. I file each tidbit away in the hopes one day I can pull from it if needed. My only relationship thus far was built on a foundation of half-truths and a lack of real, raw emotion. I was comfortable only because I didn't know any better. I was treated well and thought that *was* enough. It wasn't.

Verity and I have managed to add some of the black and white photos to the walls I had seen in the other world. Pictures taken on campus, at the café, at art installations or coffeehouses. We've included some of her fashion design friends in our outings, and they've been fun getting to know. I'm no longer threatened by them. I should never have been so worried. Along with the photos, I've made two spaces for writing rejection slips and acceptances to pin on the wall. Both columns remind me that I started in a completely opposite direction, and it showcases how far I've come. All they do is reinforce that I'm pursuing the right path for myself.

We've made this room our safe haven. And in some ways, our control center. We've collected all the information we could find about windows into another universe and pinned the articles and stories on the wall. Our walls are now decorated with colorful sketches, black and white photos, cut out paper slips, and journal articles. A hodgepodge of facets of our personalities and life together on display for all who enter here, which is usually only Jason and a few of Verity's friends. I've resigned myself to be the polite, quiet girl in my classes. As much as I'd love to branch out and meet new people, something stops me from trying. I don't know if it's because I have a fear of what's to come or a genuine lack of will to add another person in my life to keep track of. Probably a mixture of both. So, I keep to myself and pour everything I have into my classwork and writing.

A few weeks before the end of my second semester, the campus magazine editor approached me to write a monthly short story starting in the fall. A submission I had sent him impressed him, but they were already backlogged with availability and decided to hold off on printing. Flattered, I readily accepted his offer. I will get to showcase a new story each month and be a regular contributor. Music to my ears. Hurry up, fall, I have things to do and stories to write.

The day Verity and I pack up our dorm for the summer is one of the saddest days of my year. I've enjoyed this life we've created. I take snapshots of our room so I can try to duplicate its look in the fall. We won't know if we'll get the same room until then, but I hold out hope we do. Just nine months ago we were leaving home and going off to change our lives together. Now we part for a few months and try to inject ourselves back into the world of parents and childhood bedrooms. We've experienced a taste of adulthood and freedom, and it leaves a sweet taste in our mouths.

My parents are overjoyed to have me home for more than a few days at a time, and it's nice to be back with them and where I grew up. Only this time, it's no longer home to me. It's my room and my things, but they no longer feel like they belong to me. If home is where your heart is, I left my heart on campus.

I've been wary and uncomfortable around my mom ever since the day she admitted guilt. I can't fault her for what she did, or else I wouldn't be here. And I would more than likely have stayed stuck in a life with Gunner without her. It just feels awkward knowing the truth. She manages to pin me down for a lunch date on a day when I have no other legitimate plans. I knew I wouldn't be able to avoid her, being at home all summer, but unless she has answers, I have don't much to say.

I meet her at the diner and it feels like old times. The same smells of burgers and fries permeate the air, with the whirring noises of the blenders making the shakes. She keeps tapping her nails on the table which grates on my nerves after a few minutes.

"Mom, I know this isn't a casual get together like old times thing. You have something to say."

"Wow, Cassia, you don't mince words anymore, do you? College has changed you." She smiles at me, but I don't return one. "You're right. While I wish this was another casual dinner with my daughter who I've missed dearly, there is more to it." The waiter interrupts her so we order our regular meals, and then I sit back and wait for her to begin. She clears her throat and fidgets uneasily in her seat. "I have some potential news about the window that I thought you might want to hear." She brushes her hair behind her ear and takes a sip of her drink. I am feeling rather impatient.

"And?"

"It's possible you can use it as a two-way communication portal."

"What does that mean exactly?"

"You could actually communicate with Ethan in real time. Wherever he is in his world, you could find him and speak with him. Like a walkie-talkie. Or possibly even see him." My breath catches in my throat and I have trouble swallowing. Excitement floods my heart but it's paired with anxiety. I knew I'd have to see him in real life at some point, but the reality of it is hard to take in. It's silly to think that way.

"How's that possible?"

"We already know you two have a connection since you can seemingly visit each other at random. The idea here is that you can purposely seek him out and talk to him, just by thinking about that connection."

"So, just by thinking of him? That doesn't work." I feel my cheeks getting red. This is such an embarrassing topic to share with my mom.

"More like targeted thinking. And you don't have to try this right away, but I do think you should at least try. Wherever you feel comfortable. I want you to picture a window, and then I want you to focus on seeing Ethan. Just him, no one else. If you can will yourself to be where the window is, you should be able to travel there in your mind."

"I'm confused. Wouldn't the window be wherever the rift is? How can I see him in real time if it's all in my head?"

"I know it's hard to understand, but that's why I want you to try. Yes, wherever the rift is would be the most helpful as far as getting to him, but he'd have to be there to meet you. And the only way to work with him on finding it is if you can talk to each other. You might feel like you're dreaming, but it won't be while you're asleep. Just like the previous times weren't real dreams." I think of the poem that Ethan left me. He is on his side of the universe actively reaching out, but he missed *when* I would be at the coffeehouse and dorm. If he can purposefully leave me a message that sticks, then it makes sense that I can do the same. The trick is finding him in the present.

"Okay. I'll try later today. Was there anything else?"

"Cassia, I know you're confused and unsettled by what I've told you. But I want my baby back. I hope you can someday forgive me for what I've done." She sits back slumped against the booth, head hung low. I empathize so much with her that I don't want her to think I'm upset. I'm just confused. And a little fearful. The woman in front of me is a very powerful force unto herself.

"Mom, I don't need to forgive you. To be upset with you doesn't make sense because, without your act of rebellion, I wouldn't be here. And I like my life. I'm grateful for it. I can't imagine not ever getting to live it. It's just a lot to take in, you know?" She nods and looks back up at me.

"I really do want you to be happy."

"I know."

We finish up our lunch, and true to my promise, I go back to the house and lie on my bed and think of Ethan. I close my eyes and visualize a giant picture window where there are no panes of glass to obstruct my view. I bring Ethan into focus, and I concentrate on his smile and his eyes. He's such a handsome guy, and it's almost hard to stay focused on him without feeling giddy. There is no one else around, just him at the window. I imagine hearing him say my name, and then I'm not only peering at him through the window, but also seeing myself on the other side of it.

"Ethan?"

"Cassia? Is it really you?"

"It's really me, is it really you?" He laughs, and it echoes in my head.

"It's me. Where are we?"

"What do you see?"

"A window." My stomach knots up in excitement.

"When is it, in your world?" He looks down at a nice watch on his left wrist.

"Just after noon, June second." I cry out and then realize what I've done and cover my mouth in embarrassment. *"It's the same for you?"* I nod, mouth still covered. *"So, this is happening in the present?"* I keep nodding like a bobble-headed fool and make myself stop.

"My mom said to think of you at the window, and if I concentrated hard enough, I might be able to send you a message. And since I don't know how long we have, I need to say this. There is a window, an actual one, a rift. And we have to find it. Once we find it, we can see each other in the physical. I need your help to find it."

"Diana is helping you?" It catches me off guard that he is so familiar with her on his side.

"She is. How do you know her so well?"

"She's . . . helping me too." A part of me knew that because of the poem, but it's different to hear him confirm it. But if my mom is helping Ethan, why am I not also there in that world with her? Are memories of me in his world wiped from my parents, too? Do Ethan's parents exist in my world? Have they forgotten their son?

"I'll try this again soon. In the meantime, let me know if you find the location of the window. We'll need to be there at the same time."

"I will. I've missed you, Cassia." None of this would be possible if he weren't so familiar with me, but I feel cheated that he knows me more than I know him.

"Nice to actually see you in person, Ethan." He looks confused. He must not have known that I don't remember him. He tilts his head to the side and raises his eyebrow but then shakes his head slightly and doesn't say more. He reaches out toward me, but his hand falls upon glass as if we're stuck on opposite sides of a real window. I reach my hand out toward his. His hand is so much larger than mine, his arms much stronger. My body shudders as if

jolted by an electrical shock, and he's gone and I'm back on my bed, staring at the ceiling.

I did it. I contacted him in the present. I should probably tell my mom that it worked, but the mental fatigue seems to have caused physical fatigue, and I don't want to get out of bed. I roll over and snatch my cell off my nightstand and call Verity and spill the details. Excitement bubbles through her voice and she squeals with delight when I tell her he said he missed me.

"He *knows* you. Somehow when you chose Gunner, you left that world behind, I guess. Have you thought about reading anymore of your journal? The one that talks about him and the dreams?" I haven't looked at the journal in months. Since the visions had come back, I didn't think I needed to keep searching for answers between its pages.

"I haven't, but I guess I can find it in one of these boxes."

"Maybe you can add to it. You know, write out the latest information. Do you think he can contact you now?"

"I hope so. I told him how I did it. I may have only mentally found him, but Verity, I *found him!*" I can't stop myself from screaming out in joy. I don't usually get as crazy about things as Verity does, but this is cause for celebration.

"I'm so happy for you! Now that you can talk to him, maybe you both can finally find that stupid window and be together forever. None of this missing-out-on-a-life-with-him nonsense. You've had a year without a boyfriend, and it's been a fun year. But you also deserve love."

"Thanks, Ver. It's been an extremely wonderful year. But you're wrong about something."

"What?"

"I had you. And Jason. And your friends. I *had* love." She goes silent for a few seconds. "Ver?"

"Shut up, Cas, I hate crying." I burst out giggling and so does she. Love may come in different forms, but I'll never forget what the love of friendship feels like. It's just as important as any other kind of love. We hang up after I promise to find the journal, which ended up being in a stack of my notebooks for school. I flip through the pages and try to imagine being in the dream I had written about. Now that I have seen him and talked to him, I can easily add him into the images in my mind.

I visualize lying in a hammock with him. I don't know where we are exactly, but we're next to each other, and I'm hyper aware of his body touching mine. Nothing else registers for me. It's just a generic hammock, nowhere in particular. I keep going through the pages until I land on the dream of being with him in a cabin. I had been more descriptive in this entry, so I piece together what it must look like if it were real. I quiet my thoughts and meditate on the inside of the cabin. The worn sofa covered in a blue knitted throw. A rocking chair. A fire. And then it dawns on me that the table we were playing cards on must have been in this cabin. I can't place how I would know that, but the more I focus on the cabin, the more it comes alive in my mind.

The smells of hot cider, cinnamon, and pine waft past my nose. I am sitting in the rocking chair, and for some reason I feel nervous. Ethan sits across from me on the couch. I'm uncomfortable with Ethan's presence, but it's because I still can't imagine he's real. Now I'm walking down the hallway glancing at the photos of his family on the walls. I hear Ethan and Gunner talking in the next room. *How did Gunner get here?* I start to feel sick, so I race to the bathroom, but I open the door and there is nothing there.

I'm jolted awake by my own coughing, so I sit up and take a drink of water. What I just witnessed was not a dream. Those details were not at all in my journal. I put my hand on my forehead and rub my temples and look at the journal again. I read through it line by line, and there is no mention of Gunner and Ethan being in a room together. I could have fallen asleep and my subconscious took over, but I know better. I cover my face completely with my hands and steady my breathing.

That was no dream. That was a memory.

CHAPTER TWENTY-ONE

The room is quiet, save for the sound of my beating heart. I sit there on my bed, not able to sleep, not able to think. The stillness extends to my mind and I welcome it. I stare off into space, no longer conscious of my surroundings as they begin to blur in my vision. *I remember.* Only a small piece of a very large puzzle, but it fits. I wake from my trance only to focus my thoughts on the cabin. Ethan's cabin. By the lake. The more I meditate on its image, the clearer it becomes. We were there together. I was nervous because we didn't know each other that well outside our dreams. But I was also full of mixed emotions at the time. Those emotions race past my mind as each little piece of memory comes alive inside my heart. How much have I lost? How deep inside is the rest of him buried?

A small locket of my heart has been opened, and I'm eager to reveal more of its contents. What else can I remember? I flip through more of the journal entries to look for one that pops out at me. None do. Defeated, for now, I try to get as much rest as I can.

The next morning, I tell my mom what happened, and she encourages me to visit all the places Ethan and I may have gone together. I don't know where to start, but I imagine the library is as good a guess as any. We are both writers, it only makes sense we are both readers. I remember how the book changed covers when I was here, the first time I'd experienced a vision since the Trivium. I pick out *Cat's Cradle* like I had before and start reading. Words leap off the page, and I'm reminded of the time I heard Ethan's voice in the hospital. *You're my favorite.* The words echo as my eyes wander across the page. Even though I'd chosen a different life, he was still with me. Perhaps I was wrong about fate after all.

I stay curled up in the chair reading when I hear a voice speaking faintly. *So, tell me, Miss Bennet, what pray tell flaws you must have?* I look around and he is nowhere to be seen. But he was here. Before. With me. I close the book and then my eyes and think about those words. He was joking with me, being overly silly. And it was nauseating but charming. We were here, in these chairs, talking about graduation and our futures. How pretentious I was then, with my medical school aspirations casually thrown about like a trophy. And there he was, facing me with that wry smile and twinkling eyes. The memory fades back in like a long-lost friend that I welcome with open arms. My heart aches at how much I've lost. I'm thankful that parts of my memory wipe are washing away, and that Ethan is coming back to me in bits. It makes me want to visit all my favorite places just to see if there is any more recognition.

I call Verity and have her meet me at the diner. I have no idea if Ethan ever came here with me, but I'm hopeful something will happen. I fill her in on all that's happened last night and this morning, and she's eager for me to remember more.

Unfortunately, what I do tell her doesn't seem to trigger any of her own memories.

"Graduation. Verity, Ethan was at our graduation party."

"The one we went to at Athena's?"

"Yes! He was there."

"I don't remember that."

"We ran into each other there. Because he was with . . . Jason." She looks at me questioningly. We had discussed the connection before, but it still seems so foreign a concept. A friend that was completely forgotten.

"It's really sad, isn't it? Jason having lost his best friend. These things shouldn't happen, you know? You shouldn't ever lose someone you care about like that just because of some pseudoscience technology. It isn't fair. How can they justify this? With peace? With supposed happiness? But you weren't happy. My dad isn't happy. So, it's not always rainbows and sunshine and peace and love. Sometimes I think we'd be better off going back to before the Trivium. They may have had wars and crime, but at least they didn't lose people they loved in a memory wipe!" She's riled up and as fiery as her red hair. Her cheeks are flushed, and she bangs her fist on the table, making me jump. People stare at us and then decide we must be silly young people and go back to their food.

"You feeling okay there, sweetie? That's a pretty tall soapbox you are standing on." I didn't think her cheeks could get any pinker, but they redden in embarrassment.

"You know how fired up I get about certain things. Friends are one of them. I wish I could remember Ethan the way you are. And I know Jason would want to as well. It doesn't seem right."

"I guess he's still there in another world being friends with you both. Or maybe just Jason. Because in that world you chose some other guy." She rolls her eyes.

"Not likely."

"Eh, you never know," I tease. I envision Ethan sitting across from me though it leads to nowhere. I guess we didn't come here together. If we had, it probably wasn't important.

"So, nothing triggering your memory here?" I shake my head. "Want to try other places around town?"

"Where would we have gone? I've already been here and the library, I don't usually go to many other places."

"Have you tried the park?"

"No, I hadn't even thought of it. I guess it's worth a shot." We leave the diner and ride together to the park, leaving Verity's car. It's a sunny, warm summer day, and I reminisce about last summer. It's hard to believe it's been almost a year since I chose and then chose again. It's almost my nineteenth birthday. We take off down the marked path, and I'm drawn to a bench nearby. I motion Verity to come sit with me, and I lean back and close my eyes and clear my mind of outside distractions. *So, it's true. It's all real?* Ethan grabbing me as I walk away and kissing me passionately. It feels so real as if I'm experiencing it again for the first time. Why would I have ever wanted to walk away from this?

"You're blushing." Verity pops me back in the present.

"He kissed me here." She fake swoons. "Oh, stop."

"Well, how was it?" I bite my lower lip and look away. "That good, huh?" I can't do anything but smile. "So, where next? Do you want to try any other places?" I think through a list of all the places I could have tied to a memory. There are places I went with Gunner, but I don't know about Ethan.

"I can only think of one other place that could help, but it's risky."

"Ooh, where?"

"The Trivium." She gasps but doesn't try to talk me out of it. I pull up to the Trivium building and park in the visitor area. Since I know I won't be allowed inside the lab, I figure the next best thing would be the lobby. We walk in slowly, full of nerves and energy. The receptionist greets me, so I tell her we are just there to visit and see one of the paintings in the lobby. I let her know where we go to college, and she smiles and tells us we're welcome to walk around. We both feel relieved.

I pull Verity over to a painting to look at, just to make it seem like we're there for the art. The lobby brings back vague memories of being in a wheelchair and leaving. I take a seat while Verity is genuinely in awe of one particular painting. No one else is here, but thankfully the receptionist has other things to worry about and doesn't seem to mind us at all. This is where it all began. Or ended. And then began again. Here is where I made a difficult decision, and I don't understand why I chose what I did. I must have had my reasons though they are faint and far away from me now.

Pictures cross my mind rapid-fire, of Gunner and me and a life we could have had together. Of a little girl with golden hair and a hard life as a doctor. The stress worn across my face and the lack of happiness around me. And no Verity. No Jason. I remember this now. I didn't understand how it was possible to not have her in my future. I still don't. Where would she have gone? Memories of Ethan seep through, and there's only a glimpse of a life with him. Not as much detail as with Gunner, but enough to know I would be happy. And I do believe that still. That even with all the changes to my future, this is the one I'll be happy in. Verity walks over and sits beside me.

"Remember anything?"

"I remember two of my choices in the tank."

"Wow, Cas. What were they?" I tell her what I saw, but I leave the part out where she wasn't with me. I think it would upset her to know it's possible our friendship wouldn't have lasted, and that I chose anyway. It makes me feel guilty, this idea of being okay with losing her. Or maybe it wasn't something I did, but just that our lives went different directions. Of course, it doesn't show you everything, so not seeing her there doesn't mean she wouldn't have been. "I think it's great you're getting a second chance."

"I do too. Thanks for doing this with me. It's weird remembering things. It's like another window into a world that's my past, but I *lived* it, versus the windows into an alternate timeline. I kind of feel like each memory is waking me up a little like I've been hollow and sleeping and now I'm alive. It's odd to feel like a stranger to my own memory."

"It makes me wonder what I've forgotten too. If I didn't love Jason so much, I'd probably start wondering what else there was for me as well." She chuckles to herself. We both know that would be impossible. I've never seen her so happy in her entire life.

I drive her back to her car in the diner's parking lot and then head home. My mom is cooking dinner tonight, and I'm greeted with the smells of chicken and garlic. She shoos me out of the kitchen, so I head upstairs to my room. It's not long after I put my purse down that my cell rings.

"Hey Verity, did you forget something?"

"No, but I had a thought."

"What?"

"We just really need to find that window."

"I feel like I'm experiencing déjà vu." Verity laughs.

"I know, but I was thinking. If you can remember memories tied to where you were with Ethan, do you think the window is tied to where your mom met your dad?" That had never crossed my mind, but I wonder if it's possible.

"I honestly have no idea. I don't even have all the details of where they met except it was a theatre."

"Like a movie theatre or play theatre?" I try to recall the conversation with my mom.

"I would have to say theatre for a play. They met at a production."

"Well, we only have like, four of those in this area. They met here, right?"

"I think so. I'll ask tonight."

"I'll get addresses of these theatres. Maybe we can start checking them out." My heart thuds heavily in anticipation.

"Can't wait."

That night at dinner I try to coyly get details from my parents about how they met. My mom keeps one eyebrow raised at me, but doesn't ask me questions. She tells me it was a play and leaves it at that. My dad doesn't seem to recall what was playing that night, he was too captivated by my mom. I make fake gagging sounds and my dad laughs. After dinner, my mom pulls me aside.

"What are you getting at, Cassia?"

"Theories."

"Care to elaborate?"

"Verity has an idea that maybe we can find the window if we go to where you met Dad."

"Cassia, I don't know that I want you investigating that on your own. At least let me go with you. We have no idea what could happen if you find it."

"I know, mom. We have no idea what to expect. But it's time to go look. Can you remember what theatre you went to?" She folds her arms across her chest.

"No. And I'm not lying either. It was a long time ago. It was here, in this city. That's all I know. I can't even remember what play. It's hazy. I don't remember it being very good."

"You probably zoned out then." She laughs and unfolds her arms.

"You may be right. I tend to do that. Promise me if you find it, you won't try to cross it. Call me and I'll meet you there if I need to." I'm as worried about what could happen as she is.

"I promise. If we find it, we won't go near it. I'll call you first." She leans over and kisses my forehead.

"I love you, baby."

"Love you, too." She lets me go and walks back into the kitchen to clean up. If the theatre doesn't yield results, there is no telling how many other places I may need to look that's tied to my parents. Where they got engaged. Married. Went on a honeymoon. The possibilities seem endless. For now, all I can do is wait until morning, and then adventure awaits.

CHAPTER TWENTY-TWO

ETHAN

Happily ever after is for fairy tales. My story does not end with a perfect life, but it does end with an adventurous one. The ending I envision is full of laughs, arguments, compromises, love, passion, and friendship. A real life. That is all I want and exactly what my protagonist will have. I always thought it odd that stories would end when the characters got married or found each other. Though they may have experienced trials to get to the ending, isn't that ending truly their beginning?

I've had a beginning with Cassia, but I'm not ready for an ending. When one chapter is finished, another one begins. I finally confess to Verity all about Diana's past. She takes it well enough, but the information makes her even angrier than it did me. And I understand completely. I haven't enjoyed a lifetime with Cassia yet, and she blames Diana for losing her best friend. In a way, I do too, but I don't hold on to that anger because it does nothing to help my situation. Verity insists we visit with Diana to gather whatever information we can, but I have a feeling prying even more into a precarious situation will not end well in our favor.

At Verity's persistence, I agree to schedule a lunch date with Diana at the diner. A public, local place where we're known well will keep her from lashing out at us. Or that's what I'm hoping for. I pick Verity up on my way, and we arrive to see that Diana has already taken a seat in the center of the room—at a table—instead of along the edge in a booth. This gives me a feeling of foreboding. Can we talk freely in the middle of the restaurant? Was this smart maneuvering on her part? I take a seat directly across from Diana and Verity sits on my left. Sometimes I really do wonder if Verity has a truth-telling superpower—a human lie detector—and if it would serve us well today.

"Mrs. Bellerose, we asked you here today—"

"Please, Verity, call me Diana. And I know why I'm here. I gather Ethan told you everything about my past and you're wanting more answers." We're both speechless and surprised, the shock clearly across our faces. "I'm going to save you both a trip by telling you that I don't have any." Verity's look of surprise has morphed into disappointment. Her shoulders slump slightly and a frown splashes across her face.

"Diana, can I ask you something?" There must be something we've overlooked.

"Sure, Ethan. What?" She sits back in her seat and folds her arms across her chest. She's not angry as much as impatient.

"Where did you meet Cassia's dad?" She cocks her head to the side and raises her eyebrow.

"At a local theatre. Why?"

"It's just a theory. I was just wondering if where you met him might be the location of the rift." She puts her hand up to her chin and looks away as if lost in thought.

"I mean, it could be possible. That's when everything changed. But I'm not sure which theatre it was in the city—or if it's still there."

"I can look up theatres." Verity springs into action, getting her tablet and pulling up the search features. The school lets us keep one over the summer. I'm glad she brought hers. "There are not very many. I'm seeing four. Can you believe we have *four* theatres in this town?" She turns to Diana, holding up the tablet. "Do any of these look familiar?" Diana squints at the screen, then pulls out a pair of reading glasses when she gets frustrated trying to read the screen.

"Well . . ." She scrolls through the list and then back up again. "I can definitely cross off one of these. But I had friends that performed back then so I know I went to others. I remember brick walls, which would knock this list down to three. I wish I could be more help." Verity gets a small notepad out of her purse with a pen and then writes down the three locations we need to check out.

"I know this could be nothing, but at least it's a starting place." Diana reaches across the table and puts her left hand on my mine and right hand on Verity's.

"If you find this thing, don't go near it by yourself. Call me, okay? I will meet you there." Verity and I both nod, but I notice Verity giving me a strange look. We leave the diner, and Verity gets to work on mapping out the best routes to take to get to each theatre.

"First, we need to go by the Lyric Theatre Company. That's the closest one." She plugs the address into my car's computer system and the map is projected on a small part of my windshield. I follow the voice narrator's instructions until we reach an old, red brick building with a falling down sign.

"I take it this isn't still open?" Verity looks up at the sign and then gets out of the car and walks to the doors. She turns back toward me and shakes her head. I park anyway and walk up the windows and try to peer in. An empty lobby is littered with trash and storage pieces. "It looks like it's been closed a long time." We walk around to the back of the building, examining it as if it holds the missing piece to our puzzle. Even though we have no idea what we're looking for, I'm hoping we'll recognize it if we see it.

"I don't see anything. It's such a pretty building too. I wonder why it closed."

"Lack of support in the arts." She shrugs her shoulders.

"Quite possibly. It's sad."

"Ready to go to the next one?" She nods. I walk back to my car, and as I go to open the door, I'm transported to another place. What seems like several minutes later, I see my car door in front of me again. Verity is peering at me from the passenger side, so I slide in.

"What was that?" She scans my face, intent on finding something.

"I was just with Cassia."

"Oh, another vision?" Verity isn't too excited about my visions anymore.

"No. It was actually Cassia. *Now.* Today. In her world. Somehow, she brought me to a window portal, and we talked!" My body shudders, and my skin breaks out in goosebumps.

"Now? As in, you just talked to her in the *present?*" All I can do is nod. Verity sits back in her seat and cries out in delight. "Where was she? Did she tell you how to find her?" I shake my head. "Well, what then? Does she miss us?" *Nice to actually see you in person, Ethan.*

"Verity, she said it was nice to meet me. In person. As if we've never actually met." A sinking feeling hits my stomach. The pills. She had to have gone to the Trivium and taken the pills. It makes sense since in her world she didn't die there. But how would she know to contact me if she's forgotten who I am? *The visions.* She must've been having them, or gotten my messages. Maybe that means she didn't completely forget me, just our past together. That's only a slight bit of solace.

"Ouch. Geez, I hope that doesn't mean she forgot about me, too."

"She's also trying to find the rift." This seems to lift Verity's spirits.

"Did you tell her where we were looking?" I shake my head.

"No, I didn't get a chance to say much. I was a little in shock. But she's looking and said to try to contact her if I can find it."

"Well, let's hurry then and get to the next place." It takes us twenty minutes to drive to the next theatre, which is sadly under remodeling construction. We can't even get close enough to the building to do a thorough search.

"Maybe we should just sneak past the barricades?" Verity is looking for a place to get through the chain link fence but coming up short.

"I think we could get in a bunch of trouble for that. It could alert the Trivium to what we're up to," I say. She cries out in disgust.

"We'll come back to it. Let's head to the Black Box then."

"How far away is that?" She looks at the map.

"Thirty minutes or so."

"We'll need to go tomorrow then. I need to get back in time for dinner." Verity looks agitated, but she begrudgingly agrees to call it a night.

The next afternoon we take off and try our luck at the Black Box Theatre. It's a further drive from my house than I originally thought, but it's the only one to look at today.

"Well, let's hope this is it." Verity is hopeful and fidgety in the front seat. We drive across town, and because we hit the rush hour time of day, traffic nearly doubles the amount of time it takes to get there. We pull up to a newer, contemporary looking building. "Ethan, I have a feeling this is not the theatre we're looking for."

"It's a little hard to believe it would be that old. Maybe it was just refaced?" We get out of the car and walk around to the side of the building. The bricks here are much older, insinuating that I was correct in my assessment of the front being remodeled.

"I wish I knew what we were looking for," she says.

"Me too." There are a couple of doors on the back side of the building, but they're both locked. We try the front doors and they're locked as well.

"I wish there was someone here we could talk to. Everything is closed. You'd think they'd be rehearsing for a summer play or something." She peers in the windows, but they have window coverings and there is nothing to see. She stamps her foot in frustration.

"There is still that last one on the list. She could have forgotten about going there. We could try again tomorrow." She huffs loudly and walks to the car in disgust. I echo the sentiment. I look back at the building and something catches my eye. It looks like a faint blue light, and I'm drawn to it.

"Ethan, what is it?" She leaves the car and comes up beside me, looking in the same direction I am.

"I thought I saw a blue light." She looks at me questioningly but follows me as I walk back to the side of the theatre.

"Hey, I don't remember that door being there, just the ones in the back. Do you?" I shake my head because I can't get words to come out. I walk to the door and stand a few feet away from it, scanning it intently and looking for a handle. There isn't one. Verity joins me, but then she walks toward the door until she's close enough to touch it.

"Don't," I say. A faint hue of blue takes shape around the outline of the door as if it's radiating from within. I take a step closer and the light shines a little brighter. With each step, the light increases its intensity until I reach within arm's length of the door, and the door itself seems to change in front of my eyes. "Are you seeing this?" I look at Verity and she nods, her eyes never moving away from the light. I slowly reach out my hand, afraid to touch the door but wanting to know if it's solid. When my fingers are just close enough to barely caress the metal, a knob appears. Apprehensive, I turn the knob, and the door shape blurs and swirls until it's black and endless.

"This is it!" Verity screams and runs to stand right next to me. We peer into the void, and the nothingness is eternal.

"Should I call Diana?" I can't take my eyes off the abyss.

"You stay right there, I'll get my cell from the car and call her. She runs away and I hear her open the car door and shut it quickly. "Diana, it's Verity. We've found it. No, we haven't messed with it. The Black Box. Are you sure? Okay, I'll tell Ethan." She comes back beside me. "Diana wants us to come to her house tomorrow. She's sure the window will still be here, but there is something she needs to talk to you about."

"She can't say it over the cell?" I know she's right, it shouldn't go away forever, but being so close to Cassia and leaving is a hard pill to swallow.

"She said no. She sounded like this was urgent. We better get home. It's going to get dark soon." I know I need to contact Cassia and tell her where it is, so I take a few steps back away from the door and the light grows dimmer. Intrigued, I walk back to it and the light gets brighter.

"Verity, I'm going to step back from the door, and I want you to walk closer to it." She looks at me funny but obliges. As I walk away, the light dims. As she walks toward it, nothing happens.

"It's you, Ethan. You're the one causing the light. It's tied to you." I feel better knowing it will still come back, so I walk with Verity to the car. When I look at the wall again, the door is gone. It's as if it never existed.

The next morning, we drive to Diana's house, and as I pull up, I see the tinted black sedan out front. *Trivium.* Dr. Bachman, most likely. A mixture of fear and anger rises up my spine. Did she call them? Were they monitoring us already? Would they try to keep me away? We walk up to the door and Diana opens it before we can knock.

"Thanks for coming." She ushers us inside, and I see Dr. Bachman sitting in a chair. He stands as we enter and he offers his hand to shake.

"Ethan, Verity, thank you for coming." He takes a seat and Verity and I look at each other with worry before taking a spot on the sofa. "I know you've found the window, that's why I'm here."

"Sir—"

"Ethan, it's okay, but I'm here to inform you of a few things. First, we knew where the door was, but we had no way of knowing how to access it. It was being monitored by surveillance equipment, and we received a report of you being there and what happened. We feel safer knowing you are the only one who can access it. That means no one else can accidentally stumble upon this portal. But second, we also have a better understanding of what will happen when the portal opens." He clears his throat and asks Diana for a glass of water. We all sit there in uncomfortable silence until he finishes taking a drink. "I immediately called Diana when our surveillance crew contacted us about the door and asked her why you would be connected to it. She filled me in on your relationship with Cassia, and after checking your file again, it's clear you intend on bringing Cassia from another world into ours. Is that correct?" I clear my throat and nod nervously. "That would make sense as to why she was listed in your future. Ethan, I understand why you're doing this, but I want to make something clear. If you cross through that door, it will close forever. That means if you go through the door, whatever world you find yourself in will be all you have. This world will no longer be accessible. If Cassia in another world crosses into this one, she will be the one stuck here forever. And while that may sound like good news, it also means that whatever life you have here would be gone, and vice versa for her. Your friends here, your family, you would disappear and they wouldn't know why. Cassia's parents in her world would experience the same loss that Diana has experienced in this one. Those are critical choices that need to be examined, not something to act rashly about."

Thoughts swirl around my head. I hadn't thought of the consequences of seeing Cassia again. Her mom there has been helping her. Would it be right to take her away from her mom? Trading the grief from one Diana to another? And Verity and Jason, wouldn't they be upset to let her go, even though their counterparts are here? My head throbs just thinking about all the complications. I glance at Verity and she seems to be close to tears. She's probably thinking similar thoughts as I am.

"I understand," I say, thinking of nothing else to add.

"At this point, it's going to be your decision. I just caution you to think of the outcome. The rift itself poses no threat to this world as far as we know, but it will close if one of you goes through it. You took your fate into your own hands, Ethan. Choose wisely." He stands up and shakes my hand again. I walk him to the door and watch him leave, feeling numb all over.

"What are you thinking, Ethan?" I jump a bit when I realize Verity is right behind me.

"That perhaps this is all selfish and foolish." She rests her hand on my shoulder.

"I was thinking the same thing. But we need to know what Cassia wants. She should be included in the decision. Can you try to contact her?"

"I don't know how she did it. I can try." I close my eyes and think of her, those beautiful eyes and long blond hair. I focus on her smile and her laugh. And then I picture the window in front of me, like a portal of glass.

"*Ethan? Are you there?*" I see Cassia facing me on the other side of the glass, just like last time.

"*I'm here. I found the portal.*" She smiles wide and lets out a scream. For a moment I get lost in the amount of joy she's displaying and forget about the bad news. She must read my face because she comes closer to the glass, joy displaced by worry.

"*What is it? What's wrong?*" I feel my heart racing and the throes of disappointment bombarding me.

"Before I tell you where it is, I need you to know something. If one of us crosses through it, we can never return. We would be leaving our world behind forever." She steps back a bit from the glass and I see her gasp as realization hit her face.

"*My mom, where you are. Tell me why she's helping you. I need to know.*" It dawns on me that she's figured out there's something wrong on my side if I'm looking for her with help from her mother. I bite my lip, wondering what her reaction will be if I tell the truth. "*Please, Ethan.*" Her pleading wins me over.

"She's helping me over here, because . . . because you died, Cassia. And she wants you back." Tears form in the corners of her eyes and she wipes them away before they can fall. It pains me to see her upset and not be able to do anything about it.

"I knew something was wrong, I just wanted to make sure what."

"I'm truly sorry. It's why I've been trying to reach you all this time . . ." She looks back up at me and smiles a thin, sad smile.

"And Verity? Jason? They're there with you?" I nod.

"They've been searching for you, too. They miss you." She dabs at her eyes again.

"Where is the portal?"

"The Black Box theatre. On the side of the building. You'll see it when you walk closer to it. Cassia, do you know if my family is there? In your world?" She shakes her head. "Oh." It hadn't occurred to me that one of us would have to sacrifice our families and friends to be together. If my parents don't exist in her world, what could I possibly say to them—and Hannah—to make them understand why I'm leaving forever? Would I be able to let them go? Would they let me go?

"Ethan, can you meet me at the portal tomorrow evening? Maybe we can talk there first without walking through?"

"Whatever you need, Cassia. I'll be there. Six o'clock sound okay?" She nods and gives me another sad smile. I wonder what must be going through her head. Probably as many mixed emotions as are going through mine. I wave her to, she waves back, and I'm back in the room with Verity and Diana.

"Did you talk to her?" Verity asks.

"I did. I told her what would happen if one of us crossed over."

"What did she say?" Diana asks.

"She wants me to meet her tomorrow evening at six. At the door. She's hoping we can talk there. Diana, I told her the truth about why we're looking for her." Diana stands there, face going pale.

"She needed to know why she isn't here at some point."

"Diana, I know you want her back, but don't you think it's selfish to take her away from . . . well . . . yourself?" She laughs.

"I know it's selfish. I know it's terrible. And I would be hurting myself, no less! How crazy is that? And yet, I still ache to see her again. It's hard, Ethan. To know the pain of living without her, and knowing if she leaves, another me is over there going through the same grief. And even knowing that I still want her here. It's like I can compartmentalize my loss and justify everyone else's grief because I'd have my baby back. Is that wrong?" She looks on the verge of tears. Losing Cassia has aged Diana at an alarming rate. I remember the first time I met her, and how youthful she looked. I hope some of that youth could return with Cassia's presence. I notice Verity has been oddly silent, and I see that she's back on the sofa with her head resting on her hands. Her shoulders are convulsing, and I know she must be crying or trying hard not to. I go and sit next to her, putting my arm around her shoulders. She relaxes a little, and after a few minutes, she finally looks up.

"I can't do this anymore. I couldn't live with myself if Cassia left her world and came here. She would be losing everything. I don't want that for her, I just want her to be happy. And that kind of sacrifice could breed resentment, not happiness." Tears pour down her cheeks in winding streams until they drop off her chin onto her lap.

"I'll go to her side then." Verity wipes her cheeks and looks at me curiously.

"But your family, Ethan. What about them?" I feel the sadness trying to lurch its way up my throat, and I make every effort to stuff it down.

"I'll tell them what's going on. And then just hope they understand." I have to believe that a lifetime of loving Cassia could overrule the loss of the rest of my family.

"Oh, Ethan. I wasn't even thinking about *your* family. I was so consumed with mine." Diana sits down beside Verity, putting her hand on Verity's thigh. "We are a mess of a trio, are we not?" This makes Verity laugh a little, and that makes me laugh in turn.

"Indeed, we are." I get up off the sofa and walk to the door. "Diana, I'll meet her tomorrow. Do you want to go with me?" She perks up and nods enthusiastically. "I'll pick you up at five. Verity, do you want me to take you home?" She nods and gives Diana a hug before coming with me to the car. Diana walks to the driver side window, so I roll it down.

"Ethan, I can't ask you to sacrifice everything you have. I know she's wonderful—she's my daughter—but that's a huge risk. Listen to Dr. Bachman, okay? Don't do anything rash."

"I won't." I back out of the driveway, Diana waving as we drive off. Verity sits silently for the entire trip to her house. As she gets out of the car, she faces me, eyes still engulfed in sadness.

"Ethan, I want to go too. I want to see her if I can. I want to be able to give her a proper goodbye." With that, tears flow fast and hard down her face as she shuts the door and walks inside.

CHAPTER TWENTY-THREE

CASSIA

The Black Box. Ethan found it without my help, and all I have to do is go see him tomorrow. If what he said about the window is true, when one of us decides which life we want to leave, it will be forever. I'm hoping he will cross to my side, but I also know he would be leaving everything. He and his family no longer exist in this world, and there is no way to bring them all here. I think about what he said; that Diana in his world lost me—or her Cassia—and wants me home. And I understand that. I also know that my Diana would grieve just as hard if I left. What do we do? Who leaves and who stays?

I rush downstairs to find my mom and tell her the news. I find her in the kitchen, seated at the table with a hot tea on a saucer and a book in her hand. She looks up from the book and then promptly sets it down.

"Cassia, what is it? You've got a glow about you." I smile bashfully.

"Ethan found the window. It's at the Black Box theatre! He said I'd see it when I go, it's like a door on the side of the building. I'm meeting him there tomorrow evening!" She stands up so fast she almost knocks the chair over and embraces me tightly.

"Oh, sweetheart. I knew you two would figure it out, eventually. At least, I had hoped you would. What are you going to do when you get there?" She takes a step back, keeping her hands on the side of my arms.

"I honestly don't know yet. I just thought if I could see him, in person—even though it's through a door—that I would somehow know the right thing to do." She searches my face for meaning, and it must dawn on her what's going on because she grips my arms more forcefully.

"Cassia, are you saying you're leaving?" I hold back tears and take a deep breath.

"I don't know. Ethan said once one of us goes through the door, it closes forever. I don't want to leave, but I also know he would be leaving his entire family to come here. I don't know what to do. Is this relationship worth it?" She loosens her grip and lets her arms fall to her side.

"That's for you to decide. Only you can do that. Your father was worth it to me. Even knowing what I know now, I wouldn't change anything. Because I have him, and I have *you*. And you are the best part of it all. Go see him and then take some time to decide."

"Stop trying to make me cry." She laughs and then hugs me gently.

"I think you should call Verity. She'll need to know what the stakes are." I nod and walk back upstairs to my room to find my cell.

"Hey, Cas. What's up?"

"Good news and bad news." Silence for a few seconds.

"Okay. I'm not sure I want to hear this, but what is the good news?"

"Ethan contacted me. He found the window. Or door. Portal. Whatever you want to call it." She squeals and I pull the cell away from my ear.

"Wait, that's amazing news! So, what's the bad?"

"If one of us goes through it, we'll never be able to come back. The door will close. We'll be stuck on that side for good."

"I'm not understanding. Are you saying you are the one leaving?"

"I don't know. I'm going to the door tomorrow night to see him. I need to talk to him face to face if I can. I don't know what to do."

"I'm going with you."

"You don't have to do that. I'm not crossing over there and he's not coming over here. Not yet. That's a big decision we'll have to make together. And not one we'll take lightly. There's a lot at stake here."

"Cas, you aren't going alone. Besides, I want to see him too. I haven't been privy to your visions you know. I don't know what he looks like. I have to make sure he's worth it." I chuckle to myself.

"Okay then. I told him I'd be there by six."

"Jason and I are grabbing dinner early tomorrow. We can meet you there."

"You're going to drag Jason into this too?" She laughs.

"He doesn't remember his former best friend. So yeah, I'm bringing him. I'll tell him what's going on. Where is the door?"

"The Black Box theatre."

"Oh! That was on the list of places I was going to check. It'll take us probably thirty minutes to get there, so I'll message you when we're on our way."

"Sounds good."

"So, important things first. What are you going to wear?" I manage a false, exasperated sigh. "These things matter to me. You know this. Don't act like you don't. Should I come over and help you pick out an outfit?" It hadn't occurred to me to be worried about what I wear. I was just going to wear jeans and a tee. I mean, he knows me, does it matter? "Cas, don't say you're just wearing jeans." I laugh out loud. "I knew you were thinking it."

"I think it's scary how well you know me, Ver. I just don't see a need to be fancy. He knows what I look like. Don't you eye roll me over the cell." She starts giggling.

"We know each other a little too well. At least let me help with hair and makeup." I sigh loudly, not hiding my dramatic annoyance.

"Okay."

"Be over tomorrow morning." She hangs up before I can say anything else. I walk to my closet to see what I have to wear. I feel a little self-conscious about my wardrobe. A lot of jeans and tees in here, not much else to work with. I guess it wouldn't hurt to have something a little bit nicer. Like a blazer or something. Or a nicer top. Verity would freak out if I ask her to take me shopping, but I'm leaning toward it.

The next morning, she arrives exactly when she says she will and comes up to my room carrying a large makeup bag. That many makeup choices always make me feel overwhelmed. I wouldn't even know where to start.

"Ver, you're going to love this, I just know it. But I was thinking you could help me pick out something to wear." She screams in delight and jumps up and down.

"We'll do makeup last then. Let's go!" She grabs my hand and I almost stumble trying to keep up with her all the way to her car. My mom gives us a cursory glance and smiles. I manage to yell out that we're going shopping and she waves at us as we run past. Fifteen minutes later we arrive at one of Verity's favorite clothing boutiques. All the pastel colors lining the windows makes me feel faint and nauseous.

"Please don't make me wear that." She follows my line of sight and then cracks up laughing.

"You are not a pastel person. You are a jewel tone person. Never fear, I'm an expert."

"You've had one year of college." She gives me a side-eye glance.

"I'm a natural." We walk inside, and I see that color divides the different areas. It's like a rainbow threw up in here. She leads me over to some dark hues of purple, blue, and green and I feel a little less scared. She scours the racks and then starts grabbing several things at a time, handing them off to the sales associate to put in a fitting room. I watch her go around the store, picking various tops, pants, dresses, and accessories on a whim. She always looks so put together, and yet each item she wears is chosen on purpose. I just grab shirts I think are funny or witty and get them in several colors if I can. It's kind of fun to watch her work, as she glides effortlessly throughout the store contemplating what to grab and what to put back. I peek into the dressing room and the large splash of color starts to give me a nauseous feeling.

"Okay, Cas. Here you are. Get in there and then come model the pieces. I've put them together as outfits, so you don't get too overwhelmed with what pieces to match." I feel relieved. That could've taken me hours to do. I would have been left there standing in the dressing room, picking each item apart and second-guessing what to wear with it. I look at the outfits she's assembled and they're not anything I would've chosen—but that's the point. The first outfit is a dark blue blouse with intricate stitching in metallic silver threads. She paired it with dark blue dressy type jeans. This is how I know she loves me. I put it on quickly and walk outside. I get a thumbs-up from Verity, so I set that outfit on the "maybe" rack and try on another. We do this dance for an hour, me trying on the clothing and her giving me a thumbs-up or down. After what seems like forever, all the good ones are put together side-by-side so we can narrow down the options. Verity looks so serious and focused that I almost want to laugh. To her, clothing is another form of art. She can have her clothes, I'll have my words. At least I can write for her and she can dress me up. Sounds like a win-win.

"Okay, Cas, here are the top two I'm going with." She points to the first outfit, and a dress I reluctantly tried on at her behest.

"That's two though. I just need one." She shakes her head.

"You need this one for tonight," she points to the top and jeans. "And then the dress for when he comes over here and we'll celebrate." Worry hits me hard in the gut. *What if he doesn't come over?* "Cas, don't look so upset! I see it written across your face. He'll come over, just wait, and see. You're worth it." I feel a sob caught in my throat and it stings. "Cas, everyone gets a happy ending. *You* are getting a happy ending. And that ending will be a beginning. And we'll all be together."

"I want to believe that, I really do."

"No worrying now, there's plenty of time for that later." She winks at me and takes the clothing to the register. I follow and pay for everything. I'm fortunate that she's not only great at picking out clothes, but she's also wonderful with finding things on sale. She takes me home and then goes a little overboard with pulling out all the makeup palettes she brought.

"Promise me you won't go formal, Verity."

"Au naturel, dahling. I'll go simple." She hovers over me as I sit on my desk chair. It's hard to keep still, the brushes tickle and my eyelids keep twitching—much to her dismay. "Voila! You're done!" She holds up a mirror in front of me. My reflection stuns me. It's still me, but she managed to make my eyes seem brighter and my face is glowing.

"Wow, Verity. I don't know what to say."

"No thanks necessary, I'm happy to lend a hand." She gathers up all her makeup tools and puts them back in the bag. "I've got to go run a couple more errands before meeting up with Jason. But I'll see you in just a few hours! I'm so excited!" She gives me an overly enthusiastic hug that almost topples me over. We say goodbye, and after she leaves I change into the new clothes. Anxiety sets in again, and there's nothing I can tell myself to quash it. I keep thinking I can rely on intuition about all of this, but what if my gut leads me wrong?

I have nothing to do that will take my mind off what I should do next. Nothing I can think of to help me decide. I'm so worked up that my stomach is in knots and I can't eat anything. My mom had work to catch up on at the office, so I know she'll be home later. My dad is still at work and won't be home till after I'm gone. I am all alone in this house and anxious. I get the journal back out and fish through it for anything else that may help me remember. I think about the cabin. There aren't many places where a cabin would be in this town, so I grab my purse and keys and drive to the lake. Gunner brought me here on a picnic date, and I know I saw several cabins in the area. The memory of Ethan and Gunner in the cabin makes me think it all happened at the time of the picnic, but that part was wiped out of my memory. I park near the picnic tables and take off walking down the shoreline. There are many high school kids out here today. A year ago that would've been me. I already feel like I live a world far away from the one I knew before.

I reach the point where the cabins start, and I look around to see what other memory I can trigger. There's a cabin up a little way on a hill, and it feels familiar so I walk up to it. I knock on the door, but no one is there. I try the knob but it's locked. Walking around to the side, I peer in the windows, hoping to recognize it. The place is semi-empty and littered with cobwebs. I don't know what I was expecting to see, but I'm disappointed. I lean my head back and close my eyes and breathe in the smells of the lake. I imagine myself at the cabin of my memory: the aroma of cinnamon, the warmth, and peacefulness. This must be the cabin I remember. What happened to it? When Ethan was wiped away from my world, did it take his family with him? There is nothing here that is his. It's as if none of them existed. The weight of him losing his family pulls me down. My parents are still over there. Verity and Jason are still over there. Even though that Verity and Jason are different, they are still technically the same people I care about. Except missing a year with me. And they've been living a life without me for that long. Would it feel the same? Would I constantly feel guilty about leaving here?

My cell rings with a message from Verity saying she's on her way. I've lost track of time and I'm running late. I run back to my car, take a quick second to check my hair and makeup in the mirror, and then start the drive to the Black Box. Even with the air conditioner on full blast, I feel like I'm sweating profusely. My knuckles are gripping the steering wheel so tightly that they're hurting, and I chastise myself for getting all worked up. I reach the theatre without any traffic problems and park in the back.

I see the side of the building as I walk closer, but it's blank. *Where is the door?* I feel like I'm being watched, so I quickly scan the area, but no one's there. This part of town is completely empty, so much so that it's eerie and quiet. I take a step closer to the wall, and as I do, I see the outline of a door forming on the side. It's large, and steel, and the closer I walk, the more a strange blue light seems to encase it in a peculiar glow. Curious, I walk even closer toward it, and the glow seems even brighter with every step. I can almost touch the door, but I'm afraid to. Verity isn't here yet. If this door opened, and it swallowed me whole, she would never forgive me for not saying goodbye. I step back away from the door, and the glow softens. I look at my cell to see what time it is. *She should've been here already.* I pace around to the front of the building, hoping to see her car. Nothing. I try calling her and it just rings without answering. I call Jason, and he doesn't answer either. I shouldn't be impatient, but I know that Ethan is going to be waiting for me, and he's expecting me in about five minutes.

I walk back around to the back and her car isn't there either. *Where are you, Verity?* I try her again and still nothing. She would kill me if I went to the door without her, but what happens if Ethan thinks I'm not showing up? Would he stay longer just in case? Or would he leave? My cell shows it's six o'clock, so I walk back to the side and the door magically appears again. I must take the chance that I don't miss Ethan, but I'm worried about Verity too. Maybe she got stuck in traffic. Perhaps her cell died. And Jason forgot his. So many possibilities as to why they're late.

I touch the door and am surrounded by the blue light, so bright I consider getting my sunglasses out of the car. A knob appears out of thin air, and with a deep breath, I turn it. Colors swirl before me and then fade, leaving only the eternal blackness of space.

"Ethan?" I cry out into the void but hear nothing. I'm too afraid to go through the door, knowing it's a permanent decision, but I can't figure out how to get to him. I stare into the darkness, focusing my thoughts on Ethan. The darkness starts to go away, and it's replaced by an image of buildings. It almost looks like I'm gazing into a mirror, but my reflection is noticeably absent. Blurry images start to take shape before me, and I see the outline of people. Nervousness takes over my body, and I try to wipe the sweat beading off my forehead without undoing all of Verity's work. The outlines fill in with more clarity, and I scream out when I see Verity's face. She screams in response, and I look behind me to see nothing, and then back at the door to see her.

"Verity, h-how did you . . . ?" She is looking at me in astonishment, and behind her, I see another familiar face. *Ethan*.

"Cas! It's you! I've missed you so freaking much!" She starts crying and dabs at her tears with her scarf, trying to not mess up her eye makeup. "I've missed so much of your life already. It's just so good seeing you. At least one more time." It feels like I've been sucker punched in the gut. This Verity has missed out on an entire year of my life, but she's still *her*. My Verity still isn't here, and she will be kicking herself if she misses getting to see, well . . . herself.

"Hey, Cassia." Ethan walks up next to Verity, looking timid. His hands are in his jean pockets, and he's anxiously biting his lower lip.

"Hey, Ethan." We stand there silent, awkwardly staring at each other. He's not in a dream. He's not in a vision. He's not just a memory. He's not in my mind. He's here, with me. The panic I was feeling slowly subsides, and I remember what it felt like when he kissed me. Goosebumps travel up my spine and spread throughout the rest of my body. That kiss may not have been real—in the sense that he's standing in front of me real—but I know exactly how it felt. And how *I* felt. I wish I could reach out for him right now, but I know I can't. The last figure comes into focus, and I gasp out loud when I see it's my mom. But it's not *my* mom. The duality of the situation overtakes my brain, and I lose the ability to understand or reason. She is both mine and not mine. I am both dead to her and alive. A regular Schrödinger's cat. She's sobbing, tears flowing freely down her face. This must be wonderful and yet so hard for her. I want so badly to hug her. To be able to console her. To show her that her daughter is not dead, but in front of her right now.

"My baby. I never thought I would see you again. Not in this world or any other. I've missed you." I feel wetness lining my cheeks but I no longer care about the makeup or how I look.

"I'm so sorry." It's the only thing I can think of to say. I don't know which of us will go through this door. And I know I can't make promises to repair her grieving heart. To fulfill one would be depriving another. Two broken hearts do not a whole one make.

"Cassia, they wanted to see you to say goodbye, just in case it's me that comes through this door. I know that either of us will be making a lot of sacrifices, but I want you to know that I believe in us. And I believe we—us together—are worth it. If we weren't meant to be together, all of this would be for naught. I don't want to think that everything we've gone through means nothing. I love you, Cassia. And I'll do anything for you." Ethan gazes at me with a deep intensity, one I'm only familiar with in the visions. His eyes pierce through me to my heart, and I tell my head to stay quiet. Resting on intuition only, I stare back in his eyes, searching for answers. There is love there. That much is true. I feel that stronger than any other emotion imaginable. There are hints of sadness and worry. Leaving everything he knows, as well as a grieving Verity and Diana, would take a toll on him as well. I know that now.

"Ethan, how do we decide?" He shrugs. My cell rings, and I immediately silence it without looking. It rings again, and I'm forced to apologize because it's my mom calling me. She either wants to know what I've decided or is just checking on me.

"Mom, hey."

"Cassia." She starts bawling into the cell's speaker so loudly I'm forced to pull it away from my ear.

"Mom? What's wrong?"

"Are you there? At the door?"

"Yes. I am. I'm here, with Ethan."

"Go through the door, Cassia. I love you so much, honey. Go through the door! Don't come back, just go. Go to him. I'll explain things to your father as I can." My body starts trembling and I go cold all over.

"Why are you saying this? I can come home and we can talk this over."

"Cassia?" Ethan is looking at me, worried. I just shake my head to him. Verity comes up beside him, along with my *other* mom. All three are visibly concerned.

"Mom? Is dad okay?"

"Dad's fine, baby. He and I are fine. We love you. Remember when I told you I would do anything for you?" My body starts shaking and I feel even more tears about to burst through like a flooded river swallowing a dam.

"Talk to me! Why are you saying this?" I scream into the phone.

"Because I'm letting you go. You cannot stay here, sweetheart. You *have* to go with Ethan. Is Verity with him?"

"Yes, she is. Why?"

"Everyone you love is with him. And while I will miss you so very much, more than words can express, at least I'm content knowing you'll be happy. And you'll still have me. You have *me* there, Cassia. She is really, truly me. So is Verity. They may not have been around for the past year, but they were there all the years before. Diana there will have all my memories, except from after you went to the Trivium. I can live with that, Cassia. But I couldn't live with myself if I kept you here."

"But dad—"

"Dad will understand. In time. He knows what I did, honey. He'll understand. We both went after love, and all we've ever wanted was that for you too. And you can have that."

"And Verity. Mom, I still need to talk to her and Jason. She never showed up here . . ." My mom starts crying again, and my heart hurts as if it was stabbed repeatedly. Verity isn't here. Not *this* Verity. The other Verity is staring at me wide-eyed in curiosity. "Mom, do you know where Verity is?"

"Cassia, just go. And don't look back."

"Mom, where is Verity?"

"Cassia, please! I love you. There is nothing here for you but heartache." *Verity wasn't shown in my future. She hasn't called. She never made it here.*

"Mom, I can't go until you tell me what happened." I take a step back from the door, and Ethan, Verity, and Diana begin to blur. Verity cries out for me, but I can't look her in the eyes right now. "Please, momma. I'll go. I'll leave. But I can't do that without answers." I hear her blow her nose and come back to her cell.

"Cassia, Verity and Jason were involved in a car accident. It wasn't their fault. They were brought to the hospital. Your dad called me . . ." The dam breaks, and my eyes flood with tears. They were on their way to see me. This is all *my* fault. I take another step back from the door and the blur turns into outlines. I know Ethan is yelling at me, but his voice is just another echo bouncing around my mind. "They're gone, baby. In this world, they're gone." I pull the cell away from my ear and let loose as loud of a scream as I can muster. I fall to my knees on the sidewalk and bury my face in my hands. *No. No!* I hear my mom's voice calling for me and I realize I'd dropped the cell next to me.

"This is all my fault." I scream again into the emptiness.

"Baby, it's not. It's not your fault at all. She's still there, with Ethan. And she'll be living the life you two always wanted once you go through the door. It's a second chance for you, Cassia. And for her. Because she lost you there, too. Promise me you'll go. Right now."

"How can I do that? How can I promise you that? How can I leave now?"

"Go. Go where you have family. You have friends. And you have love. I could never live with myself if you stayed here and lived your life without them. They are your future, Cassia. *Yours.* You *must* go." I look back at the building, and the door is mostly gone. I know if I were to move closer to it, it would open again. And they would be there for me, on the other side. Am I living in a dream? Is this another vision? Do I know what's real anymore?

I walk back to the door and it springs into life just as I knew it would. The blue light shines bright and the doorknob reappears. I open it and after a few seconds, the other side comes into focus. Ethan is sitting on the sidewalk where I had been, Verity patting his shoulder.

"Cassia!" Diana notices me and Ethan and Verity turn toward the door. Ethan jumps up off the ground and runs to me, just slightly avoiding crossing over. Verity follows suit and stands beside him.

"You came back," Ethan says. I can only nod.

"Cassia, put me on speaker." I turn the speaker on so my mom can talk to everyone. She says hi to Ethan and Verity before asking for Diana. "Hi, me." They both giggle uncomfortably. "I know you'll take loving care of our girl because, well . . . we're the same. She's had a wonderful year at college, and I've told her all about my past. Our past. Don't let her feel guilt over leaving. We will be just fine. I don't want to lose her, but I'm glad you're there for her. Verity?"

"I'm here." Verity steps closer to the door.

"It's going to be hard for Cassia to get to know you all over again. You've lost a year of your lives together. Don't let her stop living out her dreams. Can you do that?"

"Absolutely!" She starts crying, but they're tears of joy.

"Ethan?"

"Yes, ma'am?"

"Love her. Support her. I would have loved getting to know you as a son-in-law. I'll rest easy knowing she's in your arms. You fought to find her, and any man that would go to those lengths is perfect for my daughter." He smiles sheepishly.

"I'll do my best. I promise."

"I know you will."

"Cassia? You can take me back off speaker." I oblige and hold it back up to my ear. "Promise me you will keep writing. That you'll find adventure in the everyday. That you'll live without guilt and regret. Open your heart to them. Promise me, baby." I can barely choke out words.

"I promise, momma."

"One last favor."

"Anything."

"Take a picture of you all by the door and leave your cell in your car. I want to know just how handsome my future son-in-law is, and I want to see Verity's shining face."

"Mom, it won't be the same without you."

"I'll be there! She is me! Give her a chance, okay?"

"Okay. I love you, mom."

"I love you more than life itself, baby girl. I'll see you on the other side. Literally." This makes me laugh out loud. "Now go. I'm hanging up. Bye, baby."

"Goodbye, momma." She does as she promised and hangs up. I can't leave without trying Verity's cell one more time, and again it goes straight to voice mail. I want to cry more, but I wonder how many tears can one cry before drying up entirely? Do they ever? I pull up the camera feature on my cell, and I look terrible. My face is swollen and puffy and my eyes are red. This is not a picture I want to leave, but I have no other choice. I tell the three of them what my mom wanted, and they happily oblige. The photo is of me in front of the door, but I'm grateful that they could be captured on camera through the portal so clearly. Ethan looks devilishly handsome; my mom will love that. Verity is glowing with excitement, and Diana is beaming. I forced myself to smile, but even I can tell it's not genuine. I know she will understand. I tell them to wait just a minute for me, and I walk back to my car—door disappearing once again.

I leave the cell on the front seat and grab my journal out of the back. I want my mom to have my memories. I find a pen in my purse and leave her a note on the last page. If she reads through these pages, one day she'll find my words. I leave the key under the seat and the front door unlocked and walk back to the building. I open the door to smiling faces, and it helps soothe my aching heart. These three are my family. I will never be without them again. I take one last look at my world before jumping through the door into Ethan's open arms.

CHAPTER TWENTY-FOUR

"Fate, destiny, will. No matter how you look at it, love wins in the end. And if you have love, does it matter how you got there?"
—*Ethan Rivers*

I fall into Ethan's strong embrace. He holds me tightly as if afraid to let me go. More arms surround my waist as Verity and Diana join in. They are both crying but smiling through their tears. A noise behind us shakes us apart, and we watch in awe as the door begins to close. I watch my world fade away into a blue haze and then turn into the never-ending darkness. Once the door closes, it disappears completely, as if it had never existed. It is only a building. The same one, as if I were already on this side, in this exact spot I had been before leaping. We all walk up to the wall, but nothing changes. There is no more door, just as they said would happen. I am gone from my world and now thrust into a new one. A world where I had died and yet live again. What awaits me here? How will my being here be explained? Everything is the same, it is only me that is different.

Ethan holds my hand as we walk to his car. I choose to sit in the backseat with Verity and let Diana sit in the front, so he opens my car door and kisses my forehead. I lean into him, getting to wrap my arms around him and feel his body close to mine. I hear his heart beating, and it soothes me. Did all paths lead to him? Was this truly my choice, or were we destined to find each other no matter what? I may never be able to answer that question, but right now—in this place, with him—I don't need to know. I have been dealt such strange cards in my lifetime, and I can only imagine the future holds just as much adventure.

He leans his lips to my ear and whispers softly, "I know what lies ahead is hard. But I'm so happy you're here with me." I lean back away from him and study his face. I can trace every line, count every freckle, and see each small scar. I will have a lifetime of memorizing every beautiful part of his body. He will never be forgotten to me again. I lift myself higher on my toes and bring him down to me. It is our first real kiss of my new life, and it will not be my last.

It feels strange to drive up to my house. It is mine but not. If I am going to live here, I need to tell myself that this is still mine. I never left. I never lost. My father walks to the front door as we approach, and upon seeing my face, breaks down into tears and comes running. I never told my father goodbye, but neither did *that* Cassia. My heart breaks for his loss and for my mine, and I readily accept his arms and his cries of joy. After a few minutes, we all walk inside together so my mother can explain.

Like clockwork, Dr. Bachman appears at the front door as if we had alerted him to what happened. I remember the surveillance and think it must have been the same on this side. He would know I came over and the threat is gone.

"Ethan, hello again. Cassia, a pleasure to see you alive and well." He winks at me. "I came to check on you both. I was watching the videos when you crossed, Cassia. Are you well?"

"As well as can be, Dr. Bachman. Thanks." He nods in agreement and then pulls out his briefcase and takes a seat on the sofa. Inside lies a couple of manila folders, the ones that document our futures. He glances at them and then hands our folders over to us. Ethan looks at his skeptically but then smiles slightly. Curious, I open my folder as well. It says that I chose Ethan at the Trivium, went to college with Verity this past year as her roommate, and will have various writing and editing jobs in my future. I will continue at the same college, with Verity by my side. I want to cry out of relief, but the tears are long dried up. Ethan and I swap folders, and his is almost identical to mine. Destined for writing books, college with me, a short blip about our future that makes me gasp out loud and I drop the folder.

"Dr. Bachman, can this be true? What's in here?"

"You two have forged your own path, but from here on out this is a recording of the possibilities of that path. Your files are unique in that they change as you do. I wouldn't be surprised to see another change in the future, but somehow, I doubt it necessary. According to our files, you never left this world, Cassia. You've lost nothing from the last year as far as your education is concerned." He motions for us to return the folders so we do and he packs them back in his briefcase. He stands to leave and we walk him to the door. "Ethan. Cassia. The portal is gone, and it may never be opened again. And though you may technically possess the skills to continue changing your fate, I highly recommend you proceed with caution. If you experience any side effects, please let us know."

"Wait, Dr. Bachman?" He turns back to face me. "Can I ask you why you are okay with all this? Do we not pose a threat to the system?" He shakes his head.

"The point of the Trivium is to reach happiness and be satisfied with life. Even we at the Trivium do not wish for any to despair. It's when there is a threat to peace or humanity that we will intervene. The two of you have been interesting to watch, but your choices were based on love. Isn't that all anyone wants? Who are we to part soul mates? You are very rare indeed. Good luck to you two." He nods his head and walks out to his car. I watch him leave, curious if there are others just like us that would rather change their fate. He called us soul mates. Verity once said she and I were soul mates. The fact that I am here with them both tells me you can have more than one, and I've found mine.

✳ ✳ ✳

I settle into my life in this world, never stopping to think about the mom and friend I lost. Verity and I have spent as much time together as possible. She wanted me to fill her in on the life I was leading while away at college. I tell her about our dorm, the study sessions, and trips to museums. She is sad to have missed out on my life, but she fills me in on what I missed of hers. At times it's hard to reconcile the girl in front of me with the one I knew and lost. They are the same, but different. A year can change a person, and this Verity is much more self-aware and emotionally strong than mine. But she is also mine, and over time, we bond again as best friends should. I am fortunate that she has many of the same memories of our past, it helps me accept her for who she always has been: my Verity.

For a few weeks, I could not call Diana my mom. She was so polite and understanding that it made me feel shame and guilt in return. I often wonder how my parents in the other life are doing. Are they okay? Does my father understand? I have dreams at night of being back with them, and there are mornings where I wake to familiar smells that I almost forget this is an alternate home.

Ethan and I talk every day. We are taking our relationship slow as we are learning about each other all over again. He is kind and considerate, and every day I smile to myself that he's real. While he isn't as over-the-top as my memories would suggest, he is still witty and romantic—and we have the most wonderful, deep conversations about life. We do not talk about our future. We choose to live day by day.

EPILOGUE

CASSIA

I wake up to the sound of yelling downstairs and the crashing noises of broken glass. I jump out of bed, throw on my robe and slippers, and slowly open my door. Fear envelops me though I can't imagine what there is to be afraid of. I make my way down the steps, listening for signs of my parents. All is quiet, and it's eerie. A broken vase litters the floor at the base of the stairs, so I gingerly walk over it, making sure to avoid any sharp pieces. *Odd.*

"Mom? Dad?" No answer.

I peer around the staircase into the hallway, and I gasp when I see more broken glass and ceramic lining the floor. Pieces of pottery, glass jars, and picture frames lie shattered in ruins. I call out for my parents again and am met with silence. Panic rises up my spine and my body breaks out in goosebumps. *Where are they?* I race around the house looking for signs of what happened. My parents' cars are still in the garage. Their bedroom is empty and untouched. I run to the front of the house and the door is wide open, swinging softly on its hinges to the rocking breeze outside. I feel tears coming down my cheeks as I walk to the front porch and find no sign of them. *Where have they gone?*

I try to calm down, telling myself everything has an explanation. They can't have disappeared. *Or could they? I disappeared from one life when I came here.* My cell rings upstairs, jolting me out of my shock. I jump over the broken vase and leap up the stairs, hoping to see my parents' names on the screen. *Ethan.* I answer, choking back sobs.

"Cassia! You're okay!" He half-laughs-half-cries out of relief. "I was so worried!"

"Ethan, what's going on? My parents are missing!"

"Oh no. Oh, God, no. Not yours too!" He pulls the cell away from his mouth and screams.

"Ethan! Your parents are gone too? What the hell is happening?" Desperation takes over and I feel a scream fighting its way up my throat.

"They're gone. They disappeared. I heard them scream and ran to their room, and they were just . . . gone! Hannah's gone too!" He screams again, this time in anger.

"I don't know what's happening. I heard yelling and glass breaking. There are broken things everywhere. Were they . . . *taken?*"

"I don't think so. I didn't see anyone. They were here one moment, and the next, they were gone. Poof! Into thin air. Cassia, do you think this is our fault? Could the rift have come back?" My mind draws a blank. The rift closed. I went through the door and it closed behind me. We all saw it. *But we knew there could be consequences, we were warned. Could this be our punishment for changing our stories? Could the universe turn on us by taking away ones we love?*

"Ethan, there's only one way to find out. We have to go back to where we found the door."

"I'm on my way."

ACKNOWLEDGEMENTS

TRIVIUM was born out of this idea that another me could be living a different life based on different choices made over the years. Would she have married someone else? What would her career be? Is she happy? I don't know anyone that hasn't looked back on their life and wondered . . . what if? The idea took hold of me and wouldn't let go till the very last word of the last page was written.

Even so, it wouldn't have made it this far if it wasn't for the support of my family and friends. When I wanted to give up, they kept me going. Sometimes life imitates art, and my life is no exception. I wrote a story about a girl who realized she was living the wrong life for her, and at the same time, I found that I was living the wrong life as well. But just like Cassia, I found my strength, my purpose, and ultimately, my destiny. And I would choose the same path over again if all paths lead here to this moment.

To my biggest cheerleader, my wonderful mom: I absolutely would not have made it through the darkness without your shining light. You are the reason this book made it this far. Your encouragement, love, and eternal optimism made sure that I didn't shelve my dreams. I will forever be grateful for all you have done.

To my amazing partner in life, Tj, you are my favorite. You are my Ethan. You challenge me, motivate me, and keep me laughing until I cry. All paths led to you. Thank God for that! You are love personified. The only greater love story than Cassia and Ethan's, is ours. I love you so much.

To my kiddos who struggle with loving books as much as their momma, I expect a book report about this book someday in the future. Just kidding. Maybe. You two are my everything. Trinity, this book was written for you. I wanted you to know the kind of love you deserved, but I wanted you to always pursue your dreams. You can have both. Aidan, you are my joy. My missing piece. I can't wait to see which path life takes you on.

To my Ree, my sister by choice, look how far we've come! We are doing hard things. I wouldn't know how to write a character like Verity without you. You are loyal, and strong, and you've never wavered in your belief in me. Love you.

I wouldn't be published if it weren't for my incredible launch team. We did it! Your feedback was invaluable and made this a better book than when we started. You shared my baby with the world, and I am forever grateful. Ready for book two?

Team Wayward Sisters—you ladies are my strength. Every woman should be so lucky to have such a sisterhood. I love you all. Thanks for holding my hand these past couple of years.

And to you, the reader holding this book in your hands, the success of a writer lies not in her marketing and publishing team, but in her readers. You've given me a chance to share my heart. I hope you love Cassia and Ethan as much as I do. They were written for you. Treat them well.

ABOUT THE AUTHOR

AMBER NGUYEN grew up barrel racing, writing terrible poetry, refusing to brush her long hair, and being the best tomboy she could be. Somewhere along the way, she found dresses, heels, and a hairbrush. She's a proud Sun Devil, having graduated from ASU with a BA in English. She lives in Oklahoma City with her soon-to-be-husband, four kids, two cats, and four chickens. When she's not writing, she's building furniture and selling real estate. You can keep up with her on the Trivium Trilogy website, at TriviumBook.com.

Cassia and Ethan's story continues in EMISSARY, the sequel to TRIVIUM.

EMISSARY

CHAPTER ONE

They're gone. Whatever Ethan and I did when I crossed into his universe undid something in the fabric of time. The consequences of us wanting to write our own story have led to the loss of those dearest to us. Was it worth it? Right now, my answer is a resounding *no*. This is guilt I cannot live with. I left my parents behind in one world, only to lose them in this one too. No goodbyes. No last words. Just the vivid memory of screams and crashing noises to haunt me day and night. Ethan and I aren't even close to understanding what happened and why.

Government officials from the Trivium showed up after Ethan and I first learned about the other's families. How they knew anything was wrong, and how they arrived so quickly is mysterious, but that didn't strike me as odd until after they left. Ethan had officials show up at his house too, which delayed him coming over by an hour. I didn't want to be alone while being interviewed about what happened, but I had no choice. More than anything, I wanted Ethan nearby with gentle reassurances that all would be okay.

I didn't have much to tell the officials. I relayed what I knew, but that's the only information I had to give. They gave me vague apologies and insincere promises that my parents would be found. Though they didn't blame Ethan and me directly, the accusation was implied. I had hoped to see a familiar face but Dr. Bachman wasn't with them. I wondered if he knew anything had happened or if he was no longer interested in my file. I want to know what he and my mom knew from the time before when she created the original rift. That stupid rift. The barrier between worlds that never should have been created. I can't be angry with my mom for causing it. She chose love. She changed course and set off a domino of events that led to me coming here.

In this universe, I died. When I went to the Trivium to choose my future, something bad happened, and it killed me. My mom, Diana, identified the body of the Cassia she knew. The Cassia that was me before destiny split me in two. The Trivium somehow diverged my life into two different paths. One Cassia went on to change her story, broke up with her boyfriend, Gunner, went to college with her best friend, Verity, and then found her soul mate in this world. The other Cassia remembered Ethan and for all I know, smartly chose him, and suffered for it. We'll never know because records are sealed. She was me before we were ripped apart. *Two roads diverged in a yellow wood . . .*

I still don't understand why I didn't choose Ethan over Gunner. A life of books and conversation over a life of medicine and stress. I've thought about that a lot over the past year, as I realized how happy I was pursuing writing and rooming with Verity at school. I spent an entire year of college learning who I am and what I wanted. But I also spent that time wondering who this handsome stranger was that I kept dreaming about. Ethan turned out to not be a stranger, and they weren't dreams at all. We were seeing visions of our future together, along with crossing over into each other's worlds for short periods at a time to leave messages. Breadcrumbs. To find our way back to each other. Even though Ethan and Verity have complete memories of before I went to the Trivium, my memories mostly contain the relationship I shared with Gunner. Parts of Ethan have come back to me. I know he met Gunner because a memory of them together at Ethan's cabin resurfaced. Faint, fuzzy details of the friendship Ethan and I had cultivated pop up here and there when I least expect it. I haven't been in this world long enough to ask more questions. It's still hard for Verity to talk about certain things in the past. For her, she lost me when her Cassia died. She spent a year without me helping Ethan find the rift that ultimately brought us back together. For me, my Verity in my world is no longer there. The last few minutes I had to talk to my mom before crossing over were spent in tears learning that my best friend was gone. A car accident. That version of Verity was the one I had spent my time at school with. And even though summer is almost over and it's time to go back to school, it all feels wrong. I will return as someone new, someone lost on the edge of time who never wrote for the paper, never took classes here, never roomed with Verity. Sometimes it's too much for my heart and mind to handle so I shut down and focus on the positives. And Ethan is that positive. My true north.

But now none of those problems even matter because my parents are gone. As are Ethan's. I was finally comfortable with calling this Diana, Mom. It had taken me a few weeks to wrap my mind around the words my mom had said before I left my world. *You have me there, Cassia. She is really, truly me.* And she is. She has all the memories of me before the Trivium. I have done my best to reconcile the two halves that complete my story. I am both the Cassia that died and the one that lived.

Ethan showed up to my house and helped me clean the glass right after the officials left. Broken memories of a family that had finally pieced themselves back together. We silently swept up the remains of the shattered pictures that had been knocked off the wall and entry table. The vase my mom had received as a gift from my grandmother lay in pieces at the base of the stairs. Guilt and shame covered us both as we worked quietly in tandem.

"Cas, what's this?" Ethan stared at me questioningly holding up a piece of paper. I took it from him and studied the symbol hand-drawn in black ink. A triquetra. The Trivium symbol. I turned it over and in a scrawl similar to my mom's was written the phrase, *Find Luna.*

Neither of us knew what the note meant. I've looked at it several times since then without solving any more of the puzzle. *Who is Luna? Why was this hidden in our family's portrait? Is it really my mom's handwriting?* Ethan and I have taken the past few days to collect ourselves, clean our homes, and regroup. We both wanted to be alone and relayed that info to Verity and Jason. Understandably, they were upset that we weren't ready to discuss everything and make a game plan. But that's only because Ethan and I wanted to go explore on our own. Without knowing what could happen to us, and because I'd lost Verity once before, we both agreed to keep her away for awhile longer.

And so that's the current plan. We had some time to think it over. We know we need answers. We're willing to pay whatever price it may cost us. For my parents. For Ethan's family. For the life we want together. It's time to revisit where our universes were torn apart before it brought us together. And that's what we're going to do now.

I put the piece of paper in my pocket, grab my cell, and meet Ethan downstairs. We're going back to where it all began. *That stupid rift.*